SIX

a *Novel* by

DANIEL L. MOOTS

Dedication

I would like to dedicate this book to all those who have suffered abuse in their lives, whether it be physical, emotional, sexual, domestic or any other type. If you are a victim of abuse, please seek the aid of a responsible person. If you know that abuse is happening to someone you care about, please intervene. Since I am a storyteller, let me relate a story which illustrates a form of abuse we might not consider.

Two third grade boys attended the same school and because they came from families which were considered low income, they were provided with breakfast, lunch and another sack lunch they were to take home with them so they would have something to eat in the evening. They lived in a rural area and when one of the boys realized his friend consistently had his food taken from him by his parents to eat, he devised a plan. Every day he took both their lunches home with him and then he would get on his bicycle and make the three-mile trip to take his friend the food meant for him, and they would eat together. That is a true friend.

Abuse is a social problem we have had since the beginning of time. However, we should fight to break the cycle whenever possible.

Acknowledgments

I am so grateful to my friends and family who support me in my musing. What's life without a little whimsy? Many thanks to Judi Fennell for her expertise in formatting my books. I am also very thankful to Schyrlet Cameron for inviting me into the Home Grown Book Club and giving me valuable information and guidance along the way.

Prologue

"Hold still, Charlie!" the young girl scolded her brother as she attended to a cut above his right eye. Tears from both eyes of the smaller boy streamed down his dirty cheeks, and as she worked the needle and thread, her hands smudged his face.

"It hurts Jane!" the boy whined.

"I know it does," she replied. "We have to close that cut before it gets dirt in it. You know it wouldn't hurt you none to wash your face more than once a week." She glanced over at her older brother who was watching the operation intently. "What do you think you're going to do with that hedge stick, James?"

"Whatever I need to," came his reply. Jane continued with her work as James looked around his little brother to see his back. "He's got a pretty bad cut on his shoulder, Jane. It's bleedin' a little bit." Jane kept her eyes on her work.

"One thing at a time," she said softly which comforted her little brother. "Almost done." A few seconds later she bit the thread in two and tied it off. "There. Turn around so your back is in the sunlight, and we'll take a look." The children were gathered below the cabin they shared with their father. A crooked, narrow brook meandered past them, supplying them with all the fresh water they needed for their little farm. They spent a great deal of time along this stream, individually as well as all three together. It was a comforting, safe place, unlike the cabin up the hill. "The wounds back here aren't that bad. They won't need any stitchin' but let me put some liniment on them."

"I don't like that stuff," the boy complained. "It stings like hell!" Jane put her hands on her hips.

"You better watch your swearin', little brother, or I'll wash your mouth out with soap!" she admonished him.

"Sorry," the boy uttered quietly.

"You don't act sorry," Jane said as she carefully rubbed the foul-smelling ointment on her brother's wounds. Charlie's back straightened as his sister applied it to his flesh. When she was finished, Jane hugged her little brother. "All done. I'm proud of you for being so brave."

Charlie was used to pain.

Chapter 1

Alma Zimmermann had always dreamed of having children so after her marriage to Henry Mabry in 1847, she convinced him there was no time like the present to start their family and she quickly became pregnant. The pregnancy was difficult with long days of sickness and the midwife for their area of southwest Missouri territory informed her that bed rest was necessary if she was going to keep the baby. Alma was a rule follower and, being young and inexperienced, she took the midwife's advice and when the time came for their first child to be born, she labored for nearly thirty hours before the baby arrived.

Alma was weakened terribly by the delivery and had no milk for their firstborn. Henry and the midwife had to search all over for a milking goat to produce enough milk to sustain the baby, but he thrived and was a delight to his parents. Alma, however, never regained her vigor but wanted another child so after four years she became pregnant with their second baby. The pregnancy was almost completely a duplicate of the first one and again Alma struggled mightily to give birth. The midwife feared she might lose her own life as well as the life of the child but with great resolve, Alma mustered one more push and delivered a healthy baby girl. Her health waned even more after this second child arrived and the midwife warned her and Henry that another pregnancy could take her life, but Alma had always had a desire for three children. Her husband was one of two and Alma was one of five and she couldn't explain why she felt the need to have three little ones, but she was adamant they would try one more time and then they would be finished.

The pregnancy was even more difficult than the first two and Henry did his best to make certain he knew where the midwife was going to always be in case she was needed by his wife. It was a cold, snowy January day when the labor pains began in earnest. He sent his son three miles in the winter weather to inform Henry's father of his need for the midwife, and he was able to locate her the next day. Alma was struggling to keep conscious under the strain as the pains increased and the time between each shortened. Henry was a very impatient man with a short temper, and he shouted at his four-year-old daughter to shut up as she whined and cried about wanting something to eat. He had no intention of doing anything else besides caring for his wife the best he could. His own mother was in poor health and unable to assist him. He felt quite alone and helpless as his cherished wife weakened with each labor pain.

At last, the door of their cabin flew open, and his eight-year-old son, father and the midwife entered, and she went right to work to help Alma. Henry's father began throwing more logs on the waning fire in the fireplace because his grandson was so cold he was almost in tears. The boy drew as close as possible to the fire and his grandfather threw a blanket over his shoulders. Alma's labor had lasted thirty hours again, and the midwife coaxed her into a last valiant effort to complete the birthing process. Somewhere deep within her soul Alma at last delivered another baby boy into the world but when Henry and the midwife looked down at her to show her the child, Alma had passed from this life to the next. There had been no warning, no long, last desperate breath. She had completed her earthly mission of giving birth to three children and now her spirit had flown. Each of the three adults looked at one another, hoping someone would speak but there were no words. The grandfather gathered the two older children to him, away from their mother's body. The newborn baby began to wriggle and cry in Henry's arms, and he laid the child beside Alma's lifeless body. The midwife recognized the signs of shock and guided him to a rocking chair by the fire while she tended to cleaning the baby.

After a few hours Henry's father had to leave to tend to his own sickly wife. The midwife stayed to tidy up the body for burial the next day and cared for the children as Henry knelt by his wife's lifeless body and wept. Henry had acquired several goats over the years and had a nanny goat who could supply her twins as well as the new baby with a plentiful supply of milk.

Three days after the child was born, his father came back to the cabin and Henry thought he was just coming to check on everyone. Unfortunately, he bore terrible news of his own. When he had gotten back to the cabin he shared with his sickly wife, he had found her dead in her favorite chair. This news of his mother broke Henry's spirit completely. He had struggled in a harsh wind and freezing rain to dig a grave deep enough to bury his sweet wife just two days ago. Due to his impatient nature he hated to dig any type of hole whether it be a corner post hole or a grave. Alma was a tiny lady, so he dug the bare minimum width and length but was determined to dig it six feet deep to dissuade any predators from disturbing her body.

As soon as he beat the cross into the frozen ground and removed his hat to say a few words of goodbye, he cried tears which froze as they hit the earth. When he placed the hat back on his balding head he became a changed man. He fell into a deep melancholy, and nothing could draw him out of it. He did enough to provide his children with food and clothing, but he did little else. In the years which followed his two older children had to grow up quickly and learn from their grandfather and neighbors how to plant and grow food in the garden and the fields. Baby Charlie was mostly ignored by his father. Henry blamed him for Alma's death. If he had just come more easily, he reasoned, she would still be with them, and they could be a big, happy family. He saw the child as bad luck because not only had he lost his dear wife, but he also lost his mother on the same night.

When Charlie was three years old Henry's father passed away as well, and the family burial plot grew. It was at this point Henry began to drink. He had never been a drinking man. They kept a bottle handy for severe head colds and coughs but never just swig several times a day. Their trips to the nearest town seven miles away became more frequent and Henry's purchase of whiskey became a priority for him. The oldest son had a good sense of the family's money needs and he watched as the cash dwindled due to the increased consumption of liquor by his father. It was unfair for Henry to delegate so much care to his two older children. They had to take care of their toddler brother, the chores had to be done, Henry was a poor cook, so they taught themselves how to also do that. They had school two days a week and then performed chores for neighbors for a little bit of money to make ends meet.

The older children also noticed their father was very harsh with their little brother. He would collect a swat on his rump for any minor infraction. He was a good little boy, and they felt he didn't deserve such treatment but were both fearful of their father's wrath if they should confront him about it.

The spring of 1861 was wet and dreary and the winds of the War Between the States finally blew to the neutral state of Missouri. Henry could have chosen to fight for either side but chose the Confederacy. The only reason he had for his choice was that he had no use for the Union. He felt the government wasn't doing enough for the small farmers. A dozen men in grey uniforms came to the farm to escort Henry to an encampment where he would receive his basic training. Charlie was five years old when his father left to fight in the war.

"I reckon I'll see your Uncle Nelson in the training camp. If you need somethin' go and see your Aunt Louise. I need you to stay here and take care of the animals and she don't need no more mouths to feed. You might go and check on her and your cousins every two or three weeks to make sure they're doin' alright. I don't imagine I'll be gone all that long. I expect it'll be a short war." He turned and left without even saying goodbye.

Henry was only in one battle before he was wounded in the right hip and knee and his wounds were bad enough to send him home. He returned in October of 1861, only spending six months in the Confederate Army. He was wounded in the Battle of Wilson's Creek near Springfield, Missouri. The boys in grey had their counterparts on the run and a blue-clad soldier turned and made a lucky shot, blowing off the front of Henry's kneecap. Henry didn't even know he had been shot in the hip as well until the surgeon informed him. It was incredible luck that Henry got to keep his leg and as soon as he was able to travel, he began the forty-mile trip back to his farm. In another stroke of good luck his commanding officer had given him an elderly mule to ride. The animal had become almost useless from his intense labor of pulling cannons up and down the rolling hills of the area. The major told Henry to ride him as long as he could walk and the animal surprised Henry by making the entire trip before buckling and then falling over dead.

The children had done fine in the absence of their father. The garden had done well, and food had been canned and preserved from its overflow. The hay had been harvested and so had a good crop of wheat, oats and corn. His infirmity and the children's success gave him two good excuses to stay in the cabin and drink.

Four years passed and when Charlie was ten, his brother fell in love with a local girl, and they decided to elope rather than face Henry's bad temper. Henry would not want to lose such a good worker because it meant he would have to put more on Charlie and his daughter or do the work himself. Charlie's brother confided in him the night he decided to run away. He had already said his goodbyes to their sister.

"I hate to leave you in such a bad way," he began. "Pa ain't never been the same since Ma and Grandma died the same night. I'd like to take you and Sis away from this place, but I just can't. Run away the first chance you get, Charlie. It ain't never gonna get any better. Pa's gonna run this place into the ground if he ain't careful. He's gettin' mighty close to having to sell the farm or maybe the bank will give another loan, but I doubt that. He can't pay what he owes now. Sis has a boyfriend on the side, so she'll probably run off as soon as it's legal. She might just go ahead and marry him, and they can lie about their age. That would leave you alone with Pa and he'd be in a more sour mood than he already is. I'd hate to see what he would do if he woke up from a drunk and we'd both be gone."

"Where will you go?" Charlie asked. "Where will Sis go?"

"I'm going to go where he can't find me. If I can, I'll write a letter lettin' you know where we are and send it to one of the neighbors and tell them not to give it to anybody but you. You have to promise you won't tell Pa where I am."

"I promise it," Charlie said solemnly. He was already dreading how his father might react. "Are you going to write a letter to Pa telling him you left? He'd be terrible mad with me if he asked me what happened to you, and I had to tell him the truth. He's gonna blister my butt one way or the other."

"I'll leave a note, and I'll also ask him not to take it out on you. It's me that's doin' the runnin'. I'll also tell him that his ways are ruining the farm. He ain't gonna like the things I'm fixin' to tell him but maybe it'll help. He needs to be woke up."

Charlie waited up with his brother until they were certain Henry had fallen into a drunken stupor. The two brothers hugged and when his brother shut the door quietly behind him, Charlie cried himself to sleep.

The next morning, he heard Henry hobble out the door and call for his oldest son. Charlie's sister looked at him and held her finger to her lips to let him know not to say anything. She clutched his letter in her hand.

"Where's your brother?" Henry roared. "He ain't out doing his chores and I can't find him anywhere!"

Charlie's sister walked slowly toward Henry with the paper extended. Henry snatched it roughly from her hand and unfolded it while moving toward the fireplace to see the writing. It was a short note, so it only took a few moments to read it. He swore a vulgar oath, crumbled up the paper and threw it into the fire. He rose angrily and took three quick steps toward his daughter.

"Where did he go?" he demanded and delivered a blow to her face with the palm of his hand, knocking her to the floor. "I asked you two a question! Where did he go?" This time he gave Charlie the back of his hand and sent him sprawling along the floor in the opposite direction of his sister. It was the first time he had struck either of them in the face. It was common to receive a blow to the backside or across the shoulders. Charlie looked up at his father and saw the storm clouds covering his countenance. He was almost unrecognizable when he became this angry.

"He wouldn't tell us!" Charlie's sister cried out. "He wouldn't tell either one of us!" She crawled quickly to embrace her brother to try to protect him. Charlie didn't dare shed any tears. That would have further infuriated their father. He held his sister tighter than he had ever done.

Henry stomped from the cabin and stopped at the steps to the front porch. He then did something that sent cold shivers down his spine. His father shouted repeatedly at the top of his lungs. "Why does everybody leave me?! Why?! Somebody tell me why?!" After several iterations of that lament, Henry threw himself down onto the porch and wept for over an hour. Charlie's sister wondered what he would do when she escaped him. She looked at her terrified brother but didn't utter a word.

Henry's drinking intensified over the next two years and his parents' farm was sold to feed his habit. He sent half the money to his only brother but that made him resentful. His brother was a successful traveling salesman of men's and women's clothing and didn't need the money, but he was convinced by his daughter to do the right thing. She had to watch him carefully to make certain he didn't cheat his brother out of any of his share. During this time Henry never missed an opportunity to berate his younger son over the most trivial things. Charlie strived to be the perfect child but at each minor slip he would get a switch to his rear or a kick of his father's boot. A few months after their brother had left for greener pastures the remaining children received a letter from their nearest neighbor who handed it to them privately. He had settled in the same larger town where Henry's brother lived and seemed to be thriving. James had always excelled in his schooling and had attended some advanced classes while working at a job as cashier at a large bank. He and his wife were happy and expected to have a child a year or so after their wedding.

Charlie's sister swore him to secrecy as her beau came snooping around once a week. Henry would be drinking and didn't notice but Charlie sensed a change in his sister and wondered how long it would be before she too decided to run away and get married. He didn't have to wait long.

"I hate to do this to you Charlie, but I want to be happy, and I can't be happy around our Pa," she said one evening. It reminded him of how his brother had started his speech barely two years ago. She was only sixteen and he had hoped she would wait a couple more years before she left. "I can't tell him in person so I'm going to do the same thing our brother did and leave a note. I'll also write to you to let you know where we settle down." She hugged him hard. "Pa's going to probably take it out on you. Stay strong and maybe someday you can come and live with us when you get older. You'll be welcomed."

Charlie was now twelve years old, but he felt much older than that. "I don't ever want to be like him," he began. "I'm gonna be just the opposite of him. I'm gonna be a good listener. Someday I'll be a good dad. I'll love my kids, and I won't whup 'em for no reason. I won't blame 'em for things that ain't their fault. It wasn't my fault that Ma died havin' me, was it?"

His sister had tears rolling down her cheeks. "Of course it wasn't your fault, and it wasn't your fault Grandma died the same night. She'd been sick for years. Pa's just the type that has to take it out on somebody or something and he decided to take it out on you. It was just fate. Do you know what that means?" Charlie shrugged his shoulders. "It means that things are always going to happen, and we can't do anything about it." That wasn't much of a consolation to Charlie.

They waited until Henry fell into a drunken, snoring stupor

and they shared one last hug before she crept out of the house. It took Henry longer these days to wake up from his drunk from the previous night but once the cobwebs were cleared from his head he noticed the absence of his daughter. Perhaps she was in the outhouse. He looked outside and the door with the half-moon carved into it was slightly open indicating it was unoccupied. He went out to use the outhouse and then looked around for her afterward. She was not performing any of her usual chores and he instinctively knew she had also abandoned him. He reentered the house and stared at his youngest son.

"Well, what's the story? She's gone too ain't she?" Charlie approached his father much like his sister had approached him when their brother left, a note from his sister in his right hand. Henry took it rather calmly and held up a recently lit candle to see the writing. It was short and sweet, much like the letter from his older son two years ago. She had run off with a friend of the young woman his son had run off with. Charlie had not read it because his sister had asked him not to. It contained something he would not know for years. His sister confided in the note she was three months pregnant. A shotgun wedding. Henry knew the boy and felt sad they were leaving the area. He was big and strong and would have made a good farmhand. Better than either of his own sons. Henry didn't say anything. He slumped in his chair and worked on braiding a piece of rawhide.

"I'll go do all the chores," Charlie announced as he began walking to the door.

"Fix us some breakfast after you gather the eggs. Make them the way I like them, or you'll be sorry," Henry said matter-of-factly to his youngest child. Charlie had no idea how to make eggs, and he certainly didn't know how his father liked them. That was always a chore performed by his sister. It didn't seem like a good time to mention that, so he made his way to the chicken coop to pick up the eggs their hens had laid since the day before. What he found was a fat black snake which had not only eaten several eggs but had consumed at least one baby chick. The hens were making a terrible fuss and Charlie grabbed a big rock and pounded the serpent to death. He picked it up and carried it off a few paces and found five eggs left. It would be enough for him and his Pa. He took the basket of eggs back to the house.

"What took you so long, boy?" his father asked while still braiding.

"There was a snake in the coop. He ate a few eggs and one baby chick. I killed him with a rock and took him off a ways," Charlie explained.

Henry looked at his son skeptically. "You'd best get a fire going in the stove. I'm hungry."

Charlie could build a fire in the stove. He had done it many times and was successful in his first attempt. He put the cast iron skillet on the stove and looked at his father. "How do you like your eggs?" he asked. A storm cloud quickly made its way across Henry's face.

"How long have you been living in this house, boy?" he asked. "Ain't you paid attention to anything? You have to start with some lard in the pan. Your brother knew how to make eggs the way I like 'em. Your sister did, too. Why don't you know how to do it? You're nothing but a worthless, stupid curse on this house and on me! I bet there wasn't no snake because you're a liar to boot!" Charlie realized what his father had been braiding as he stood up from his chair. In his right hand was a whip. The handle was made of wood and there were three rough rawhide braids attached to it. Each braid was three feet long. "In the Bible they called this a scourge. If you don't straighten up, I'm gonna tie some bone and glass to these braids just like they used to do back in the old timey days. That'll open you up good!" Henry advanced toward Charlie. "Now, lean over that chair right there. I'm gonna teach you what'll happen to you if you don't stop being a sluggard!" Charlie knew there was no use fighting his father. It would only make matters worse. He leaned over the chair as he had been instructed, and the whip came whistling down on his back. The first blow made him cry out and lose his breath. The next two came swiftly after the first and his father was satisfied. "Now, I'm going to show you one time and one time only how I want you to fix my eggs. If you don't do them right, you'll get the whip again. That's a promise you can take to the bank."

From that day forward Charlie did his very best to stay busy during the day while his father was semi-sober. He was forbidden to attend school any longer because there was simply too much to do on the farm. He didn't keep track of the beatings he received, but they averaged two or three each week. His worst beating occurred because he fell asleep in the sweet corn patch one night while guarding it against racoons who always seemed to sense when the corn was ready to harvest. He was an honest boy and even though he knew it would be a horrible punishment, he admitted to his father what had happened. The raccoons had made away with about half the corn harvest, and they had been so sly he never heard a thing. His father was infuriated and added the promised bone fragments and pieces of metal and glass to the whip, and it tore open his flesh when it was applied to his bare back. Charlie had to contort his body to reach all the wounds and apply some liniment to them to keep them from getting infected.

Charlie turned fifteen years old in January and in late March he had spent the entire day from sun-up to sundown plowing and planting their biggest garden ever. He was exhausted from his labor but still fixed his drunken father something to eat before falling face down on his bed and going fast asleep. He was normally a light sleeper but, on this night, he slept hard, barely moving from his original spot. He was having a wonderful dream about playing with young nephews or nieces. He didn't even know if they existed because his brother and sister had never sent for him to come live with either of them. In the middle of his deep sleep, he was awakened by the familiar sound of the dreaded whip whistling down upon his back. He cried out in pain and held his arm out to try and fend off the frenzied blows from his father who seemed enraged but shouted things that made no sense to Charlie. A piece of metal from the whip ripped open a gash on his left arm and Charlie struggled to get to his feet, still holding that arm out to protect his eyes. The cabin was bathed from the light of a full moon, but he still ran into the potbellied cookstove in the middle of the room. The cast iron skillet was still on the stove, and he grabbed it. He had been so tired he had failed to clean it so he knew he would suffer another beating because of that. His father was cursing him apparently because he wasn't landing any heavy blows with the whip. Charlie had no idea what had brought the attack on. Henry didn't need much of a reason to beat his son. The pain from the whip was excruciating and the thought occurred to Charlie that his father meant to kill him. His drinking had never been worse, and the beatings had intensified. Charlie had finally had enough. He waited for the precise moment when his father reached his whip hand back behind him to generate another blow and Charlie swung the heavy skillet as hard as he could, connecting with the left side of Henry's skull. Charlie heard the sickening sound of the skull being caved in and Henry collapsed as if he had been shot. Charlie stood over him panting. He could feel the blood flowing down his back from multiple wounds. He had a foreboding thought as he stood there looking at the lifeless form of his father. He thought how much trouble he would be in for wearing his work shirt to bed and getting it ripped by the whip but that was no longer a concern.

Charlie held his hand in front of his father's nose and mouth to see if there was any breathing and there was none. He took the three fingers of his right hand and applied them to the left side of his father's neck to detect a pulse and there was nothing. He sat down heavily on the edge of his bed and slowly removed his shirt. He didn't want the cloth to stick to his wounds. He sat there for several minutes, his mind racing. The magnitude of what he had done swept over him, but he did not cry. He hadn't cried since his sister left. He got up and lit several candles and he stared at the crumpled body of his father. Henry stunk because he rarely bathed and now there was the added stench of death on him. Blood poured from his skull and his nose and spread across the floor like streams overflowing their banks. Adrenalin overcame exhaustion so he managed to move his father's body from the floor to his bed and covered him with a sheet. He sat back on the edge of his own bed and attempted to lay out a plan for the morning. He could take anything of value from the house and light the cabin on fire. Everyone would just think Henry had fallen asleep drunk as usual and knocked over a lantern or candle and died in the flames. He could simply bury Henry in the family plot and tell everyone he drank himself to death. Everyone who knew him wouldn't doubt the validity of that tale. However, if someone dug up the body, they would find he had lied and then he would probably stand trial and hang if convicted. Did they hang boys his age? He doubted it but it didn't seem worth taking a chance.

He finally decided to make the trip into town in the morning, find the constable and tell him his story, the truth, and maybe also convince the town doctor to come out and examine the body. Charlie had the scars to prove his father's abuse of him. The cuts from that night would still be fresh. Henry had built a reputation as a drunkard so that might also help Charlie's case. He once again applied liniment to all his cuts. There wasn't a single place on his back he couldn't reach because he had done it often enough. Once that had been accomplished, he laid back down and slept peacefully for the first time for as far back as he could remember. There would be no more beatings.

Chapter 2

Charlie awakened to the crowing of one of the several roosters on the farm. The things which had happened the night before seemed like a bad dream until he looked across the room and saw his father's body under the sheet. Henry's right arm was exposed and hung down almost to the floor. Charlie had no appetite and decided not to waste any time. He saddled the horse he had gotten from his grandfather's estate and pointed him in the direction of town. Along the way he thought he should have left a note on his father's body, explaining what had happened and he was on his way to town to tell his story to the local officials. He soon decided that it was a foolish notion. No one ever visited them. No one wanted to be around Henry, not even the most benevolent people. He was a base individual, and he also smelled awful. Charlie put his fine horse into an easy lope. His grandfather was an excellent judge of horseflesh and had raised harness racing horses years ago. This tall buckskin he had named Sandy could keep this pace all day and not raise a lather. They made it to town after one hour and he made his way to the constable's office first. He tried the door, but it was still locked. There was a bench in front of the office, so he sat down, put his hat over his face and closed his eyes. He was still spent from the night before. Just as he dozed off, he heard the door open, and he looked up to see the constable walk out. He was a medium sized man, sturdily built. Charlie noticed he had a square jaw and looked like a law man.

"You waitin' for me?" he asked Charlie, who stood up.

"Yes sir, I am. My name is Charlie Mabry. My family farm is seven miles west and a bit north."

"I know where your family lives." The constable's name was Warren Heisner, and he had been elected a number of years ago. Apparently, he did a good job since he still had one. Either that or no one else wanted it. The town was known to be a quiet, law-abiding place filled with people who simply wanted to work and earn an honest living. "What is it I can do for you, Sonny?"

Charlie liked the fact he was direct and to the point. He decided to do the same. "I came to town to report a death in the family." Charlie waited expectantly for Constable Heisner to question him.

"Who died?" he asked bluntly.

Charlie always told the truth, and he was determined to do that today. "My Pa. My Pa died."

Warren didn't seem too surprised at that news. "What happened? Did he drink himself to death? Did he get drunk and fall off his horse and break his neck? What happened?" he repeated. Everyone knew about Henry's propensity to drink too much.

Charlie hadn't rehearsed what he was going to say about the fight. He took a deep breath and began. "It was me. I'm the one that killed him."

The constable looked at Charlie carefully before he proceeded. "What do you mean you killed him? Why would you do that? Was it an accident?"

"I can honestly say I never intended to kill him," Charlie said convincingly. "He attacked me with a whip in the middle of the night, and I grabbed a frying pan and hit him so hard with it that it killed him. It caved in his skull. I was just trying to get him to stop hitting me."

"Good Lord," Warren muttered. "Whatever possessed him to beat you with a whip?"

Charlie didn't have to think about that question. "My Pa always blamed me for my Ma dying because she died having me. We found out later that my Grandma Mabry died that same night. My brother left five years ago, and my sister left three years ago.

He took all his anger out on me. I've got the scars to prove it. Do you want to see?"

Warren put his hand out to stop Charlie from unbuttoning his shirt. "I do want to see them, but I want us to go over to the doctor's office and we'll both take a look together."

Charlie nodded and turned around back the way he came and walked beside the constable. He had passed the doctor's office on the way to see Constable Heisner. They didn't have far to go and Heisner opened the door and allowed Charlie to enter first. The doctor sat at a messy desk, reading a thick book. Charlie had been in this office twice before, once with pneumonia and once with a broken arm which his father had caused. Charlie remembered that day well. He had been seven years old and was sitting on the rail fence of the corral watching his brother work with a yearling colt. Charlie had finished his chores thirty minutes before but that wasn't good enough for Henry who walked by and pushed him off the fence onto the hard ground inside the corral. Charlie wasn't expecting it, so he fell awkwardly with his arm pinned under him. His brother had run to him to check and see if he was hurt and saw instantly the arm was broken.

"Charlie's arm's broke, Pa," he announced. Henry shook his head.

"A fall like that shouldn't break an arm," he said disgustedly. "The stupid kid can't even fall right." He thought for a minute. "I guess you'd better load him up on the wagon and take him to see the doc in town. Tell him I'll pay him the first chance I get."

The brothers took their time getting into town that day because every time the wagon was jarred by a hole, or a rock Charlie would wince or even cry out in pain. Charlie remembered the antiseptic smell of the doctor's office and he couldn't detect much of a change all these years later.

"Well, hello Charlie," Doctor Burlington greeted him. "I haven't seen you in years. You look fine today. What seems to be the trouble? Hello, Heisner."

"Doc. Charlie has something he wants to show the both of us,"

Constable Heisner said. The doctor appreciated a good puzzle or riddle, so he said nothing but waited as Charlie pulled his suspenders off his shoulders and unbuttoned his last good shirt. All his other shirts had at least one cut in them from his father's whip. His shirt was half tucked into his pants so when he got unbuttoned all the way, he didn't remove the shirt completely. He simply pulled his arms from the sleeves and let the shirt hang down. He was facing the two men, so he slowly turned to present his back to them. At first neither one of them uttered a word. They made no sound at all for several seconds until the doctor finally spoke.

"By God, Charlie," he began. "Who did this to you?"

Charlie stood still, allowing the men to come closer and examine his scars. He had not bathed that morning, so the newest stripes were particularly shocking. There were four or five deep fissures which all started along his right shoulder where they were the deepest and crossed all the way over to his left shoulder area where they were shallower.

"Come on over here and sit on my examination table and let me bring in some more light so I can see your back better," the doctor said as he gently directed Charlie to the table in the middle of the room. "Swing your legs over and face the other wall." Doctor Burlington lit a lamp and hooked it over an arm of a tall wooden stand next to the table. The doctor muttered to himself as he examined Charlie's back with gentle fingers. "There are several of these wounds that are going to need a few stitches each so they can heal properly. It's going to hurt like the devil and you're too young to give any whiskey to."

"I'm used to pain, Doc," Charlie said matter-of-factly. "I reckon I can handle a little more if you think that's what you have to do."

"I'm going to wash your back real good before I get started. There's a whole lot of dried blood back here." He poured some water into a kettle and set it on the wood stove by the front door of his office. A fire was already burning and his coffee pot on the stove began to drown out some of the other smells in the room.

"Mind if I pour myself a cup, Doc," Constable Heisner asked.

"Help yourself. I'll just be over here slaving away while you enjoy my hospitality."

"Much obliged," Heisner said, and the doctor looked Charlie in the eye and shook his head.

"Are you a coffee drinker, Charlie? Would you like a cup?" he asked.

Charlie shook his head. "I like the smell of coffee, but I never got used to the taste. As I recall my father was kind of put out about that, too." He stopped and reflected a bit. "It didn't take much to cause him to raise his hand against me."

"So, your Pa did all this to you?" the doctor asked. "I'd like to take a whip to him and see how he likes it."

"I'm afraid you're too late, doc," the Constable said. " And besides that, you'd have to stand in line behind me. Charlie tells me his father woke up in the middle of the night and took a whip to him while he was laying on his stomach in his bed. Charlie grabbed the nearest thing he could find and hit his Pa with it and caved in his skull. Henry's body is back at the cabin. Charlie came in to tell me what happened."

Doctor Burlington was busy preparing needles and sutures now that he had prepared Charlie's back. "What did you use to hit him with?" he asked.

"A cast iron skillet," Charlie replied, wincing as the needle pierced his flesh for the first time.

The doctor was skilled and worked quickly. "That would certainly do the job."

"I need you to do three things for me, doc," Heisner said. The doctor didn't answer him, so he continued. "First, I need you to tell me those wounds came from some kind of whip. Second, I need you to come meet the judge with me before he leaves town so you can tell him what you think. Third, I need you to come with me and Charlie to look at Henry's body and make sure the boy is telling the truth. Since you're also the coroner you'll need to make out your report once you've examined his body."

The doctor was tying off the first batch of stitches. "Business isn't exactly jumping through the window today so unless something changes, I can go with you whenever you're ready."

"Much obliged," Heisner said. "Charlie, when the doc finishes with you, I want you to come down to the hotel. That's where we'll find the judge and we can talk to him together and you can show him your back. I'll see you in a bit."

"Yes, sir," Charlie said as the doctor finished the second opening. "I have money to pay for all this work you're doing on me," he announced. "I found my Pa's whiskey money."

"Oh, no, you keep your money," the doctor said. "I'll just charge it to the town or to the county, whichever one has some funds."

In ten minutes or less the doctor sent Charlie on his way and told the boy he was going to gather what he needed for the trip to his cabin and then he would go to the livery stable and have his buggy prepared. He would be ready when his companions were.

Charlie walked a few blocks to the only hotel in town and entered the door to the lobby. His back felt stiff from the stitches, and he walked carefully so they would not open. Constable Heisner was deep into a conversation with a man in a black suit with a white shirt and black bolo tie. The man had wavy white hair on his head and a trim white beard. Judge Dandridge motioned Charlie over to the table and extended his hand to the boy.

"Charlie, I'm pleased to meet you." He took Charlie's hand and shook it firmly. "The constable tells me you have something gruesome to show me." There were no other people in the lobby except for a nosy clerk who kept his eye on the boy. Charlie performed the same ritual as before and showed his back to the judge. "Doc must have thought these few were deep enough to need stitches. I'd like to hear your whole story, Charlie, if you don't mind."

Charlie started with what he had been told about the night he was born. He related to the judge about the broken arm incident and countless other times his Pa had beaten him or whipped him. He lamented the times his brother and sister left home, leaving him alone at last with the man who despised Charlie. He finished his speech with the actions of his father the previous night and what Charlie had done to his Pa.

"Doc and I are going with Charlie to the farm after we're done here," Heisner informed the judge. "Doc can examine the body and then we'll bury Henry in the family plot." The constable looked down to his feet for a moment before continuing. "Charlie, I hate to pile more trouble on you, but I was going to come out to your farm this week to see your Pa. The bank has foreclosed on your property. Your Pa hasn't made a payment in several months and the president of the bank wants his money one way or the other. I'll try and buy you some time to get your affairs in order at the cabin before I serve the papers on you. I sure apologize to you for giving you more bad news."

"It's alright, Constable Heisner. You're just doing your job," Charlie replied. He wasn't surprised at the news. His father had squandered his share of his inheritance from his parents on strong drink. He had begun dipping into his own funds after that. Nothing much was coming in at the moment, so the remaining money disappeared every time Henry made it to town. He would sell a hog on occasion, but it was never enough to keep up with his insatiable appetite for liquor.

"It sounds like a self-defense case to me," the judge said to the pair. "How old are you now, Son?"

"I'm fifteen, sir," Charlie answered.

"He's still a minor so if you and the good doctor find what Charlie has said to be true when you examine the body, just write it out and I'll sign it the next time I'm in town. Charlie, I wish you well from here on out. Do you have any idea what you might do next?"

Charlie had given that some thought on his ride to town. "I have a brother in Springfield. I've lost track of my sister. I don't know where she might be. Maybe I'll see if I can live with my brother and his family a spell until I'm old enough to strike out on my own."

The judge shook Charlie's hand once more. "You're a tough young man. I'm sure you'll figure out what to do with your life. Good luck to you. Before you leave town perhaps you should check at the post office to see if one of your siblings has written you a letter. Maybe your sister has tried to contact you to let you know where she has settled."

For some reason that had never occurred to Charlie. "Thank you, sir. I'll do that right now."

Heisner told Charlie he would meet him at the livery stable as soon as Charlie had checked for any mail. The boy walked down the street a short distance to the busy post office and waited his turn. When he was next to be served, he asked if there was any mail for anyone in the Mabry family and to his surprise there were four letters addressed to him and his Pa, two from his brother and two from his sister. He sat on a bench outside the post office and opened each letter with a pocketknife he had gotten as a Christmas gift from his grandfather Mabry. His grandfather was a kind man and never once had he blamed Charlie for the death of Charlie's mother or his own wife. After opening the letters, he read the ones from his brother first. To his surprise Charlie found out that he was an uncle. His brother and his wife were the proud parents of a baby boy, and they hoped Henry and Charlie would make the forty-mile journey to Springfield to meet his wife and new son. The second letter repeated the request for a visit and included some details on what the little boy was now able to do as he continued to grow. Charlie opened the first letter from his sister, and she informed her father and him that they had settled in western Kansas in a town called Garden City. Ironically, the man who had gotten his sister pregnant had apparently repented of his sin and had become a pastor of a small church in that community. She also requested they consider a visit to their humble home because she had given birth to a boy and was pregnant again and wanted them to meet her husband and their child. The second letter announced the arrival of a baby girl. Charlie took the letters and put them in his saddle bag when he got to the livery stable. The doctor and Heisner were waiting for him and since Charlie hadn't removed his saddle from his horse, they left immediately to make the seven-mile trek back to the Mabry farm.

Upon arrival, Charlie led them into the cabin, and the doctor wasted no time removing the sheet covering Henry's body and began to examine the head wound.

"You must have swung pretty hard to bust his skull like that," he said as he continued moving Henry's head from side to side, looking for any other wounds. He stripped the body looking for bullet holes or stab wounds but found nothing else. He poked and prodded at Henry's nearly naked body, turning him over to check him thoroughly. The doctor concentrated on Henry's liver area. "His liver feels as tough as a boot. It's a wonder he was still alive. Maybe he was pickled." After fifteen minutes or so the doctor had completed his autopsy. "He died from the blow to his head, that much is certain. It's my opinion he would have died in the next few months from liver failure or a heart attack. The man was a serious alcoholic. I don't have any reason to misbelieve anything Charlie has told us, Heisner. He's a minor but there's not a court in this territory that would blame him for what he did even if he was of age."

Heisner nodded his approval. "Charlie, let's find a couple of shovels and see about burying your Pa if Doc is done with him."

Burlington shook his head slightly. "I'm done with him. I'm going to write it out as a cut and dried case of self-defense resulting in a massive head wound to the deceased."

"Then you, me and the judge are all in agreement. Charlie, you don't have anything to worry about. I'll see that you get one week from today to get everything you need from this place and then you'll have to vacate it. The bank president won't like that, but he can just wait. I think he already has somebody interested in buying the place. It wouldn't take much to make it into a fine home for someone who will take care of it."

The constable and Charlie spent the next two hours digging a suitable grave for a man who didn't deserve any favors, and the three men struggled to get the heavy body from the house to the hole in the ground. Heisner fashioned a wooden cross as a marker with Henry's name on it. Charlie didn't know when Henry was born so they only put the date of his death on it along with his name. After the burial the two men set off for town and they wished the boy well again. After they were gone Charlie began going over the entire cabin inch by inch to see if there was anything of value, either monetary or of sentimental value. He didn't feel there could be anything worth remembering about this place.

Charlie did find a few keepsakes belonging to his mother and he packed them into a flour sack. He also kept the whiskey money he had discovered and found a few other silver dollars and some paper money hidden under a floorboard in one of the corners of the cabin. He had been extremely lucky to have stumbled upon a loose board. He wondered if perhaps his father had hidden the money in a drunken state and had forgotten where he had put it.

After his perusal of the cabin, he made his way to a workbench in the small barn and among the tools strewn across the top of the bench were also a few old pistols belonging to his father and grandfather. There was also an old single-shot carbine and an eight-gauge shotgun laying out on the table. The carbine and shotgun were in good condition, recently oiled and cleaned. The pistols on the other hand were a hodge podge of pre-Civil war guns and a couple of newer models. Some had cracked handles, and some were just in pieces amongst the other weapons. Charlie had never been allowed to inspect the guns and was not trusted to own one yet, but he had secretly wanted to look at them and feel them in his hand and now he had the opportunity. There was no one to stop him.

He began by taking apart the pistols which were still intact and arranged the different pieces of six or seven old pistols in separate piles. One pile consisted of cylinders, another with barrels, another with handles and so on. The light was poor in the barn so he lit a lantern and once he could see better, he inspected the different piles. He would pick up each cylinder and roll it in his hand, trying to feel a difference in each one and he would put the cylinders back on the table in order from best to worst in his opinion. He examined the barrels next to see which one had the best feel and had the least amount of wear. He looked through each barrel to make certain they were straight and true and ranked them as well. He ran an oily piece of cloth through each barrel. After a few hours he was ready to begin building the best pistol from the best pieces from each pile. He selected a yellowish handle and attached the truest trigger action and cylinder and barrel. He put in a new looking firing pin, loaded the cylinder with six cartridges and took the gun outside. He held the gun up to look down the barrel to the small sight at the end of it, aimed at a tree about ten paces away and squeezed off a shot. Not only did he hit the spot he was aiming at, but the weapon also felt like an extension of his arm. He was proud of what he had accomplished because the gun had a good feel and good balance to it and was accurate as well. His grandfather had a belly holster so Charlie decided that it would be the weapon he would carry on his person. He had to scrounge around for a suitable scabbard for the shotgun but when he was done around midnight, he had an arsenal of two large pistols which would ride in a double saddle holster, his belly gun, the carbine along with the shotgun he was afraid to even try and shoot. It was his grandfather who had told him that he would rather have something and not need it rather than need something and not have it. He found enough ammunition for each weapon to have a dozen shotgun shells, two dozen bullets for the carbine and over two hundred rounds for the pistols which were all the same calibers. He found a brown pouch, just the right size to house the ammunition. He blew out the lantern and went back into the cabin to sleep. He would take the time to eat when the sun rose.

Chapter 3

When Charlie awakened the world seemed a much brighter place. The roosters were crowing, one of the cows mooed loudly, begging to be milked. Birds were singing their happiest songs, and the sun was creeping up from the east. It would be a good day to start his journey. He attended to the cow to give her some relief and after drinking a little of the milk he poured the rest into the hog trough as a treat. He decided to stop by his aunt and uncle's homestead to tell them what had happened, and he also intended to give the three cows, one ram, five ewes and their lambs to them. They could have the chickens and hogs as well. They wouldn't last long without someone watching for chicken hawks, coyotes and snakes. He hated the thought of simply abandoning them so once he had everything loaded on Sandy, Charlie headed west a few miles to the farm of the only relatives within forty miles. His uncle didn't trust Charlie or any other boys for that matter to be around his two youngest daughters so Charlie knew the visit would be brief.

"Don't bother gettin' off your horse, boy," his uncle Nelson said, meeting him fifty yards from the cabin's front door. "What do you want? Make it quick and then skedaddle."

Charlie didn't blame his uncle for distrusting him. He had heard stories from several boys when he was still in school about the second to youngest of the five children. She was two years younger than Charlie, but it was easy to see she was going to be a beauty. She seemed to know it as well and used her good looks to get anything she wanted. She happened to come out on the front porch to throw some dishwater out onto the ground and when she recognized Charlie she waved at him. Charlie completely forgot why he had come to their home.

His uncle looked back over his shoulder and saw what Charlie was looking at. "You get yourself back in the house, girl! Go and help your Ma!" He turned back to Charlie, an exasperated look on his face. He couldn't trust her at all. Just two weeks ago he shot a load of rock salt into the rear end of a sixteen-year-old boy who had tried to lure his daughter into the hay loft behind Nelson's back. He considered it a challenge to keep his daughter pure, no matter how hard she tried to cast purity aside for the sake of excitement. Charlie considered his cousin might end up a saloon girl someday. Or worse.

Nelson had lost all patience with Charlie. "Boy, I'm gonna wear you out if you don't tell me what's on your mind!"

Charlie came to his senses with the threat. "No, sir. I don't believe I'm ever going to let anybody wear me out ever again." Charlie matter-of-factly removed the piece of leather that held one of his saddle pistols in place and rested his hand on the handle of the weapon. Nelson's expression changed quickly. He had heard rumors about how his brother-in-law treated the boy.

"Rest easy, Son," he said calmly. "What is it you wanted to tell me?"

"I've already seen the Constable, the doctor and a judge in town, and I told them what I did."

Nelson was confused but urged Charlie to continue. "What did you do, Charlie?" he asked.

"Pa beat me nearly half to death a couple of nights ago while I was asleep in my bed. I defended myself and hit him with a skillet and killed him. The judge said it was self-defense and they're not going to charge me with any crime. He's buried back in the family plot and the constable told me he was going to serve papers on Pa to foreclose on the farm. Pa spent almost all his money on strong drink. The doc also told me Pa's liver was nearly done so that would have killed him soon. Anyway, I came to tell you so you could go and claim all the animals and anything else you might want. I'm headed to Springfield to see my brother. I'll never come back here."

Nelson stared at his nephew. His mouth was open in shock. "Good Lord! I can't believe you went and done that to your Pa. I know he was rough as a cob but maybe you should have thought about running away instead of killing him."

Charlie smirked at his uncle. "I was pretty sure you wouldn't offer me a place to stay. I didn't know where my brother or sister were until I checked the mail when I was in town yesterday. My brother is in Springfield with his wife and baby boy, and my sis is somewhere in west Kansas with her husband and their boy and girl. I'm on my way to my brother's place now. I can make it there sometime tomorrow."

Nelson continued to gawk at his nephew. "I didn't even know they was gone," he said.

"Nobody comes around much. Why would they? Pa smelled worse than a pen full of hogs and he'd curse anybody that did try and visit." Charlie pulled the reins to his left to turn Sandy. "I just wanted to offer the critters to you. I hate to see some varmint come in the night and pick 'em off. I'll leave that up to you, though. I'll be on my way now."

The shock was still heavy on Nelson, and he waved feebly at Charlie's back. Charlie trotted Sandy down the lane to the road he could take to the east a ways before turning south a bit and then back east. That would lead him to the main road which would lead him to Springfield. It was a forty-mile trip, and he figured he could make it easily in two days. He hated to backtrack, but it was necessary to see to the care of the animals on the family farm. Once he and Sandy got back to close to where they had started from, he felt a sense of relief. The trip was a joy. He had never been allowed to go anywhere except to school two days a week when he could attend and when it was in session. He smiled most of the way that first day and he found that camping out was soothing to him and he slept hard that night.

Once he got to Springfield he had to ask directions to the address on his brother's letter. Even though Springfield was huge compared to what he was used to, he found the little house rather easily. He tied Sandy to a rail before climbing the three steps to the front door. He knocked and heard a small child crying inside. There was a female voice speaking soothingly to the little boy and at last the door opened revealing an exhausted looking young woman carrying a small red-haired boy in her arms. She looked Charlie over carefully before speaking.

"Is there something I can do for you?" she asked. Charlie hoped he hadn't awakened the boy from a nap. His mother certainly looked as if she could use one herself.

"I'm sorry, ma'am," he began. "Would this be the Mabry home?"

"It is," she replied, bouncing the sobbing child on her hip. "Who might you be?"

Charlie remembered his manners and removed his hat. "I'm Charlie. Charlie Mabry. I believe your husband is my older brother."

The young woman's head snapped back a bit in shock. "Oh, my goodness!" she exclaimed. "I can see the family resemblance. Come on in! James will be home from work soon. He's in for the surprise of his life." His sister-in-law's name was Charlene and Charlie's nephew was William. He liked her right away and found her easy to talk to. Charlie sat on the floor and let William crawl all over him while he and Charlene conversed about his trip to Springfield from the old home place. He deflected any personal questions until his brother James arrived. Charlie felt the time had gone by quickly and the front door opened suddenly, and James broke into a huge smile upon seeing his brother.

"I wondered whose horse that was!" he exclaimed, crossing the room to embrace Charlie. "I can't believe it's you!" James picked up William who extended both arms to his father. "When did you get here?"

Charlie reached out and patted his nephew on the back. "No more than twenty minutes, I reckon. This boy is fine, just fine."

"You must have gotten my letters," James stated. "I never got any letters back, though."

Charlie shook his head. "Pa was never one to do much writin'," he said. "Maybe you should sit down before I tell you what I have to."

James took Charlie's suggestion and sat by Charlene. "Didn't Pa want to come? I only saw one horse."

"That's what I need to tell you," Charlie began. "I'm sure you've had letters from Jane. She's someplace called Garden City, Kansas. After you two left Pa started beating me worse and worse." Charlene apparently knew about her father-in-law's habits. She didn't seem surprised at the news. "He was drinking all the time, spending every penny on whiskey and such. A few nights ago, I woke up with him whipping me with this awful thing he called a scourge. I defended myself with a frying pan and after I clubbed him with it, he died." James and Charlene were dumbfounded. "I didn't mean to kill him. I just wanted him to stop. I told my story to the constable, the doc and a judge who was in town. It was the judge that said it was a clear-cut case of self-defense. The constable also told me the bank was foreclosing on the farm because Pa hadn't paid anything at all against the loan for months. The constable gave me a week to clear out, but I couldn't wait to get out of there. I left only two days after I busted Pa's skull." Charlie hesitated a moment before adding one last thing. "Me and the Constable buried Pa next to Ma in the family plot."

James had conflicting feelings about what his brother had just told them. Their father had never done more to him than a few earned swats on the rear for some misdemeanor. He was ashamed that he never tried to prevent Pa from administering such terrible punishments on his little brother. To make matters worse, he had left the first chance he got. There were nights he awakened with a nightmare about what might be happening back at the farm to Charlie. It was his innate fear of his father which prevented him from ever coming back. "My lord," was all he could manage to say. "My lord."

Charlene sat quietly through the story, at times shaking her head in disbelief. Tears rolled down her cheeks and she reached out to take William from her husband.

"I found some money I think Pa forgot that he hid and took it. There was a little bit of his whiskey money left. I spent hours taking pistols apart and saving the best pieces to build three good ones. There was an old single-shot carbine and Grandpa's eight gauge cannon out on the workbench in the barn. I went to Uncle Nelson and offered our farm animals to him. I sure hope he went fast to get the pigs and chickens at least before the coyotes have 'em for breakfast."

"What did Uncle Nelson have to say when you told him all this?" James asked.

Charlie shook his head. "He didn't even know you and Jane had left. It had been a fair number of years since our families had got together for big dinners like we used to. Nobody wanted anything to do with him, including me, but I didn't have much choice." He saw James's head dip. "I don't mean no disrespect toward you or Jane. I would have done the same thing if I was in your shoes."

"You boys need to let your sister know about this news," Charlene reasoned.

Charlie had been thinking about that on his way to their house. "I've decided she deserves to hear it in person, not by a letter. I've got to figure a way to get there and let her know. I've got a hankerin' to see her two kids and meet her husband." He turned to address Charlene. "You were acquainted with him, weren't you?"

Charlene nodded her head. "We grew up in the same area about three miles apart and we were closer to the school across the way, so we went there. Me and my brothers and sisters spent many hours playing after church with him and his five brothers. They were a rough and tumble bunch. I remember his Pa being one of the foulest mouthed people I have ever known. It's kind of surprising to me that he became a preacher."

"You're too young to make that kind of a trip on your own, Charlie," James said. "Maybe you can find somebody who's going west that way and strike up with them. If you're serious about going, I'll start keeping my ear to the ground to see what I can hear."

"Until then you're staying with us, and I won't take no for an answer. Maybe James can help you find some work to do until you can head to see Jane," Charlene ordered.

Charlie easily settled in with the young family. He would go searching for work during the day and help his brother and sister-in-law with chores around the house in the evening to pay for his keep. It felt good to lay his head down at bedtime and not have to worry about suffering his father's wrath in the middle of the night. He couldn't grieve for his mother since he never met her, and he refused to grieve for his father who was the basest sort of a man. Inside of a week, Charlie found a job sweeping and cleaning for the local gunsmith. Before long he had demonstrated his ability to deftly repair pistols, and Mr. McConnell paid him two bits for every gun he fixed on top of the money he was already making. Charlie used his regular pay to keep Sandy boarded at the livery stable and he saved his extra money for his upcoming trip out west. Sometimes his customers would tip him with some extra money for a job well done. He gave that money to Charlene because he felt guilty about imposing on them. He wanted to pay for at least some of the food he was consuming.

Little William loved his Uncle Charlie. Charlie would whittle in his spare time, and he made tiny wooden farm animals for his nephew. It was fun to hand him some new figure, tell William what it was and make the sound the animal made. The little boy was a quick learner, and he would make the noises repeatedly until it became an annoyance to his parents. Charlie just snickered when Charlene would give him a look that meant she wished he wouldn't be so helpful.

Charlie had never known such an ease of life. After six weeks of his employment, his brother James came home from work with exciting news. "I know you can ride a horse, but can you rope?" James began. Charlie nodded his head because he liked to practice throwing a rope at the pump back at their cabin. He felt he was proficient enough at the skill. He wondered about the question. "The reason I ask is a man who has a big ranch north of town came into the bank today. He opened a new account and deposited a fair sum. I overheard him say it was for supplies and to pay men to help him drive a herd of horses somewhere in eastern Colorado to a fort. The army is in need of good horseflesh, and he said his were some of the best. He's going to be at the saloon tomorrow looking to do some hiring. It wouldn't hurt for you to go down there and fill out an application."

Charlie furrowed his brow. "Why would I do that?" he asked.

"Because eastern Colorado is next door to western Kansas where Garden City is," James explained. "If you could get hired on, you could help take the horses to the army and then backtrack to Garden City. He's a tall, slender man. He'll be easy to spot."

It all sounded good, but the practical side of Charlie was skeptical. "Will they even let me in the saloon? I'm sort of underaged. I doubt he'll want to hire somebody who ain't even sixteen yet."

James gave him a knowing grin. "Here's something I've learned about looking for employment. Don't worry about your credentials. Just march in and ask if you can apply and if they tell you that you're too young at least you can count that as experience you can use later on. I'm not trying to get rid of you. You're welcome to stay as long as you want. I hope you believe that. You're a big help around here and you pull your weight. It's just that I know you want to see our sister, and this seemed like a good possibility."

Charlie let out a big sigh. "What time do I need to be there?"

Charlie made his way to the saloon and noticed several flyers advertising for help nailed on posts as he walked. The pay seemed more than fair. One dollar per day plus good food and there was also a possibility of a bonus when they delivered the horses. Each man might also earn an additional five dollars if they arrived without losing any of the animals. There was already a line outside the saloon door at eight o'clock in the morning. The man in front of him sensed Charlie's presence and turned slowly to look down at him. He was standing on the first step to the saloon but would have towered over Charlie without the aid of the step. Charlie was happy the man didn't say anything to him or laugh at him. As each man filled out his application, he either walked back out the way he came or drank a cup of coffee in the saloon. The men who walked past Charlie gave him a surprised look but just like the man in front of him, no one spoke. It made Charlie squirm.

When he made it as far as the swinging doors Charlie could see two men sitting at a table. One had to be the owner because he met the description James had given. The other was a black man with the broadest shoulders Charlie had ever seen. He finally could hear some of the conversation coming from inside.

"This is my right-hand man Big Jim," the wiry man said. "If you get hired, you'll be taking orders from him. Ultimately, I'm in charge but Big Jim takes a lot of responsibility off me. If you have a problem with that don't let the door hit you in the butt on the way out."

The line had moved a lot more quickly because most of the men refused to fill out the application because they would not work for a black man. Charlie had hopes that might help his chances. The man in front of him was so big Charlie could not be seen by the men sitting at the table.

"What about you?" the owner of the horse herd asked as the man in front of Charlie took his turn. "Do you have any qualms about working with Big Jim and doing what he tells you to do?"

The big man shook his head. "The only time I'm gonna have any problems taking orders from anybody is if that man was a durn fool and asked me to do somethin' ignorant. Then I'd have a problem. My rule is I won't work for a man who asks me to do something he wouldn't be willing to do himself."

The owner's name was Max Dunham, and he liked what he heard from this man. He asked about his experience with driving horses and some other questions. "I'll let you know if you're hired by the end of the day. I'll post the names outside the saloon."

The big man walked to the bar for a free cup of coffee and Charlie suddenly felt exposed.

Dunham grinned at the sight of this young boy applying for a job. "Well, Big Jim, it looks like we may need to throw this one back so he can grow some more." Jim smirked at Charlie.

"I think I hear your Momma callin', boy," Big Jim said. "You better go see what she wants." Charlie stood his ground. "She probly wants you to feed the chickens or somethin'."

"I know you're just funnin' me Mister but my Ma is dead and so is my Pa. I need to find a way to get to Garden City to my sister." Charlie suddenly had a thought. "Maybe I could help your cook. You wouldn't even have to pay me."

Dunham was intrigued by the boy's persistence. "Why don't you just take a stagecoach to Garden City?"

Charlie shook his head. "I'm mighty attached to my horse. I got him from my grandpa, and I don't mean to give him up."

Dunham and Jim looked at each other. Dunham liked this spunky kid. It took a lot of guts to walk into a saloon and ask for work.

"I've got a new cook on this drive," Dunham stated. "The last one fell head over heels for a saloon girl in Wichita and one of her many lovers shot him dead. I don't know how this new man will take to having a helper if I do decide to take you on." Dunham stroked his chin as he considered. "I'll tell you what I'll do, boy. I'll ask the cook what he thinks. If he's dead set against it, then the answer is no. If he doesn't care, then maybe I'll add your name to the list. What is your name anyway?"

Charlie couldn't believe his ears. "Charlie Mabry, sir."

"Well, Charlie Mabry, what else can you do?" Dunham asked. "I know you've got your own horse."

Charlie was so excited he couldn't think at first. "I can rope, and I've got my own guns. I'm a pretty fair shot."

Dunham nodded. "Come back around 5:00 this afternoon. The names will be posted out front. Once I make my decision, that's it."

Charlie reached out to shake the hand of both men. "I'm mighty grateful for the opportunity," he managed and then fled the saloon to go to the bank to tell James. When he finished there, he went back to the house to let Charlene hear the story. It seemed to take forever for 5:00 to finally arrive but he was there when Big Jim came out to nail the piece of paper with the names on it to one of the posts in front of the saloon doors. A dozen or more men were with Charlie to see if their name had made the list. There were five names on the list and beside each name was the word 'drover', but after their names was Charlie Mabry, cook's helper. He wanted to see his name on the list, but he didn't really expect it to be there. He had to stare at the list for a minute, rub his eyes and then read the list again. It also mentioned they would be leaving in three days. Charlie was elated and ran off to tell his brother and sister-in-law the exciting news. He had found his way to reach Garden City.

Chapter 4

The next three days passed by slowly for Charlie. He would miss being with his brother and his sister-in-law and his nephew. He realized that this was a golden opportunity that might not come again any time soon and he had better take advantage of it. Each day he would go down to the holding corrals and assess the fine horses he would be helping escort to Colorado. He also met three of the five drovers along with the cook who put him to work hauling the supplies he purchased from the general store to his double wagons. There had to be some grain for the working animals plus all the foodstuff for the men. The first wagon was longer than the second and it was the shorter wagon that would haul the supplies needed for the animals. The cook had once run out of water on a drive, so he took no chances and had four large barrels of water on that same wagon, two on each side. Four sturdy mules made up the team which would pull both.

The three drovers were tolerant of Charlie. They told the boy to stay out of their way and they would get along nicely. When Charlie asked the whereabouts of the other two drovers, Dunham and Big Jim, they simply smiled and walked off without answering and Charlie didn't see any of those men until the morning of departure. The cook told Charlie he had spoken with Mr. Dunham, and the herd would move out at daybreak on the third day after the interviews had been completed.

Charlie was too excited to sleep the night before and he was ready to go an hour early. His brother and sister-in-law had anticipated that and were up as well to see him off.

"Here's a letter to Sis from us," James said. "Ask her to write us when you get there and maybe you could add some news about your trip. We'd be happy to hear from you."

"I'll do it," Charlie replied. "Thanks for bein' so good to me and all." He shook his brother's hand and got a hug from Charlene. William was still asleep. "Give my nephew a hug from his uncle Charlie for me, will you?"

"Sure thing," James assured him. "Do what the bosses tell you and you'll be all right. Good luck."

Charlie felt himself getting emotional, so he tipped his hat to them and walked out the door with all his gear. He had already settled with the livery owner and Sandy was in one of the stalls waiting for him. He had checked her shoes the day before, but he felt the need to do it again and they were snug. He saddled her, added all his weapons, swung himself up and backed her out of the stall before pointing her to the horse pens. The cook was already there to fix a breakfast of biscuits with butter and honey plus bacon and scrambled eggs. Coffee was in abundance to wake everyone up. Big Jim was next to arrive to make certain everything was in order and five minutes later Dunham came trotting up on a fine bay gelding. One by one the drovers led their mounts to the gathering place and Charlie got his first glimpse of the two drovers he hadn't met yet. One was the big man who he had stood behind when he applied for the job. The other was a tall, slender cowboy who puffed on a cigarette as he ambled up.

When each man had gotten something to eat, Dunham began to speak. "A couple of you men look like you've already been rode hard and put away wet." The two men who had gotten there after everyone else looked down to the ground and grinned while the other drovers snickered. "I wonder what you've been up to." This statement elicited another laugh but then Dunham became serious. "We're going to Fort Garland in the Colorado Territory. From here it's about 740 miles. If we can make thirty miles every day we can make it in twenty-five days. We'll take every Sunday off, not because I'm a religious man, but it's a good way to measure out some rest. You can catch up on your sleep then. There's four Sundays between now and when we should get there so that makes a grand total of twenty-nine days, give or take. I reckon the safest route will take us through Joplin, up to Wichita then Pratt, then all the way across to Dodge City in the Kansas Territory. From Dodge City it's a pretty straight shot to Fort Garland. I want to keep a nice, steady pace. Don't push 'em too hard or the cook wagon won't be able to keep up. Our cook for this trip is Hank Beltcher and one of his rules is that nobody steals anything from the cook wagon. If you want somethin', just ask him. Any questions?"

The men were paying strict attention to Dunham's words. "You take your orders from me or Jim. Our word is final. Anybody have a problem with that?" There was some muttering of agreement. "All right then. Let's get us to Colorado."

Hank instructed Charlie the way he expected his cooking utensils to be stowed, and they were ready to roll within five minutes. Sandy was tied off behind the second wagon and Charlie settled in beside Hank who slapped the mules gently with the reins and they began a slow walk westward. Dunham brought a fifteen-year-old mare named Alice out of the corral next and she fell in line with the wagon. Charlie looked around the side of the wagon to watch the proceedings.

"That's the only mare in the whole herd," Charlie said to Hank. "Why is that?"

Hank spit tobacco juice over his side of the wagon. "Alice is sort of a lead horse. She'll set an easy pace, and all those geldings will follow her as easy as can be. She's a mighty good swimmer too. When we come up on a river to cross, she'll just walk in like she's walkin' on the ground now. She never misses a beat. Mr. Dunham's been offered a mighty fine price for her but she's too valuable to sell. It might seem like five drovers ain't enough for a hundred horses, but truth be told, we could probably have left two or three of those drovers behind and been just fine. Mr. Dunham don't like to take chances, though so that makes twenty horses per man. I reckon if we run into any trouble, it'll be nice to have as many as we do."

Just as Hank had predicted, the herd settled into a peaceful pace. On the second day, Charlie untied Sandy and allowed her to walk with the rest of the horses. She gravitated toward walking with the only other female in the group and Charlie enjoyed watching her and Alice move easily down the trail. It was as if they had known each other for years. Charlie became accustomed to waking up pre-dawn and helping with breakfast. His main job was to clean up afterward and he had to learn to do that with a minimum amount of water due to Hank's paranoia, but Charlie was a rule follower, and he wanted to do a good job. He and Hank had to get everything cleaned and put away so they could get out in front of the herd. It wasn't quite so hectic in the evening and when the men who weren't watching the herd relaxed after supper, they sat around the fire and smoked and played cards before turning in for the night.

One of the things Charlie enjoyed most was listening to the cowboys who drew night hawk duty singing and talking gently to the herd to keep them calm.

"It ain't the quality of the singin' that's important," Big Jim told him one night. "Them horses just want to know somebody's there. It gives 'em some comfort." Charlie tried to listen to and memorize the songs in case he was asked to be night hawk at some point. He had lived a sheltered life and knew no songs. He especially enjoyed listening to a man who always whistled instead of singing named Eugene who could take a lively saloon song and turn it into a comforting tune the horses seemed to love. He had a quality to be admired. A couple of the men couldn't carry a tune in a bucket, but it was like Big Jim said. It wasn't the quality that was important.

Chapter 5

"Bath day! Laundry day! Who's first?" Hank cried out as he poured more hot water into one of two oversized washtubs. Charlie had been hauling buckets of water from the slow running stream below the camp for the last two hours on their first day off and Hank had been busy heating the water. He thought perhaps they would be doing laundry, but he wasn't anticipating having to take a bath. Mr. Dunham was attending to the herd, and all the other men were lounging on their bedrolls after breakfast.

"I'll go first," Big Jim announced. "Then I can spell Mr. Dunham when my clothes is dry." Jim looked directly at Charlie. "Boy, you come up here with me and old Jim'll show you other fellas how to do this." Jim began by slipping his suspenders off his wide shoulders before unbuttoning his shirt. He was facing the men as he stripped the rest of his clothes off. "When you get nekkid, you need somebody else to check you for ticks. We don't need nobody comin' down with tick fever so check everywhere. When you get sat down in the water that same man'll pour a bucket of water over your head and watch for lice. If we find any lice Hank here will shave your head. Ray, you ain't got no worries."

The men chuckled because Ray was already shaved bald. Big Jim lifted his arms and nodded for Charlie to check his armpits for ticks. Of course, that wasn't the only place ticks might congregate, and the men chuckled again as Charlie had to check between Jim's legs.

"I don't see nothing yet," Charlie said, and Jim slowly turned in the water to face away from everyone and when he showed his back to Charlie the young man was startled by what he saw. None of the other men uttered a sound but they all stared at the big man's back and shoulders. Whip marks were everywhere on his flesh, but the worst thing was a huge 'X' which stretched from shoulder blade across and reached to just above the buttocks on the opposite side. It hadn't been whipped into Big Jim. It had been cut into him with a knife.

Charlie tried his best not to be alarmed at what he saw. He was somewhat thankful he noticed a tick attached to Jim's rear. "Jim's got a tick back here," he announced to Hank.

"Use these tweezers and make sure you get all of it," Hank commanded.

"Me?"

"You're his partner, ain't you?" Hank asked.

Charlie did the job carefully because he didn't want to have to do anything more with it. Once he removed the tick he held the tweezers up to Hank for his approval.

"That's fine, Charlie," Hank said. "Finish checking him and we'll put something on it when he gets done with his bath. Gather up his clothes and wash them good."

Charlie obeyed as Jim scrubbed himself vigorously with the hot water and strong soap.

"Soon as you hang up my clothes it'll be your turn kid," Jim said.

"My turn? Why can't I just bath in the stream?"

"'Cause I said so, that's why." Jim continued his scrubbing. "I know you boys is dyin' to know about my scars. I could feel your eyes on me. My last master was a fine man but the one before him whupped me and cut me for runnin' off one too many times. I reckon I should be happy he didn't just go ahead and hang me. I know he thought about it long and hard."

"Where was you at Big Jim?" one of the men asked.

"I was on a plantation just outside of Jackson, Mississippi. I got to where I didn't care if I lived or not, so I took off. I got about five miles before the dogs run me down. They tied me to a tree and whooped me nearly half to death and that 'X' was what they called the mark of Cain. Somebody told me that was in the Bible somewhere. It weren't the first time I felt the whip on my back."

Charlie listened intently as he scrubbed Jim's clothes on the washboard. He knew there was no fighting the bath. If he chose to resist, the men would simply grab him and tear his clothes from his body. It was going to be degrading either way. He wondered what the men would think of his own scars. He hung up Jim's long underwear, shirt, trousers and socks on a line which he and Hank had run earlier in the morning. Just as he finished, Jim stood up and stepped out of the tub to begin drying off.

"Your turn kid," Jim said. "Start shuckin' them clothes off."

Charlie glanced at the other men who were already snickering. He sat on a rock and pulled his boots and socks off. He undressed the same way Jim had done but before he removed his long underwear, he walked behind the washtub facing away from the men. He thought if he showed them his back perhaps they wouldn't make fun of the fact he was much less endowed than Jim. Charlie took a deep breath, unbuttoned the front of his underwear and pulled them off his shoulders. He heard one of the men utter an oath under his breath. He allowed the garment to fall to his feet and stepped out of them and into the water. Jim had never seen a white person with whip marks, and he couldn't speak for a moment. He noticed some of the wounds had been stitched.

"Who done this to you, Charlie?" he asked, and it was the first time Big Jim had called him by name.

"My dear old Pappy gave those to me."

"What did you do, aggravate him?" one of the other drovers asked.

"He was aggravated at me from the day I was born 'cause my Ma died givin' me life. He blamed me for her death."

Hank came over and examined Charlie's back. "I'd have killed him if he done that to me," he said.

Charlie stared straight ahead at the prairie. "That's what I did," he said. "I killed him one night with a cast iron skillet up the side of his head."

Jim began the task of searching Charlie for ticks and he took his time, examining the worst of the wounds. "One of you boys go and get Mr. Dunham. He needs to see this." The youngest of the drovers jumped up and got on his horse and left quickly but not so fast as to spook the herd when he found the trail boss. Five minutes later Dunham rode into camp, irritated by the fact that the routine had been interrupted. One look at Big Jim caused his anger to dissipate. As he walked closer to Jim and Charlie he could see the stripes on the boy's back.

"His Pa's the one what done this to him for somethin' that weren't his fault," Jim stated.

Dunham was stunned. "What did he think you'd done to deserve this?" he wondered.

"I was born," Charlie said simply. He went on to explain to Dunham and the others in a little more detail what had happened to him in his young life. He admitted he needed to come on this adventure to see his long-lost sister in Garden City, but he intended to finish the job he was hired to do and then he would backtrack from Colorado.

Charlie was finally allowed to sit down in the warm water and bathe himself while Jim personally washed his clothes. All the men treated Charlie with great respect from that point forward. He didn't take advantage of his situation. He simply wanted to be one of the men.

Chapter 6

The day after bath day, Dunham drew Charlie aside. "I want you to start learning how to drive these horses, young man," he began. "You've got a fine horse yourself so you might as well put him to use. You can start by riding drag with Poke. Give the herd a wide berth as you ride back to him and tell him I said he's with you today. Don't let him feed you too many lies."

"Yes sir!" Charlie exclaimed. He was excited to do something more useful than helping Hank with the cleaning. He would still make himself available as the cook's helper, but he liked the idea of learning something new. He filled a spare canteen with water, saddled Sandy along with his saddle pistols and made his way to the back of the herd, following Dunham's instructions so he wouldn't spook the horses.

When Poke saw Charlie coming toward him, he stood up in his stirrups. "Look who it is! What are you doing here kid? Did Hank throw you out of the wagon? Did you steal some sugar?"

Charlie didn't want to seem too excited as he pulled Sandy beside Poke's little sorrel. "Close. Mr. Dunham is punishing me by sending me back to learn how to ride drag from you."

"My lord," Poke said as he shook his head in disbelief. "What did I ever do to deserve this?" he joked. "Dunham sure has a sense of humor, I'll say that for him. Well, here's all you need to know about riding drag. You eat dust all day for one thing. For another thing you have to deal with knot heads like that tall gray near the back." Poke nodded his head toward his nemesis. "Here in a little while he'll start forgettin' he's supposed to stay with the herd. He'll start taking himself too serious and he'll meander off to the right until he's on his own. It's the drag's job to hurry him along back to the rest of his brothers before he starts gettin' others to follow his lead. He's a bad influence, that one is."

"And Mr. Dunham pays you just to do that?" Charlie chided back.

Poke didn't miss a beat. "It ain't just that. Another one of my jobs is to keep things light around here. Otherwise, the rest of you boys would get too bored to do any work."

Charlie laughed. "Say, I know Poke ain't your real name. I read a dime novel before we left on this drive, and it said that men and even women sometimes change their names out west. They do that because if they get in trouble with the law and they use their made-up name it would be harder for the law to pin some charge on to them. Is that what happened to you? Are you runnin' away from doing something awful?"

"You bet! I'm wanted in fifteen counties back in Missouri! And that's just countin' the women that want me!" Poke smiled at his own joke.

Charlie was persistent. "C'mon! You can tell me. I won't let anybody else know. What's your Christian name?"

"I'll give you a little hint," Poke began. "My momma named me after a famous writer. Maybe you were named after a famous writer, too. Why, the man you share a name with was so good, the king or queen of England made him into a knight! Sir Charles Dickens was his name. You ever hear tell of him?"

Charlie was enjoying the banter. "Sure, I've heard of him. We read some of his stories when I was in school, but I doubt my Pa named me after Mr. Dickens. My Ma and him must have already agreed on a name for me before I was born else he would have named me Mud." Poke found that funny. "At least tell me why they call you Poke. Is it because you poke fun at everything?"

"That's only partly true. You see, my Ma worked on the wrong side of town, if you know what I mean." Charlie's blank look told Poke he had no idea what that meant. "She wasn't exactly a respectable lady with a respectable job." Charlie still didn't understand. "She sold her favors to men, Charlie. She was a prostitute!" Charlie blushed. "Some of my early recollections of childhood was when men would come around my Ma wantin' to buy a poke from her so I just kind of adopted that as a nickname."

Charlie looked down at Sandy's mane. "I guess I don't know much," he mumbled.

"It ain't my job to tell you about the birds and the bees," Poke said with a smile. "You should ask Mr. Dunham. He's in charge of you. Don't ask any of them other boys. They'll tell you nothin' but lies. Why, there's no tellin' what kind of foolishness they'd fill your head with."

Charlie knew he had turned red as a beet from embarrassment. "So, which famous writer are you named for?"

Poke was enjoying leading Charlie on. The gray gelding was beginning to lag toward the back of the herd and Poke pointed at him. "What'd I tell you? He's got the wanderin' eye. I'll give you a hint since you've had some schoolin'. Poke cleared his throat and sat up straight in his saddle. "'Go west young man.'"

Charlie looked toward the gray. "I've heard that somewhere in one of my books. My Pa made me drop out of school because he was so drunk all the time, he couldn't tend the farm so it would have been from a few years ago." Charlie thought as hard as he could, but nothing came to mind. "Can you give me another hint?"

Poke simply smiled at him. "He's probably more famous for being a newspaper writer than for writin' books like Mr. Dickens done. As far as I know he's still alive."

"Horace!" Charlie exclaimed. "You're named after Horace Greeley!"

"Shhh!" Poke said while waving his hand at Charlie. "You promised not to tell the others and you're practically shoutin' it from the rooftops!"

Charlie could see the two men on the left flank and the two men on the right. They weren't even looking at the two riding drag. "Sorry," he said. "I'll keep my promise, Horace."

"I can already tell I should have kept my big mouth shut!" Poke said. "I don't never want to hear you say that again because it might slip out sometime and one of them others with big ears might hear it!" Charlie just grinned at him. "I ain't proud of it so that's why I go by the name of Poke. Now go convince that dumb gray to join up with the rest of his friends." Charlie obeyed and worked the gray slowly back into the rest of the herd. He didn't know Charlie, which might mean he would be harder to work with next time.

Over the next four days Charlie became acquainted with each of the other drovers. There was the extremely large man he had met first and everyone called him Slim, which Charlie found amusing. His real name was Frank Bryant, and he hailed originally from Jefferson City, Missouri. The third day Charlie rode with Raymond Kahre whom the men just called Ray. He was from a town not far from where Charlie's farm was located, and he had a wonderful singing voice which was pleasant to the horses as well as the men. It was a rich, pure baritone but he had enough of a range to sing bass as well as some tenor if it wasn't too high. He and Big Jim would sometimes sing together before turning in for the night. They knew many folk tunes as well as spirituals. When they sang by the campfire, the man riding night hawk wouldn't have to sing to the horses. He would just listen as they did to the harmonies of the two talented men.

The fourth man was a quiet sort. Try as they might, the other men couldn't draw him out to say more than a few words at a time, but Charlie still liked him. His name was Curtis Eugene Richardson, and he hailed from a little town east of Springfield. He was a no-nonsense type of man, but he wasn't rude or unfair in his judgements. He would rather listen than talk and the other men would rather talk than listen, so he balanced things out some. He measured his words so when he spoke the other men paid attention but if they tried to bait him into an argument, he would go silent, and no amount of coaxing could get him back in the conversation. Charlie felt that was wise.

The fifth man was the only one who was hard to get along with. He was from Tennessee and because of his upbringing he disliked Jim. He hated taking orders from Big Jim and more than once already Mr. Dunham had reminded him that he had agreed to do whatever he or Jim ordered. Charlie could tell it stuck in his craw to swallow his sizable pride. His name was Matthew Wharton. He had dark eyes and always wore a scowl on his face. He also had no chin to speak of and it gave him a suspicious look. It was a long day when Charlie had to ride with him, and he learned nothing from the experience.

"You ride with me today boy," Big Jim said on the last day before their next break. Jim and Dunham traded places each day, one riding scout and one riding point and it was Jim's turn to ride scout so the two rode off a mile or so ahead of the herd. The job was to check for water for the herd and generally to make sure the path was clear or at least make sure there was nothing unexpected in their way.

The two rode in silence for the better part of an hour and Jim observed Charlie riding easily on his fine buckskin. He thought he detected a slight smile on the boy's face.

"What you smilin' about?" he asked.

Charlie was a little embarrassed at getting caught. "All my life except twice I was either gettin' beat or worried about gettin' beat. The first time was when I spent time with my brother and his family for a few weeks. That was nice. I ain't never spent much time around a little kid before and I really liked my little nephew. The second time is on this drive. I like the work, and I like being outside and I like almost all the men I'm around." Jim had to smile about the final part of Charlie's statement.

"I bet I know who you talkin' about," Jim said. "I don't like that Wharton neither. He got them black, beady eyes. He hate me, that's for certain."

"Why did Mr. Dunham hire him?" Charlie wondered.

"He had more experience by a few years than them other boys," Jim replied. "I argued with him about it. I don't trust him but whenever Mr. Dunham ask me why, I can't answer him. It's just a feelin' I got deep down. That wasn't enough for Mr. Dunham, so we ended up hirin' him, beady eyes and all."

They rode a few more minutes in silence before Charlie spoke up again. "Why did you men hire me? I didn't have no experience."

Jim thought about that for a moment. "Mr. Dunham is a good man," he began. "Him and his wife never could have no children of their own, so they adopted three. They adopted a white girl, a Mexican boy and a little black boy is the youngest. Them kids love they momma and daddy and Mr. Dunham and his sweet wife love them back. I wouldn't say he felt sorry for you for wantin' to get to Garden City to see your sister, but he got a kind heart and just wanted to help. You been pullin' your weight in this outfit so just keep that up and you be fine." Jim thought further on the subject. "Maybe since you're older than his kids he can study you and see what it's gonna be like when his own kids get to be your age."

Chapter 7

The following day was Sunday and another bath day and laundry day. Charlie was clean and content, so after he finished doing the laundry he lay on his blanket with his head resting on his saddle. His comfort zone was invaded by Wharton sitting down beside him, coffee cup in hand. The other drovers were engaged in a game of cards.

"I reckon we may see some tomorrow," Wharton said in a low tone as he got settled. Charlie had no idea what he was talking about. "You ever see a real live red Indian before, boy?" It was the first mention of Indians on the trip.

"No. I ain't seen one."

"We'll be startin' on the last half of our trip tomorrow," Wharton pointed out. Dunham's got a big trunk in the feed wagon filled up to the brim with all kinds of beads and cloth and ribbon and other such things to keep the Indians happy."

"How do you know that?" Charlie inquired.

"I watch everything, Sonny. I watched when the wagon was bein' loaded and everything else was pretty normal except for all the gifts. What we have to hope for is that we don't run into any hostile tribes. He'll tell you that the dangerous ones live farther north or south from our route. My thinkin' is that they could move for one reason or another and we could run smack dab into 'em. I don't believe they'd care for him handing out some doodads for us to have safe passage to deliver horses to soldiers that might be coming out after them mounted on good horseflesh."

Charlie considered what Wharton was telling him. "What kind of Indians do we have to worry about?" he asked.

"Oh, there's Comanches and Apaches to the south. There's Sioux, Cheyenne and Pawnee to the north. I'm sure there's more than that but those are the main ones. The ones I've run into were friendly enough but they're always expectin' you to give them somethin'. I reckon that's why Dunham loaded up that trunk. Maybe they'll keep us from losin' our hair."

"Losing our hair!" Charlie exclaimed. "What would Indians want with our hair?"

Wharton grinned a sly grin. "It's called scalpin'. They take their knife to the top of your forehead and cut the hide along with the hair past the slice. And then they lift it off your head. Sometimes you're still alive when they do that. That's what I've heard anyway."

"Why don't you stop scarin' Charlie, Wharton?" Poke spoke up and to Charlie he said "Don't you worry about gettin' scalped Charlie. Mr. Dunham's made this trip more than once, so he knows what he's doin'. Why don't you come over here and let us teach you how to play cards?"

` Charlie was grateful for the invitation and got up, leaving Wharton by himself. The disagreeable man settled down in his bedroll with his hat over his eyes. He needed to sleep since it was his turn to be nighthawk. Hank had to kick him awake to feed him supper before he went on his way to relieve Dunham.

Charlie watched him until he reached his horse and rode out of sight. "I wish he was more like you fellas," he said.

"You mean smooth actin' and good lookin'?" Slim asked and everyone had a good laugh over that statement.

Hank had overheard them. "Charlie, you need to pull yourself away from them good lookin' fellas and give me a hand with supper if it ain't too much trouble."

A day off gave Hank more time to rustle up a better meal and that night was no exception. He made a hearty beef stew with dumplings and deep-dish apple pie for dessert. Charlie thought it was funny that Wharton had only received beans with a slice of bread.

"Eat hearty men," Dunham said. "It looks like we may have some rain moving in so there might not be any hot meals for a day or two. I'm sure Hank will do his best but he ain't no magician. Charlie, if there's rough weather, I may need you to ride double drag and watch for strays. They tend to get a little nervous when there's thunder and lightning. Otherwise just watch for any signs from the other men to see if they could use a little help." Charlie nodded his understanding. "Get a good night's sleep, men. If we lose some time to bad weather, I'm gonna want to make it up somehow so we may have to push them a little harder."

Charlie took his place closest to the fire when it came time to bed down. He craved the warmth. There were times on the farm when he couldn't keep up with the wood chopping due to having to perform all the other chores by himself. He didn't like waking up to a cold cabin simply because he had to conserve the wood to cook with. Wood wasn't plentiful on the prairie, and it had become one of his daily tasks to search for and gather what they needed for the day. Buffalo chips made a fine fuel, and the sage brush was good as a fire starter. The horse herd had been well behaved the last two days, and he was able to go off and gather enough to store in the feed wagon to get them through a couple of days of cooking.

Charlie dozed off to the sounds of snoring men and the crackling of the fire. He was lying on his right side facing the wagons and sometime during the night he noticed movement around the chuckwagon. He didn't move because of his fear that perhaps a wild Indian might be ransacking the wagon for anything of value. Hank slept under the chuckwagon, but he was such a sound sleeper he never moved as the figure entered the wagon from the front. Charlie was frozen to the ground and didn't know what to do. Maybe he was still asleep and this was a dream. He closed his eyes as much as possible but was still able to see. He didn't want to be detected by whoever was in the wagon. He felt that his eyes were as big as pie platters before he closed them halfway. He concentrated as much as possible on the sounds from within. He could hear some kind of scraping noise, but he couldn't identify it. The wagon pitched slightly as the figure stepped out of it and Charlie was shocked when he recognized the man responsible. It was Wharton. Charlie was surprised he would abandon his post to come back to the wagon for something. He had taken quite a chance leaving the horses unattended. Perhaps he had seen something and had come back for another weapon. All the extra guns, including most of Charlie's were in that wagon. No harm was done as Charlie heard him once again begin singing off-key to the herd. Since it proved to be someone he knew, Charlie went back to sleep and slept soundly until Hank woke him up to assist with breakfast.

Chapter 8

There were storm clouds to the northwest as soon as it became light enough to see them. There was no lightning, just dark, foreboding dark blue clouds and they were headed their way. Charlie took his cue from the others and broke out his winter coat and placed his rain slicker over it. No one wanted to get their clothes wet if a fire couldn't be built that evening. The general store in Springfield only had one size fits all for slickers so it covered every bit of him. He decided that it could be beneficial.

"Charlie, I've changed my mind, at least until the rain hits," Dunham said. "You go ahead and ride scout with Jim and if you find wood just set it along the trail and we'll pick it up and put it in the wagon. Once the rain starts you come on back and I'll put you where I need you. This is liable to be a real toad strangler."

Dry wood was going to be like gold and Charlie searched diligently. He would end up riding alongside Jim again after taking a little detour now and then jumping off Sandy and placing some limbs by the side of the trail as he had been instructed. As he looked behind him, he noticed the herd was strung out much further than normal. They seemed to sense the rain coming and were already slowing down.

"I seen somethin' funny last night Big Jim," he said as they rode alongside each other.

"What you talkin' about? What did you see that was so funny?"

Charlie almost wished he hadn't opened his mouth, but it was too late now. "I don't like the man, but I would hate it if I got him into any trouble, but Wharton left the herd last night and was doing somethin' inside the chuckwagon." Jim looked at him sternly.

"What did you see him doin'?" he asked, a concerned look on his face.

"I couldn't see a thing, but I heard a scraping noise inside the wagon. It only lasted a couple of minutes or so and then he run off back to the herd." Jim's expression didn't change.

"Now you listen to me and listen to me good," Jim began and his tone chilled Charlie more than the dropping temperature. "Ride easy back to Mr. Dunham and fall in by his side. When you get there to him you need to tell him just what you told me. Don't make no big fuss about it, just tell him plain." Jim paused for a moment to let Charlie absorb the instructions. "Is you hearin' what I'm sayin' to you?"

Charlie had never seen the big man so serious. "I hear you Big Jim. I'll do just what you say."

Jim turned in his saddle to look behind him, but they were all lagging far behind. "I feel like a fool 'cause I was the one what spelled him during the night. That means he ought to be ridin' drag this morning. That's good. You go on now and do what I told you. Don't leave nothin' out!"

Charlie nodded and put Sandy into a mild trot back to Mr. Dunham. He followed Jim's orders precisely and swung Sandy to Dunham's right side and rode along with him.

"What's wrong Charlie? Did Jim find something and send you back to report?"

"No sir. He sent me back to report on something all right but it's about something I seen last night when I was supposed to be asleep." Dunham just looked at Charlie without saying anything, so Charlie continued. "I seen Wharton leave the herd and get into the chuckwagon. I heard some kind of scrapin' sound, but I couldn't see anything inside 'cause it was pitch dark in there. He told me before he laid down to sleep yesterday afternoon that there's a big box full of things to give to any Indians we might see to keep them happy. I figured he was looking in there to see what all we had for them."

Dunham didn't change expression. "I appreciate you telling me and Jim that, Charlie. I want you to understand something though, and this is awful important. The rain is going to start in the next ten minutes or so and I need you to go back, and ride drag along with Wharton. Don't tell anybody else what you told me and Jim, especially to him. I can't stress that enough. This news you just gave us stays with us three, nobody else. Do you understand me, Son? Don't tell him you saw him last night at the wagon and don't tell him you passed this information on to us. Swear that to me now." Charlie saw the seriousness on the face of Mr. Dunham.

"I swear it, sir," he replied.

"Good. Here's what's gonna happen now. As soon as it starts raining, I'm going to ride back to the chuckwagon and tie my horse to the side. Wharton shouldn't be able to see me from back in the rear. I need to check something in the wagon but if he does see me and asks you what's going on you just tell him you don't have no idea."

"Yes sir. That ought to be easy 'cause I don't have no idea what you're going to be doing."

Dunham smiled at him. "Good boy. Here she comes."

The raindrops began slowly at first, but it didn't take long for them to intensify and soon visibility was cut in half. Dunham nodded to Charlie to indicate it was time for him to go ride another drag position behind the herd and Charlie trotted Sandy back to where Wharton was. The man looked questioningly at Charlie as the boy came close.

"I'm supposed to ride drag with you until they tell me otherwise. Mr. Dunham's worried about the storm," he announced to the suspicious man, but Wharton simply nodded at him, rain pouring off the brim of his hat.

Dunham made his way slowly back to Hank who was surprised to see him. He was even more surprised when he transferred over to the seat beside him and tied his horse to the wagon.

"Just keep goin', Hank," he said. "I need to check something in the wagon." Hank knew enough not to try and ask questions, but he wore a perplexed look on his face. Dunham tried to be careful but there were only so many places he could hide the lockbox with the money for purchasing supplies and paying the men at the end of the drive. He knew Wharton wasn't looking to see what items he had bought to barter with any Indians they might come across. He was looking for the money. The box was under some blankets and the first thing he noticed was that the lock was still in place. The light was poor due to the darkness brought about by the storm, but he looked carefully at it anyway and couldn't find out if it had been tampered with. He dug in his inside vest pocket and found the key to the box. Jim had the only other key. He inserted the key in the lock and turned it, noticing that it turned with more difficulty than he remembered. Perhaps he was just being paranoid. He thought he might not have detected anything if he hadn't known there was the possibility of tampering.

It was just as difficult to see inside the box due to the darkness, but Dunham turned the box to what little light there was and what he saw made his body tremble. There were eight men to pay, and he allowed for thirty days to make the drive. That came to two hundred and forty dollars plus he brought another one hundred dollars for supplies. Without taking the time to count he noticed the five twenty-dollar gold pieces for supplies were all missing. He wondered why the thief didn't take all the money when he had the chance and then made a run for it. He decided that Wharton believed he hadn't been seen and was waiting for the best time to get away. What a fool. The perfect time would have been last night. He could have taken the entire box and made away with it while he was on night duty. The only thing that made sense to Dunham was that there was a new moon in the sky, and he would have had to be careful as he fled. Dunham and Jim could have caught him the next day with ease. Dunham put the lock back on the box and placed it under the blankets again and made his way to the seat of the wagon.

"Don't tell anybody what I was doing, Hank," he instructed. "That's an order. It's important."

"Too late. Curtis was riding flank over on this side and he seen your horse tied to the wagon."

Dunham looked over at the drover as he performed his job. "He should be okay. He barely puts more than two words together at a time, but I'll say something to him."

Dunham took hold of the reins of his mount and slid easily on to him. He rode slowly up to Curtis and ordered him not to say anything about seeing him in the wagon. Curtis simply nodded and touched the brim of his hat to acknowledge his understanding of the order. Dunham looked to the rear of the herd and Wharton and Charlie were struggling to keep stragglers on pace. It was going to be a long, hard day.

The cold rain persisted all day and they were fortunate to make around two-thirds of their goal for a normal day, but it still put Dunham in a more sour mood than he was already in. He had to replace Curtis on nighthawk duty because the quiet man wouldn't sing. He would only whistle and the constant rain prevented him from making a sound. Ray would have to replace him for the first watch and Slim would still be his relief as planned.

Hank's mood was no better as he and Charlie struggled to get the fire started under Hank's protective canvas covering the back of the chuckwagon. The wood wasn't wet. The humidity was causing the issue they faced. Dunham finally snapped at Hank to stop wasting time and matches and ordered him to make a cold supper of beef sandwiches and cold beans with no dessert. That put everyone else in a foul mood except for Jim and Charlie. Charlie liked sandwiches and there was less to clean up after a cold supper.

Dunham had been stewing all day about how to handle the Wharton situation. Confronting him would be tricky. He had to make certain to get the money back before everyone bedded down in case the thief made a mad dash out of the camp and caused more hardship in tracking him in the wet conditions. He couldn't allow Wharton to stay on after he retrieved the stolen money. As bad as he hated to, Dunham would pay the man for time spent even though he was a thief but then he would dismiss him into the night. Both Dunham and Jim watched Wharton like a hawk to see if they could tell if he had the stolen money on his person or had hidden it somewhere else. The men milled about in misery from the rain, and they lined up for their food.

"Men, I have some disturbing news," Dunham began. "I check the money box from time to time. I can't say why I do that. If I don't get into it to pay for supplies, it ain't going anywhere but that's just the way God made me." The men managed slight smiles. "I suppose maybe I checked it 'cause we're going to come into a town in the next couple of days and we'll need to lay up a few things. The problem is when I checked it today there was at least a hundred dollars missing. I haven't taken the time to count it yet but all the twenty-dollar gold pieces I had for supplies are gone." He looked at the men to see if he could detect anything from Wharton, but the man had a blank look on his face. "I trust Jim and Hank came with good references and I know he wouldn't steal from me. But one of you did steal from me. I've already talked to young Charlie, so I don't believe he did it. The thief knew how to pick a lock. I can see that it was messed with when I examined it under the light of a candle just a little while ago." Dunham looked at each man in turn for just a few seconds. It'll go easier on you if you just admit it and return the money. Which one of you stole the gold?"

Curtis looked at Dunham and now understood what his boss was doing in the wagon earlier in the day. The other men stole glances at each other. Everyone except for Wharton. He stared at his boss with something resembling hatred or indignance.

"You know in Old Testament times they used lots sometimes to find out a guilty party. It could take some time, but they cast the lot on each man until they narrowed it down finally," Dunham explained.

"And then when they found him, they throwed stones at him until he was dead," Jim added.

"Yes sir, that's just what they did. I'm a fair man, though. When I find out who did it, I'm going to pay them for time spent and then ask them to leave immediately. I don't want to see their face again because if I do see their face, I'm gonna kill him. We'll just agree to cut ties."

Dunham was beginning to lose patience. "I see we have nobody who wants to admit their guilt. All right. Jim, start searching each man."

Jim was closest to Poke, so he searched him first. After that, he checked Slim, then Ray, then Curtis and finally Wharton. He was surprised when he found nothing on him.

"All right," Dunham said. "Check their saddle bags." Jim started in reverse order. He was surprised again when Wharton's saddle bags did not contain the stolen money. Curtis was next, then Ray, then Slim and finally Poke. When Jim stuck his hand in one of Poke's two saddle bags, he felt the coins. He pulled out some of them and showed Dunham."

"Oh no!" Poke exclaimed. "I don't know how those got there Mr. Dunham! I'll swear on a stack of Bibles that I didn't take that money! I don't know how to pick a lock. You've got to believe me, Mr. Dunham! Somebody must have put the gold there!" Dunham was taken aback by this turn of events. Charlie's story made perfect sense to him, and he trusted the boy. Wharton must have planted the gold in Poke's saddle bag in case his own were searched. Dunham hadn't wanted to drag Charlie's name into the discussion, but it had become unavoidable.

"I know you didn't take the gold, Poke," Dunham said. "The money was taken last night while Wharton was on nighthawk duty." He shifted his full attention to the perpetrator. "You left the herd during the middle of your shift didn't you Wharton? I know you did it because Charlie saw you. He got a good look at you when you left the wagon. He heard you making some kind of scraping sound. That sound was you picking the lock. You must have planted the money in Poke's saddle bag in case I ordered a search before you could make off with it." There was no change in Wharton's expression, but everyone noticed he wasn't denying it. "I asked myself this morning when I found out the money was missing why you just didn't take the whole box and carry it off while you were alone on nighthawk. There was a lot more money to be had. I know you didn't leave it out of the goodness of your heart."

Wharton stood in defiance before his accuser. "Too dark," he simply replied. Dunham was surprised at the statement because it gave him the answer to his question, but it was also an admittance of guilt. Dunham offered a wry smile.

"Did you find all ten gold pieces, Jim?" he asked. Jim jangled them in his huge hand.

"Yes sir. I got all ten of 'em right here."

"Put them back in the box for me Jim and draw out the fifteen dollars I owe this thief."

Jim was gone only a couple of minutes and dropped a five-dollar gold piece and a ten-dollar gold piece into Dunham's open hand. Dunham then threw the money at Wharton who never moved, and the coins glanced off his chest into the mud. He bent down and retrieved them, taking the time to rinse the mud off both coins in a water puddle. He slipped the coins into his pants pocket.

"I guess I should be grateful you didn't hang me or shoot me," he said as he turned to get his saddle.

"Don't tempt me," Dunham said, glad to nearly be done with him.

Wharton expertly saddled his horse and mounted him. He walked him around the picket line and looked straight at Charlie. "Nobody likes a snitch, kid!" He spurred his horse as hard as he could and aimed the animal right at Charlie. The mud prevented Charlie from getting out of the way and the big animal slammed into him, knocking him three or four feet sideways into the mud as Wharton rode off. The blow didn't knock Charlie out completely, but he was stunned and his shoulder burned like it was on fire. The rest of the men in camp were so shocked they didn't have time to draw their pistols and shoot at Wharton.

Hank wasn't just the cook. He was what passed as a doctor for the drive. He pulled the boy out of the muck and began checking him to see what was wrong. The boy held his left arm up to his waist with his right hand. Hank quickly checked to make sure the collarbone was intact and then he ran his hand down Charlie's left shoulder and found it to be completely out of place.

"Jim, you hold him tight now. I've got to jerk his arm and get his shoulder back in its rightful spot. Charlie this is gonna hurt like thunder, but it's got to be done."

Charlie was fighting tears. "I know," he managed and just as he said that Hank placed his own foot on Charlie's left hip and tugged with all his might on his left arm. The shoulder jumped back into place and Hank was relieved he could once again feel the boy's shoulder blade. The shock caused Charlie to cry out, but Jim held him close.

"Take the pain, Charlie. Take the pain. I know you done took lots of pain in your life. This ain't so bad now, is it?" Jim's calming voice helped.

"Poke, fetch me the whiskey bottle inside the wagon above the sugar box. I should have given him a shot before I yanked his arm. I apologize for that Charlie, I really do. Now take a big slug of this and it'll help you with the pain," Hank said. Charlie obeyed and the liquid burned all the way down to his toes. He didn't notice it making him feel better right away but maybe it would help him rest.

The men made over Charlie and fixed a place for him to sleep in the dry of the feed wagon. They had used enough of the feed to allow Charlie to fit snugly, and Hank stayed by his side until the boy fell fast asleep.

Dunham motioned Jim to join him under the canvas of the chuckwagon. "It's bad enough we're down one man but now

Charlie won't be able to help either. It's been a long day. You take the early nighthawk duty, and I'll spell you in a while. We'll figure things out in the morning." Jim nodded his understanding and hurried off to perform his duty.

Poke approached Dunham with hand extended. "I wanted to thank you for believing me when I said I didn't steal that money, Mr. Dunham."

Dunham shook the man's hand. "Don't thank me. Thank Charlie. You can do that when he wakes up in the morning."

Chapter 9

Charlie awoke in the wagon to Hank's pleading. His shoulder ached terribly.

"Wake up boy," Hank said. "I need you to try and eat a little somethin' before we get started. If you thought Dunham was in a bad mood yesterday wait till you see him this morning."

Charlie noticed the rain still poured down from the heavens. He was dry inside the canvas of the feed wagon, and he was truly grateful for that. Out of his line-of-sight Charlie heard Mr. Dunham using words he never could have imagined coming out of his mouth. Dunham was mad at the weather, mad at the circumstances of the day before and mad at what promised to be a long, slow day. In between swear words Charlie heard the threat of no day off this coming Sunday so they could make up for lost time. Charlie felt guilty for being unable to help his friends.

"Eat this oatmeal, Charlie," Hank ordered. "It'll stick to your ribs." Hank tried to spoon feed the thick mixture to Charlie.

"I can do it," Charlie said as he took the spoon away from the cook. He took a big bite even though he didn't care for oatmeal because he knew he needed something. "Can we rig some kind of a sling so I can at least ride and lend a hand?"

"I'm way ahead of you." Hank produced a white sling and slipped it over Charlie's head and under his bad arm. "That shoulder needs rest so you can just forget about ridin' a horse until I say you can. Chances are you'd fall off and hurt yourself worse and then there'd be more hell to pay from what I'm callin' the angriest man on the face of the earth right now. The more you rest the faster you'll heal up. Then you can help. The only time I want you out of this wagon is to relieve yourself. I'll help you do that right now and then I'll check on you every couple of hours. Get a move on. We have got to get started."

Charlie didn't have anything else to do but sleep and eat but after two days he took his case to Dunham to try and help the exhausted men.

"I've had plenty of rest the last few days," Charlie argued with Dunham as Hank listened in. "Maybe I can help more than you think. I'm still a little scared to try it but I volunteer to take an all-night watch with the herd. They're mighty tired too I guess so I don't think they'll give me any trouble. The rain is finally over. I won't have to ride except out to the herd and back in the morning. That would give all of you a break you need so you can catch up on your sleep."

When Dunham heard Charlie's request it made him realize he had been kicking himself for hiring a lout like Wharton and he had been taking that decision out on the other men. Hiring the boy had proven to be a fine choice and he felt vindicated. He still had misgivings about letting him take on such a large responsibility. Jim walked up as Dunham prepared to give Charlie his decision.

"How sound is he Hank?" Dunham asked the cook. "Is his shoulder healed enough to sit his horse all night?"

"I've been workin' his arm some the last couple of days, and it don't show no sign of popping back out. The muscles in his shoulder have healed enough to hold it in place. As long as he don't overdo it I think he'll be fine."

Dunham put his arm on Charlie's good shoulder. "Son I truly do appreciate what you're offering to do. That being said you're too young. I can think of a dozen things that could go wrong and how would you be able to handle them even if you were whole? No, I think we'll trudge through this spell of bad luck we're in. We've only got about two whole weeks left and then we'll be at the fort. You rest one more day and then we'll see about letting you sit your horse and help herd for a few hours the next day."

"Can I say somethin' Mr. Dunham sir?" Jim asked.

"Speak your piece Jim," Dunham returned.

"How about me and Charlie do the nighthawk job for a few nights? I'd bed down right out by the herd so if anythin' went wrong, I could help right quick. If Charlie needed somethin' I'd be handy. I'll take another blanket from the feed wagon, so I don't need no fire to keep me snug. When Charlie gets to feelin' better, he can help them other boys drive the herd."

Dunham saw the wisdom in Jim's idea. To make up for time lost they were going to have to push the horses a little past nightfall each day until they reached their destination. It wasn't that he would get more money for bringing the animals in on time. He just hated being late. If he ever did business with that fort again, he didn't want them to remember him by being the rancher who didn't get there when he said he would. It was bad for business.

"We'll try it tonight and see how it goes," he said, and Big Jim smiled at Charlie. The boy was just happy to be contributing again.

Charlie was right about the herd being tired. After supper Big Jim found a spot on a knoll where he made his bed and could see the boy and the horses. Charlie eased Sandy into the middle of the animals, and he settled into his saddle and began to talk to the herd at first and then a little later he attempted his first song. His voice was weak and quivery, and he hoped Big Jim was already asleep, so he didn't hear but Jim heard him and smiled. He knew that Charlie had made up his song about good horses compared to bad horses, quiet horses compared to noisy horses, and he sang to them about their new job in the army. Charlie had picked out the gray gelding in the light of a half-moon. He was pleasantly surprised that the troublesome animal was content to stand close to the others and sleep.

The job proved to be boring after the first couple of hours and when his time was up, he crept Sandy through the other horses, talking to them quietly so they wouldn't become startled.

He made his way to Jim and shook him awake. Jim told him not to sleep on the hill but to go back and claim his spot in the wagon and when breakfast was served, he was ready to do his job as drover. It was very satisfying, and his sore shoulder mended so quickly he was almost back to normal in just a few days.

The third week ended with Dunham keeping his word about working on their day off. He found himself looking over his shoulder a dozen or more times each day, expecting Wharton to come in with a gang and try to steal the money and the herd. It would amount to a fair sum. Even though he was tired like the rest of the men he would ride back the way they had come at the end of the day checking to see if they were being followed. Sometimes he thought he saw a campfire in the distance but that could be anyone. The nearest town of any size was fifty miles away and he knew that Wharton would need some time to get to a town, hire some thugs and get back. Dunham toyed with the idea of getting within three days of the fort and sending Big Jim to go and fetch some soldiers just in case. Some of the horses were green broke and Jim was a fine horseman. He could have a fresh mount and get there and back in three days since the herd would also be making its way west.

Jim had been contemplating the same thing so they picked out the gelding who looked the sturdiest of the lot and still provided the speed he would need. They were fortunate to pick one which was more than half broken and it didn't take Jim more than an hour to get him calmed down enough to ride.

"I'll see you in three days," Jim said as he rode west. Everyone knew why he was leaving except for Charlie.

"Mr. Dunham is a might worried that Wharton might come back and try somethin'", Slim explained.

"You mean by himself?" Charlie wondered.

"No, he's too big of a coward to do that. He'd have to find a good-sized town and convince some men to join up with him. Money is a mighty powerful bait for bad men," Slim said. "I've never been out this far west, so I don't know anything about where the towns are of any size. I wouldn't get too worked up worryin' about that scoundrel. Just the same I can't get past the feelin' we're bein' watched."

Slim's statement made Charlie uneasy, and he wished he had the instincts of the older men. For some reason he had started this trip expecting each day to be like the one before it but that certainly wasn't the case.

Chapter 10

It had been two days since Jim had left the herd to go to the fort. They were only six days away from the end of the rainbow. Mr. Dunham still rode scout, but he stayed much closer to the other men and the herd than he previously had. It was a cloudless day with a light blue sky as far as the eye could see. The men were engaged in their jobs with Curtis on the right front flank of the herd when half a dozen red Indians on a ridge appeared suddenly about twenty yards from his position. When Curtis finally saw them, he almost fell off his mount. The men wore buckskins, and each wore a band on their heads to tame the long black hair each possessed. They carried long lances and had bows over their shoulders and quivers of arrows on their backs.

"Mr. Dunham!" Ray called out because all Curtis could do was stare with his mouth open.

Dunham turned and saw the newcomers and immediately trotted his mount back to where they stood on high ground. He held his hand up at shoulder height and the red man in the front of the group did the same. Charlie watched Mr. Dunham make some hand motions directed at the man who appeared to be in charge and then was surprised when the Indian made hand motions in return. He had never heard of such a thing and was fascinated at the back and forth between the two men. Soon Mr. Dunham turned his horse toward the feed wagon, dismounted and motioned Ray to help him unload the massive trunk which held the items he had brought along on the trip to trade with the

Indians. It wasn't locked so he lifted the lid to reveal bright colored cloth, materials of all colors, ribbons of gold, silver and scarlet and multitudes of various sizes of beads. Dunham had also packed several pounds of tobacco.

As the leader got down off his pony Charlie wondered what Mr. Dunham was going to receive for some of the goods they were both sorting through. The Indian he was bartering with reached into the trunk and pulled out an oddly shaped hat with a feather attached to it. Dunham allowed each of the men to select something from the bounty if it wasn't too big such as an entire roll of ribbon. He measured some gold ribbon off and used his knife to cut a length for one of the braves who seemed keenly interested in it. He accepted it with the look of a satisfied customer. After each man had accepted a gift of some sort Dunham pointed back to where the drive had already come. He made some other hand signals, and the six red men got back on their horses and made their way back to the east.

"What was that all about?" Poke asked.

"Help me with this trunk again will you Ray?" Dunham requested. The trunk was scarcely any lighter and the two men struggled to get it back in the wagon. "That was an Arapaho hunting party. Did you see the way they painted their horses? It's one of the ways you can tell what they're up to. I just traded a few trinkets for their help. They're going to go back the way we came to see if we're being followed. I gave them sort of a description of Wharton."

"What did you tell them to do with them if they found 'em?" Slim asked.

Dunham remounted his horse. "I just asked them to chase whoever they found back the way they came. The hair on the back of my neck has been standing up for a while. I haven't actually seen anybody yet. Maybe our friends there were the ones making me anxious. Let's get everything moving again." Before turning his horse back to the front, he called out to Charlie. "How're you doing back there Son?" Charlie looked down at his left arm in a sling.

"I'm doing okay. Just a little sore is all. Mr. Dunham, sir, I've never seen hand language like that before. How did you learn it?"

Dunham grinned at him. "It's called sign language, not hand language and I learned it in the army. It's what they call a universal language. That means anybody can understand it no matter what other language they actually speak. I'm not as good as some are at it. I just kind of make it up as I go along but they seemed to understand me."

Charlie was fascinated with that notion. "Do you think you could teach me?" he asked.

Dunham turned his horse to head back to the front of the herd. "Not on this drive. Maybe when we get to the fort and rest a few days but not until then. There's too much else going on."

Charlie questioned the other men at supper about sign language and the only one who had any knowledge of it at all was Hank, so he showed the boy a few hand gestures and what they meant.

"How do you know old Hank there is telling you the truth?" Poke was always the instigator and tonight was no exception. "He may be tellin' you to say to some Indian to stand in front of a chargin' buffalo or somethin'!"

Hank was finishing stirring the stew pot and he pointed the large wooden spoon at him. "Poke, you brainless horned toad! If you were talking to an Indian about buffalo the sign would be like this." He sat the spoon down and put his hands on either side of his head and raised the index finger of each hand. He bent over slightly to make it appear like one of the buffalo they had seen on the drive, and he even moved his head around and pawed the ground with his right foot. This amused the drovers, and they raised a raucous laugh. Slim's big belly bounced up and down and he nearly fell over from his seat on his blanket. Dunham was watching the horses until Curtis could finish his meal and take his place.

"I sure am glad you straightened us out on that Hank," Poke said through his tears. "That's some mighty useful information!"

Hank looked at Charlie with exasperation and shook his head. "I'm afraid it's useless. You can't teach these boys nothin'". He spooned some stew onto a plate and brought it to Curtis. "Eat this and get out of my sight so I can have Mr. Dunham come back to camp. It'll be nice to have an intelligent conversation for a change." Curtis accepted the plate and as usual said nothing in return. "I'll tell you one thing. If we ever get attacked by red Indians and they tell us they'll spare our lives if one of us lets them cut out one of our tongues I'm gonna elect Curtis. He never uses his anyhow."

The men laughed again, this time at Curtis's expense but he simply glared at the cook. He wolfed the food down, walked over and threw his plate and fork into the wash bucket and mounted his horse to relieve Dunham. A few minutes later Dunham rode into camp, unsaddled his mount and Charlie went over to brush his horse for him.

"What did you boys say to Curtis? He's always in a bad disposition but it was even worse tonight."

"Hank insulted him is all," Poke answered. The other men fought to keep their composure.

"What did you go and do that for, Hank?" Dunham asked his cook. Hank wasn't happy with Poke, Ray and Slim as they turned Dunham against him. He didn't want to defend himself because he believed he wasn't in the wrong, so he threw the wooden spoon on the ground and pulled his apron off and tossed it into the chuckwagon.

"You can get your own supper!" he snapped as he walked away disgustedly.

Dunham shook his head as the three remaining drovers got on their feet and made their way to the cook pot. "I don't know if I can take too many more days of this. If you boys don't want to cook your own meals, I suggest you lighten up on Hank. Charlie, you relieve Curtis tonight. I'll bed down where I can see you like Jim did."

Chapter 11

Twenty miles behind the herd the six Arapaho braves crouched in a buffalo wallow and watched the same number of men huddled around a fire. The leader surmised these must be the ones the white man with the horses had asked them to scatter. It was only an hour since sundown and these white men had settled in to eat. He had been thinking as they rode along what they might do once they came upon this party. There was no need to kill them. That would only make the white soldiers angry, and they might seek revenge. These men were not soldiers and their horses did not bear the soldiers' brand. They were fine animals however and he surmised the best thing to do would be to steal the horses from these men and put them on foot. That would satisfy the man up the trail and it would give them six good horses to take back to their village. His chief would be proud of him, and he would be a hero to the rest of his people. They all would be. He became lost in his daydreams until one of his companions nudged him for instructions. Silently he told them they would wait to see if the white men posted a guard or if they would be foolish and all go to sleep at the same time. He indicated they would wait to see what happened in the camp before they acted.

After their meal the white men produced a bottle and began drinking and passing it around. Each man drank and that meant each man would fall asleep with no guard. Their watchers simply had to bide their time until these irresponsible men drank so much, they would no longer be able to keep their eyes open. Darkness fell and the men began speaking more loudly than before and their laughter could be heard from far away. Their fire began to burn out so the last man who could stand threw some more sticks on it until the flames licked upward again. He then passed out next to the fire and the braves crept out of their hiding spot and over to behind the white men's horses. There was only one of the braves who had ever stolen a white man's horse before, and he expertly grabbed the muzzle of one of the animals to keep it quiet. The rest of the horses moved from side to side, reacting to strange men handling them but they were subdued easily, and the lines were cut. They had no use for saddles, so they began walking quietly back the way they came leading the stolen stock.

The braves had made it about halfway back to their own horses and did not notice the sleeve of the man who had passed out by the fire was smoldering. There was no wind, so the smoke from the cheap jacket went straight up. The sleeve finally caught fire, and the pain jostled its owner. He sat up suddenly and began to swear loudly while slapping his arm against the ground to put out the flames. This commotion awakened the other men, and they sat in a stupor watching the proceedings. A couple of the men laughed at their comrade's predicament and one of them fell backward in his glee. When his eyes adjusted to where the horses should be he noticed in his fog they were gone.

"Our horses is gone!" he shouted. All the men struggled to their feet and stared at the spot where they had tied their animals. The braves stepped up their pace to try and disappear in the darkness but the last one in line was detected by one of the white men and he drew his pistol.

"Indians!" He took no time to aim and fired into the darkness. His hurried shot turned out to be lucky and he hit the trailing brave in the back between the shoulder blades. The other men began filling the dark air with lead, but their shots weren't as fortunate. The next to last brave in line collected his friend's stolen horse and they all disappeared into the dark prairie. The white men were struggling to follow on foot and by the time they got to a point where the braves had collected their own horses it was too late to stop them. They could hear the whooping and hollering the braves made as they led the stolen horses away.

Wharton looked wide-eyed into the darkness in the general vicinity of the sound of hoofbeats and squeezed off one more useless shot from his pistol. They would never be able to retrieve their own horses while on foot and the herd of Mr. Dunham was too far ahead of them. Every mile they would try to follow only put them in a more perilous situation and farther from the safety of any town. He had failed at yet another robbery attempt and this time it could cost him and his fellow thieves their lives. To the west lightning brightened the sky and there was a ten or twelve count before the thunder rolled across the prairie, shaking the ground. Ten miles away and moving fast he thought. It would be a powerful storm that would pile on to their misery.

Two of the braves returned a little later to retrieve the body of their brother. They carried him out to where one of the white men's horses stood and they draped him across the back and led him away to join the others. It wasn't fitting to leave him behind for the animals of the prairie to devour. He would be given a hero's funeral.

Chapter 12

The thunderstorm which poured buckets of water on Wharton and his thugs was only a light sprinkle on the horse herd as they began another day of trudging across the prairie. Five more days remained on their journey and Dunham wasn't certain how many days they had been in Colorado Territory. His best guess was three days but there were no boundaries between the Kansas Territory and Colorado. The men were in a much better mood now that Wharton was gone.

Big Jim hadn't returned when he said he would, and Charlie and the other men could tell Mr. Dunham was concerned that something might have happened to him. They only had to wait one more day and Jim arrived with an escort of a dozen soldiers from the fort.

"I was beginning to worry about you," Dunham said. "Did you run into some trouble?"

"Nah. Not really. I spotted a pretty good-sized bunch of Indians along the way, so I had to make a long trip around 'em. When I told the colonel at the fort about that, he sent these soldier boys along with me. I don't think he was so much worried about us as he is about his horses he's buyin'. They be addin' lots of new soldier boys and they ain't got no horses to ride."

"You did good, Jim. We'll fix their horse situation pretty quick," Dunham stated. "Did the colonel have anything else to say?"

"No sir. He didn't seem too happy talkin' to me. He was from one of the Carolinas. They still fightin' the war between the states down there."

Dunham wasn't surprised. "They'll be fighting that war for decades I'm afraid. Well, let's push the herd a little harder the rest of the day. How many more days to the fort, Jim?"

"Four more days, Mr. Dunham," Jim replied.

Dunham wasn't afraid to put the soldiers to work but he left the night hawk duties to his drovers. They had made it this far and he was unwilling to allow green hands to watch over the horses after the sun went down over the next few days.

When the fort finally came into view Charlie was surprised to see several Indian lodges outside the gates. The Indians living there just stared at the men and horses as they walked past. A uniformed man of medium height walked from his quarters to greet Mr. Dunham. Charlie didn't know the difference in rank.

"Mr. Dunham, I presume," the soldier said as he extended his hand.

"Pleasure to meet you, Colonel," Dunham replied. "Here are your new mounts. What do you think of them?"

The colonel nodded his head enthusiastically. "They are a good-looking bunch. I dare say they make our current horses look mighty bad. Did you make it here with all one hundred?"

"Minus one, I'm afraid. Broken leg from stepping in a prairie dog hole so I had to shoot it." Dunham looked around at the facilities. "Do you really need all these animals, Colonel? It doesn't appear that you have the room for them."

"We'll keep half and take the other half to another fort about a hundred miles from here. I don't suppose you'd want to take on that chore for more pay?"

Dunham shook his head. "No, Sir. I don't believe we'd want to do that. I'll be happy to get the agreed upon price."

"I understand. There's a town about fifty miles from here, but you and your men are welcome to stay here for a night or two before you head back or do whatever else you've got on your mind," the colonel offered. "I have the money in the safe in my office."

Dunham agreed and he paid the men what he owed each of them including a five-dollar bonus for the success of the drive.

Charlie had never seen so much money. Dunham collected what was owed to him just before they left two days later, and he placed it in the strongbox in the wagon. The men said their good-byes to each other as they left the fort. The drovers had decided to go to the town they had been told about and Dunham, Jim, Charlie and Hank with the wagon directed themselves east to head back to Missouri.

"Charlie, would you like to know what those men are going to do with their hard-earned money?" Charlie nodded. "They'll start out by drinking a large amount of liquor. Then they'll visit a house of ill repute if there is one and then they'll get in a card game with a bunch of experienced gamblers who will take whatever funds they have left and if they're lucky they might get through a whole week before they go broke. Then they'll have to find another job. Maybe they can go back to the fort we just left and beg the colonel to let them drive the horses to that other fort. Then they'll take that money and do it all over again. Men like them never learn."

"If I didn't have to drive the wagon, I would have probably joined them," Hank said, and the others laughed.

"Charlie, we're going to escort you to Garden City so you can look your sister and her family up. It isn't that far out of our way back home. Maybe Hank can have a little fun while we're there. I'll watch him to make sure he doesn't lose everything," Dunham joked, and Hank simply shook his head.

Chapter 13

Garden City proved to be a busy little town and Charlie decided the best thing he could do would be to find the church and introduce himself to his brother-in-law. Mr. Dunham paid to have all the horses boarded at the livery stable and Charlie left them to start his quest. The church wasn't readily visible, and Charlie began walking to what appeared to be the center of town. He decided to search for a little while before asking for directions. He was too excited to wait very long. He was taking in the sights of the town when he spotted two elderly men playing a game of checkers outside the general store on the boardwalk under the overhanging roof.

"Excuse me," he began. "Could you point me in the direction of the church here in town?"

"What do you want to know that for?" one of them asked, his eyes never leaving the board.

"I'm trying to find my sister. She's married to the parson here," Charlie explained.

Both men looked up at Charlie. "Is that a fact?" the other man asked. "It seems kind of strange that you said you were looking for your sister. Are you lost or something?" Charlie knew he had to be civil to get the information he needed so he didn't reply the way he wanted to.

"No, it's just that first my brother ran off to get married leaving me and my sister at home with our Pa. Then she ran off and got married and left me alone with my Pa, so I haven't seen her for a few years and I ain't never met my brother-in-law. I hear

I have another nephew and a niece." The two old men looked at each other and one of them struck a match and puffed his pipe back to life.

"We ain't much on goin' to church," the other man said. "Our wives go though. They just go on and on about that preacher and how he can preach the bark off a tree. They hardly ever mention your sister and their little kids, though. My wife sure gets mad at me if I say anything about Pastor Gunderson. To hear her talk, when God wants to take a day off, he just turns the reins over to the pastor."

"That ain't what we hear, though," the man with the pipe chimed in. "There's plenty of rumors goin' around about that man."

"Rumors? What kind of rumors?" Charlie wondered.

"Oh, it ain't nothin' too bad. Not like he's got another woman on the side or anything of that sort," the first man said. "It's just that either that boy of theirs is the clumsiest child you ever saw or there's somethin' goin' on inside the home." Charlie's blank look at them told the men he didn't comprehend their meaning. "Let's just say that if you get enough beer into our town doctor, he'll forget all about the doctor and client privilege and tell you all kinds of information." Both men laughed and Charlie was growing tired of the way they were leading him on.

"I don't understand what you're gettin' at," Charlie blurted out. "What are you trying to tell me?"

The second man puffed hard on his pipe to get it to draw the way he wanted it to. "The boy has had a busted collar bone, some bruised ribs and a black eye all in the last few months. Somebody said your sister couldn't come to church because of the shiner she had under one eye."

Charlie was seething as they described the injuries to his sister and nephew. It sounded much too familiar to him. "Where do they live? Can you point the way to me?"

The two old gossipers finally grew weary of their game with him and gave Charlie directions to the church and there was a little clapboard house beside it which served as a parsonage. He opened the gate to the yard and walked up to the porch but before he could knock on the door he heard a noise behind the house in the backyard. He went around the house and saw his sister beating a rug which was hanging from their clothesline. Charlie watched for a moment to work up his courage before he finally addressed her.

"Jane."

She turned quickly to see who had spoken and at the same time a small boy ran over to her and clung to one of her legs. Charlie was embarrassed when he realized he was still wearing his pistol. Jane had a look of shock on her face.

"Baby brother? Is that really you?" Jane picked up her son and raced to Charlie to embrace him. "Oh, my goodness! How did you get here? It's such a long trip!"

Charlie was shocked at how much she had aged. He noticed she had one tooth that was chipped but he reasoned that could have happened in many ways. He looked down at the wide-eyed boy. There were a few bruises on his arms, but he knew boys have lots of opportunities to get those.

"Oh! I'm so excited I forgot my manners!" Jane exclaimed. "This is your nephew, Joshua. Joshua, this is your Uncle Charlie. Can you say hello to him?" The boy cowered behind her skirt and refused to acknowledge Charlie. "He's just being a little shy is all. He'll come around. Come on in and I'll fix you something cold to drink and you can tell me all about your trip. Your niece is napping right now. Her name is Rebekah."

For the next hour the pair exchanged information about each other. Charlie explained about their father's death, and she didn't seem surprised. He told Jane about their brother and his family living in Springfield. Then he told her all about driving the horses across the prairie to the fort in Colorado and everything he had seen and experienced. She told him about how her husband had tried his hand at lots of different jobs but could never seem to find what he was supposed to do with his life and then he claimed he had gotten the call to be a preacher and that was what he had been doing for the last three years. Charlie noticed Jane kept looking at the grandmother clock which was sitting on a table by the fireplace.

"Maybe it would be best if you left before he gets home," she finally explained. "Where are you staying? I'll send for you after I tell him all about you."

Charlie was perplexed. "I was hoping to stay with you for a while before I leave to go back to Springfield. I've decided that's where I ought to live at least for now."

"I want you to stay with us for as long as you like," she nervously explained. "It's just that my husband doesn't like surprises. It would be best if you let me smooth it over first."

"How many hotels do you have in this town?" Charlie asked. Jane held up one finger. "I'll either be there or the stable. I don't have anywhere else to go. I'm here with three of the men from the drive and they're probably already settled in at the hotel. They're going to be moving on to Missouri in a day or two. I don't necessarily have to go with them."

"Good! I'll come and find you when I've had the chance to talk to him."

Charlie left the house and made his way to the hotel. When he asked for the room numbers of his friends, he was told they weren't checked in there. He checked the saloon next but only Jake was there. Charlie entered the establishment under the watchful eyes of a dozen men and several saloon girls.

"I just checked at the hotel, and they told me none of you were staying there," Charlie said.

"That's because they won't take men of Jim's kind," Jake explained. "That made Mr. Dunham mad as a wet hen so they're down at the stable bargaining for us to have a place to sleep for the night before we up and leave tomorrow morning. I suppose I'll sleep there with them but that doesn't mean you have to. Why don't you take a room at the hotel?"

Charlie was angry at that news. "I don't want to stay where Jim ain't welcome. I'll sleep in the stable too."

"Of course, they wouldn't let Jim come in here to drink

either," Jake added. "It's funny. This didn't seem like a two-bit sort of town, but I reckon it is."

All four slept in the stable that night. All but Jim had eaten at the local restaurant, and they brought something back to him because it was clear he wasn't welcome in any of the establishments in town. Charlie told about his experience with his sister and that only served to make Dunham angrier.

"Something just isn't right in this town," Dunham said. "It appears the whole town is made up of bigots and hypocrites. Charlie, we'll be leaving in the morning. I've had my fill of this place. I hate to leave you alone, but I understand you want to get to know your sister and her family better. You'll find a safe way to get back to Springfield."

In the morning, they shook each other's hands, and the men took their leave of Garden City. Charlie decided he might as well be comfortable, and he rented a room at the hotel halfway down the street and he waited there for three days before a boy of about ten years of age found him and gave him a note from his sister. She informed him he couldn't stay with her and her family, but she invited him to supper that evening at seven o'clock so her husband could meet him. Charlie felt that was such a strange thing. He and Jane had always cared greatly for each other. She had tried her best to protect Charlie from their father and that usually ended badly with him taking his anger out on both instead of just his younger son.

The afternoon dragged on but Charlie at last washed himself and walked one hundred yards or so to the house. He walked to the door and hesitated before he knocked. The door opened slowly, and Joshua looked at him shyly from behind it. Charlie nodded toward him as he entered. He could see Jane as she labored in the kitchen. She turned when she realized he was at the front door.

"Charlie! Come in! Welcome!" she said enthusiastically but Charlie thought she acted very agitated and nervous. "Come in and meet my husband!" She gestured for him to come forward to where a large man sat lazily in a padded chair. "Charlie, this is Jared. Jared, this is my brother Charlie. As much as I've talked about him you should feel like you already know him."

Charlie extended his hand. "It's nice to meet you, sir." Jared didn't offer his hand to Charlie. He simply stared at him, sizing him up. There was palpable tension in this first meeting and the only one who seemed comfortable with it was Jared.

"Are you saved, Charlie?" he asked. Charlie was confused.

"Saved from what?" Charlie wondered. There was no compassion in the man's eyes. Charlie felt it was more like an accusation in his gaze. It made him extremely uncomfortable.

"Saved from your sins, that's what. I know all about your Pa not ever taking you kids to church so you could hear the truth from God's Word." He patted a large Bible on the table beside his chair. "That was his fault but if you've never darkened the door of a church since you've been out on your own then that's your fault. It's just one of the things that makes you a sinner." Charlie finally realized he still had his hand out and he let it drop to his side.

"What are some of the other things that make me a sinner the way you see it?" Charlie asked.

"It's not how I see it. It's what the Bible teaches us. I can tell just by looking at you that you're full of hate, pride, covetousness and you're probably experiencing lust of the flesh already." Jared hesitated for a moment. "Your sister let me read your letter. She didn't want to, but I convinced her."

Charlie didn't like this man. There was something very false about him. "How did you convince her?" he heard himself ask. The question made his sister fidget as she stood behind her husband.

"Let's just say I'm pretty persuasive," Jared answered. "You're a greater sinner than just about anybody I've ever come across because you're also a murderer. You murdered your own father." Behind him, Jane let out a little whimper. "Shut up woman!" Jared screamed.

"I was defending myself against an evil man. I doubt that God the Father would blame me for that. On the other hand, it don't trouble me none that he's barking in hell right now and forever more. I suppose that makes me a sinner too, don't it?"

"Yes, it does. You should get down on your knees right now and beg for forgiveness before it's too late."

Charlie grew bolder as his anger grew stronger. "So, you believe it was okay for my father to beat me without mercy and blame me for something that wasn't my fault?"

"The Bible teaches that if a man spares the rod, he spoils the child. Maybe your Pa was trying to help you and not hurt you. Did that ever occur to you?"

"No. The only thing that occurred to me was how much he hated me. Hate was what drove him to do the things he did."

"Please! Let's just go in and have our supper," Jane pleaded.

Jared finally moved from his spot and turned to face his wife while he was still sitting. "Don't make me tell you again woman! I told you to shut up and I meant it! Do you want me to show your brother how much I mean it?" He started to rise. Joshua began to cry, adding to the confusion in the house. "Stop your whining boy! You know what happens when you whine!" The young boy took two steps backward while Charlie took one step toward him to defend his sister and nephew. He wished he had brought his pistol with him. Charlie glanced around the room to see if there was something he could use if he had to.

"What do you think you're going to do, boy?" Jared asked, leering at him.

"You're the evil one," Charlie said calmly. "A good man would try being kind. All you know to do is the same thing our Pa did to us. You just blame my sister and your children for how much evil is in you and you take it out on them by beatin' 'em. You're nothin' but a big, fat hypocrite!"

"Look kid. I don't want to get in a pissing contest with you," Jared said as he moved closer to the edge of his chair.

"It's too late for that," Charlie answered. Jared moved with surprising quickness for a man his size and he hit Charlie with his fist hard enough to knock Charlie all the way back to the front door. Charlie recalled hearing both his sister and Joshua scream before he lost consciousness for a moment. Then his baby niece began to cry as well. The next thing he knew Jared was hovering over him menacingly. The room was spinning, and Charlie remembered a time when one of his dogs was attacked by a larger dog. Charlie's dog lost the fight and lay on his back submissively as the larger dog stood over him threatening another attack. It was a bad memory because Charlie had fled the scene rather than come to his dog's defense. He considered it a cowardly act.

"Do you have anything else you want to say to me you little squirt? Speak up or did I break your jaw?" Charlie moved his jaw around and felt it with his right hand. It wasn't broken. "You need to leave my house and never come back. Don't you dare tell anybody about this little incident. I'll just call you a liar and the good people of this sinful town will believe me."

Charlie rolled over to his left side and struggled to get up. Jared never moved. When he got to his feet he had to lean against the door because the room was still spinning but that sensation passed after a few deep breaths. Joshua ran across the room to embrace his mother.

"You don't want to see what I'm going to do to punish my wife and son," Jared said with a look of anticipation in his eyes. It hurt Charlie to leave and as he opened the gate, he heard the screams from his sister and nephew as the punishment began. Charlie wondered how long it would be before Jared would begin to beat his little girl as well.

Charlie stood at the gate waiting for the ground to stop moving. When he could focus at last, he looked around to see several people looking at him from the safety of their own porches. They were staring at him with pity, and it made his anger rise again.

"What are you all looking at?" he shouted as the sounds of abuse came from the house behind him. "Why doesn't somebody do something about this? Can't you see what he is? Can't you hear what he's doing to my sister and her little boy?" The people stared at him a bit longer and then turned to go back to the safety of their homes.

Charlie stumbled back to the hotel. His first thought was to strap on his pistol, go back to the house and break down the door and shoot Jared to death. He wondered if they hung young men of his age. It was the only thing he could think of that might save his blood kin. He suddenly felt very ill and vomited into the wash pan in his room. He barely made it to the bed before he passed out.

Charlie woke up to a terrible headache. The sun was shining through his window directly on his face. Normally he would welcome the warmth but not this morning. Somewhere outside a dog barked and children laughed. Each sound caused a new pain to course through his head. He struggled to the window to look up at the sun to judge what time it was and immediately regretted the decision. The sun bore through his eyes and caused an intense pain in the back of his head. That scared him enough to want to go see the doctor about it. He walked on unsteady legs to the wash basin and remembered he couldn't use that to splash his face, so he poured some water into his hand and threw it toward his eyes.

He slowly made the descent from his second story room and had to sit on the bench outside the hotel for a few minutes to get his bearings. He looked up and as luck would have it, he saw the shingle outside the doctor's office diagonally across the street from the hotel. He took a deep breath and began the difficult walk in that direction. He ignored the horses and wagons and other pedestrians crossing in front of him and that earned him several curses and one man on a wagon threatened him with his whip.

At last Charlie made it to the door and walked in. The brightness of the sun caused his eyes to have to adjust to the relative darkness of the room but when he could finally see he stopped immediately. On the doctor's table was Joshua and the doctor was busy stitching a cut under his eye. Jane saw her brother but didn't say anything.

"Be with you in a few minutes," the doctor said without

looking up. His back was to Charlie and Jane was on the other side of the table. "I'm about to get this young man fixed up." Charlie hadn't noticed at first, but Jane's arm was in a sling and there was a cast on her arm.

"Is it broke?" Charlie asked.

"Is what broke?" the doctor returned.

"I was talking to my sister. Is it broke?"

The doctor finished the last stitch, cut the suture and tied it off. He turned and looked at Charlie. "Your sister?" He looked back at Jane. "You didn't tell me you had a brother around here."

Jane looked at her brother. "He's not from around here. He's just visiting. You were about to leave town weren't you, Charlie?"

"What else is wrong with my nephew, Doc?"

The doctor raised Joshua's shirt to expose a wrap around his midsection. "He's got some bruised ribs, just like your sister does. I'm also treating him for a possible bruised kidney." He rolled Joshua gently over to his side and pulled his underpants down slightly to expose the discoloration on his buttocks.

Charlie moved forward to get a better look. "What did your husband use on his butt? It sure wasn't his hand."

"I had to take some splinters out of his rear end," the doctor said matter-of-factly. "My guess is a piece of firewood. Would that be right, Jane?" Jane's back straightened.

"That's none of your business, Doctor. None of this leaves this room. Aren't you bound to secrecy with your patients?"

"That's true. I'd love to walk down to the sheriff's office right now and tell him all about the injuries to you and your son. Most people in town know your husband is an abuser. I know you're scared of him and scared of what he might do if you reported it but if you don't stop it now, you'll be miserable the rest of your life which might not be that long." He rolled Joshua onto his back and helped him sit up. "You should just talk to the law, pack your things and leave. The people of this town would give you enough money to buy two tickets away from here."

"I want you to leave with me, Sis," Charlie chimed in.

"Leave with me and if he comes after you, I'll shoot him. I'll shoot him as dead as he can get."

Jane began to weep. "I made a vow to him when I married him. For better or worse and all that. God would never forgive me for leaving him. I made a promise."

Charlie moved around the table to embrace his poor sister. "Please come with me. We'll go to Springfield and live close to our brother and his family. It'll be safe there. Your little boy didn't make no promises and neither did your little girl. If you won't come, then let me take him with me and save him. I don't have no way to take my niece." Jane couldn't speak but she buried her head in Charlie's chest and shook her head.

"I can't," she said through her tears. "I'm bound to stay with him as a family."

"I thought just a little bit ago that I could go up and get my pistol, walk into the church and blow him to hell. Maybe they wouldn't hang me because of my youth."

Jane's countenance changed to anger toward her brother. "You'll do no such thing! This is not your problem, Charlie, it's mine. You need to just leave!"

Charlie wasn't willing to give up. "I'm gonna let the doc examine me. Then I'm gonna go gather my things and walk down to the stable and get my horse. If you change your mind, meet me there. I might have enough money to buy a buggy and another horse for you and Joshua to ride in and we'll leave this God-forsaken husband of yours behind. You won't believe how happy you'll be to make that right decision. If you're not there, I'll take it that you chose to stay, and we'll never see each other again."

Jane picked Joshua up from the examination table with her good arm and sat him on the floor. "Give your Uncle Charlie a hug good-bye," she ordered, and the boy complied. He clung to Charlie like he didn't intend to let him go but Jane finally pulled him away and walked out the door.

"Do I get to say good-bye to Rebekah?" Charlie asked. Jane shook her head.

"She's at the church with Jared," Jane replied as they walked out the door.

Charlie sighed as the doctor patted the table for him to have a seat. "They won't be in town long. I have it on good authority there's about to be a come to Jesus meeting where that rotten soul is going to be asked to leave the church. There's only about twelve people that go regularly anymore. Everybody else got tired of him telling them how they were all bound for hell while he beats his wife and son within an inch of their lives."

The doctor looked at the bruise on Charlie's jaw before examining his eyes. "Your jaw's not broken or fractured but I can give you something for the pain. You've got a slight concussion. Let me guess. You're suffering a splitting headache, especially in the sunlight. Would that be about right?" Charlie nodded slightly.

"Why doesn't anybody in this town do something for my sister and her kids? Is everybody that afraid of him?"

The doctor helped Charlie sit up and get down from the table. "She won't press charges against her husband and yes, everybody else but the sheriff is afraid of him. In fact, the sheriff is the one who is getting rid of him before he shoots the charlatan himself." He made his way to a cabinet full of bottles and containers and measured some pills out into his hand and slipped them into a small envelope before handing it to Charlie. "Take two of these in the morning and one at night before you go to sleep. Be sure and take them all until they run out. That's some powerful stuff I'm giving you. You understand the instructions, don't you?"

"Yes sir," Charlie answered. "Two in the morning and one at night. I'm much obliged to you for your kindness. How much do I owe you?" The doctor scratched his face before he replied.

"Oh, I'd take a dollar if it doesn't strap you too much for cash." Charlie dug the coin out of his pocket and handed it to him. Charlie turned to leave the office. "You know she's not coming to the stable, don't you? Maybe things will be better where they end up next." Charlie looked back at him one last time.

"You and me both know it will only make things worse."

Charlie went back to the hotel to gather his things but before he left, he found paper and a pencil in the small desk in his room. There was even an envelope, and he carefully wrote a letter to his brother explaining everything about their sister, niece and nephew. He knew the doctor was correct. She wouldn't join him. He folded the paper carefully and slipped it into the envelope. He paid his bill, apologized for the mess he had left and asked for directions to the post office. When he got there, he posted the letter and made his way to the livery stable, straining his eyes to hopefully see his sister and her children waiting for him. He walked slowly to give them more time, but they never came.

Chapter 14

Prairie life agreed with Charlie. He was used to fending for himself as he grew up. He was reluctant to even kill one of the hens on the farm because he was afraid of running out of food. The chickens and pigs were emergency meals, so he taught himself how to make traps for rabbits, squirrels, quail and prairie chickens. He wasn't allowed to use guns in his early years but now he had three handguns, his carbine and the eight-gauge shotgun at his disposal. His first attempt at using the shotgun on game resulted in the jackrabbit he had seen exploding into hundreds of tiny pieces. He didn't want to use the carbine for hunting because he couldn't afford too many bullets for it. That left his pistols but with a little practice he had become quite proficient in his aim. He spotted a dozen prairie chickens behind some tumbleweeds before they spotted him. He took careful aim and fired at the small head of one of the birds and scored a direct hit. Luck was with him that day as the bullet also removed the head of a second bird directly behind the first. Charlie wished there had been someone with him to witness it but there was no one for miles around.

It was a good day because there was a small stream nearby plus plenty of cottonwood trees for shade and it was close enough to nightfall to make camp in this favorable spot. He was a little sorry that he had killed two birds because one was more than he could eat in two meals. Some varmints close by would get an easy meal, but Charlie thought he might as well dress both birds and once Sandy was tended to, he began the task of picking the feathers off the pair. He built a fire, found some properly shaped twigs to make a spit and skewered the birds over the flames and coals. A bit of fat would occasionally fall from the meat and the fire would sizzle. It was a satisfying sound and reminded Charlie of the times he would sit in front of the fireplace in their cabin back home and wait for the crackle of the fire.

Charlie's melancholy was interrupted by a slight rustling from a thicket directly in front of him. He put his hand on the grip of his belly pistol and focused on the brush. There was no sound but whatever was there remained concealed for there was clear ground surrounding the thickness and he hadn't seen anything cross them. He noticed what appeared to be cloth of some kind as he stared into the different areas of leaves and wood. The meat needed to be turned so he attempted to do that while still watching.

"These two birds sure do smell good," he said out loud. "That was the luckiest shot I've ever made. Two birds with one bullet. Too bad some of this meat is gonna go to waste. I sure can't eat all of it myself." There was still no movement, but Charlie concentrated on the spot where he had last seen the faded blue of what he was certain was some type of clothing. He sniffed the air loudly. "Not only was that the best and luckiest shot I ever made but I do believe this is the best game I've ever roasted. Yes sir. It's gonna taste just as good as it smells. They sure is plump." Still nothing. "I'd be more than happy to share. You can come on out now. Don't be afraid."

The brush moved again and at long last a figure appeared. To Charlie's surprise it was a young white girl in a one-piece light blue dress. She had long black hair and wide brown eyes. She looked half-starved and stood about thirty feet away from Charlie and stood silently.

"It's alright. You can come on ahead. I won't bite." Charlie was a very patient individual and knew she wanted to come and eat so he let her take whatever time she needed to be able to trust him. Finally, she took a few cautious steps toward him. "That's the way. Come on over and have a seat by the fire. Supper will be ready in no time." Charlie put his hand out in her direction and after stopping for just a bit she proceeded on toward him and sat down just close enough to feel a bit of the warmth from the flames. "My name's Charlie. What's yours?" The girl drew her knees up and rested her chin on them, but she didn't respond. Charlie turned the spit a little bit more. "You don't have to tell me your name if you don't want to, but I may have to make one up for you if you don't tell me pretty soon." The girl continued to size him up, seeing if he could truly be trusted.

Charlie unsheathed his knife which made the girl scoot backward a bit, but she relaxed a little when he reached over and cut a leg and thigh from the first bird and placed it on his only tin plate. He handed it in her direction but allowed her to come to him for it, which she did after a few seconds. "Be careful," he said. "It just come from the fire so it's gonna be mighty hot. Don't burn your mouth. You might try blowin' on it before you try to eat it." The girl took his suggestion and blew quickly on the meat before tearing a piece off and blowing on it again before putting it in her mouth. She looked at Charlie with what appeared to be gratitude before beginning to devour the meat. "Don't make yourself sick by eatin' too fast now," Charlie advised. "Is that okay or would you like some white meat instead?" She didn't answer but he was certain it didn't matter. She was too hungry to care.

Charlie preferred the white meat, so he cut a big portion of the breast off, and it was so hot he almost dropped it on the ground. He removed his kerchief from around his neck and used it to hold the meat while he also blew on it to cool it off a bit. When he took his first bite, he closed his eyes and savored the flavor. It was truly the best cooking he had ever done, and it made it more enjoyable to share it with this unexpected guest. He let out a satisfying sigh. "Now that's good eatin'".

"Sure is," the girl said, and Charlie was shocked that she had spoken. "I'm sure glad you come along, mister. I was so hungry I thought I was just gonna dry up and blow away."

"I ain't hardly no mister," Charle corrected. "It don't appear I'm much older than you. What are you? About ten or twelve?"

The girl took another big bite. "I'm twelve. This is the best chicken I ever tasted!"

Charlie was grateful for the compliment. "Thank you kindly," he replied. Charlie looked all around. "Where in the world did you come from? What are you doing out here in the middle of nowhere? Where are your people? Don't tell me you're out here all by yourself."

The girl tossed the bones over her shoulder and licked her fingers. "You sure do ask a lot of questions. Could you cut me off some of the breast meat?" Charlie was taken aback by her statement. A few moments ago, she was acting like a scared rabbit and now she was putting him in his place and asking him to wait on her, but he obeyed and sliced off the rest of the breast meat from the bird they had been eating. She took it from him and didn't bother putting it on her plate. She devoured it in just a few bites.

Charlie took the other leg and thigh and began eating that while he watched her. "I'm feedin' you, ain't I," he said defensively. "I think that entitles me to some information. Let's start with your name."

The girl surmised there was nothing to worry about by just telling him her name. "Angela," she simply said.

Charlie nodded his head. "Angela," he repeated. "Well, that's a start anyway. How is it that you're out here all by yourself? Are your people over that rise over there?"

"If you put the rest of that bird on my plate, I'll work on pickin' the bones," she said, and Charlie once again complied. "I don't have any people out here. I'm all by myself," she said as she began tearing tiny bits of meat from the bones.

Charlie felt exasperated. "You ain't exactly a wealth of information, girl. That just causes me to ask more questions such as what happened to your people? You didn't just appear right here out of nowhere. You had to have come from someplace." Charlie stopped and stared at her, waiting for some sort of explanation. She looked at him closely, trying to determine if he could be trusted and if so, how much.

"I ran away," she finally said, further exasperating Charlie.

"Ran away from where? Ran away from who? How long have you been out here by yourself?"

Now it was Angela's turn to be exasperated. "I haven't had anybody ask me this many questions in my whole life!" Charlie muttered something under his breath and cut some more breast meat from the second bird.

"Well, I ain't had this much conversation in a long time so I guess that makes us even," he said as he decided to allow her some time to get used to him. "I was kind of happy there for a little while to have some company but now I ain't so sure."

Angela's mood changed and Charlie noticed it. "If I tell you something, will you promise not to take me back?" Charlie wanted to ask where he promised not to take her back to, but it was clear she was tired of his questions, so he simply nodded his head.

"You have to say it to make it a real promise," Angela demanded.

"All right. I promise then."

Angela was satisfied with that and took a deep breath. "I don't have any family. I'm an orphan and I ran away from a home for girls." She looked all around her. "I ain't exactly sure which direction it is but I've been gone for three days. This is the first food I've tasted since I left. I found some berries, but I wasn't sure if they was poisonous or not so I didn't try them." She waited to see how Charlie responded to her news before she continued. "I don't think I should tell you any more just now."

Charlie was surprised there would be an orphanage out here on the prairie. The towns he was closest to didn't have one and he supposed maybe Springfield or Wichita or other big towns might have an orphanage but there wasn't a town for miles from this place. It didn't make sense to him. He wanted to know more but felt the door was shutting.

"Seems like an odd place for an orphanage," he said. Charlie pointed with his knife at the second bird, but Angela shook her head and continued picking at the remains of the first. "I come through here a few weeks ago with a horse herd going west to a soldier fort in Colorado territory and I don't recall there bein' a town anywhere near here." Angela concentrated on her task with the bird.

"It's about twenty miles from any town," she said. "It's way out in the country."

"I swear," was all Charlie could manage. It was clear Angela was done talking for now. "I reckon you can use my bedroll to sleep in, and I'll throw my coat over myself. I'd better collect some more firewood." Angela jumped up as if she was on fire.

"I can do that!" she exclaimed before bolting off to do the chore. It only took her a few minutes to gather more than they would need. "I'm sorry I was kind of rude earlier. If it wasn't for you, I might have died all alone out here and nobody would even care." She sat down on the bedroll Charlie had prepared for her. "Somebody would have found my body and wondered who I was and where I'd come from. Maybe they would have said some nice words over my grave."

Charlie smiled at her as he got his coat ready to act like a blanket. "We should get some sleep. We'll talk about things in the morning."

"You mean things like what you're going to do with me?" she asked with concern in her voice.

"Well, that thought did cross my mind," he said as he settled down for the night. Sandy let out a soft whinny behind them. "Good night to you, too, Sandy," Charlie replied as he placed his hat over his face. "Good night to you as well Miss Angela."

Angela smiled as she laid her head down. She found it humorous he had said good night to his horse. It was comforting to be by the nice, warm fire. It was also comforting to know she had found someone who could help her. She slept soundly all night.

Chapter 15

Angela woke to bright sunshine and birds singing in the tree the pair were camping under. She was lying on her left side away from her companion, so she rolled over and Charlie was sitting up, rifle resting on one of the branches he had used for the spit. It was pointed down the slight grade past where she had been hiding in the brush. She looked in that direction but did not see anything.

"There's somebody snooping around down there," Charlie said without even looking at her. Angela strained her eyes but still could not see anything stirring.

"I don't see anybody," she said. "How many are down there?"

"He's out of sight right now but there's only one that I saw for sure."

Angela reached between them for Charlie's canteen, poured just a little water in the palm of one hand and then splashed her face to wash the sleep from her eyes. She hoped that it would help clear her sight and she trained her eyes the same direction Charlie was peering.

"He was leading a horse that looked like he was on his last legs. He was carrying a rifle. It was a white man, and it looked to me like he was trying to find some tracks," he said allaying the possible fear Angela had of Indians. Angela's heart beat faster and her breaths were strained. She wondered if Charlie could hear her.

"I reckon I ought to go down there and see what he wants," Charlie said and started to stir from his position.

"No!" Angela said, a little too loudly and she looked down

the slope to see if her voice had been heard. "What I mean is, maybe there's more than one. Why don't we just leave them be?" she pleaded.

"Maybe he can tell us where the nearest town is," Charlie reasoned. "I need to find some place for you to stay. Maybe there's a church and a preacher who could help us. Better yet, maybe they've got some law that can give us a hand. I'll go down there and ask. After all, I'm pretty good at asking questions ain't I?"

Angela had to make Charlie understand. "It might be he's looking for me! I can't explain everything to you now, but I just can't go back there. Please, I'm begging you! Don't make me go back!" Charlie could see the terror in her eyes.

"All right, all right. How about you hide, and I'll go talk to him and I won't tell him you're up here? How would that be? That way I could still ask him about a town, and he wouldn't mind telling me."

Angela could see the wisdom in that idea, and she nodded her head. She had nothing to gather so she went back to her stand of brush to hide again. Charlie saddled Sandy as quickly as he could, placed the carbine back in its scabbard and removed the leather thongs which kept the big Navy revolvers in place in their saddle holsters. He eased Sandy down the hill toward the last place he had seen the stranger and kept his eyes wide open. As many rolling spots as there were to the bottom of the hill it would be easy to be bushwhacked. When he got about fifty yards from the lowest point he saw him. The man was still on foot allowing his mount to graze a bit as he surveyed the surrounding area. He was dressed all in black except for a dingy white shirt. He seemed alarmed upon seeing Charlie riding toward him but when he saw how young the boy was, he relaxed.

"Howdy Mister," Charlie began. "I seen you from my camp up the hill a ways and it looked like you were missing something. Did you lose a stray?" The man had a sharp beaklike nose and thin face. He was a skinny man with suspicious eyes.

"Howdy yourself. You ain't seen a girl about twelve years

old, have you? She's a runaway and her mother and me are worried sick about her. She's sort of a wild one if you know what I mean. This ain't the first time she's run off." Charlie hated to lie but he felt it was called for this one time.

"A young girl you say? No, I ain't seen anybody for days until I spotted you. Do you have a cabin around here?" Charlie asked convincingly.

"We live about nine miles up this creek to the north. Got a big house there and a farm. If you see her, will you tie her up and bring her back home? She'll probably try and run off from you too after she tells all her lies. Or, if you're headed to town maybe you could haul her there. They got a marshal there that could lock her up for safe keepin'". I'll eventually make my way to Hays, and I can check and see if she's there. The prairie might have already got her by now."

"How do I get to Hays?" Charlie asked, excited about the existence of a town with a marshal in it.

"Follow this creek east. You'll run right into it," the man said.

"I'm beholdin' to you," Charlie said. "My name is Charlie Mabry."

"Elmer Bigby. Pleased to meet you, boy. Mind what I said about that spitfire of a girl. She's a handful."

"I'll be sure and do that," Charlie said, and he touched the brim of his hat as he turned away. "By the way, how far is it to Hays?"

"I'd say ten or eleven miles," Bigby said pointing down the creek.

"I'll go back and break camp and head for town, but I'll keep my eyes peeled for her. What does she look like?"

"Long black hair, brown eyes, blue dress. Her name is Angela." Charlie turned and trotted Sandy back to collect his things. He saw Angela out of the corner of his eye but didn't want to look directly at her in case Bigby was watching. He casually collected his bedroll and canteen. While he was keeping himself busy, he spoke in low tones to the girl without turning toward her.

"He said his name is Elmer Bigby. Does that name sound familiar?" Charlie asked.

"He's the one I'm running from!" Angela replied. "Him and his sister CoraLu run an orphanage for girls. They make us work all the time and if we don't act the way they want, they beat us!"

"They beat you? How many girls are they at this orphanage?"

"There's twelve of us countin' me," Angela said.

Charlie kept working and thinking. "He told me where it was. What I need to do is get you to the marshal in Hays and bring him back out here to see for himself. The problem is Bigby looks like he's headed for town too. Somehow, we've got to sneak around him to get to the marshal before he does. He says if we follow that creek east, we'll run into Hays. We'll have to see if we can figure out a way around him and keep track of that creek. You can help me watch for it while we ride. When I get on Sandy you walk on her other side so he can't see you if he looks up here. When it's safe I'll swing you up here behind me."

Angela followed Charlie's instructions and after thirty minutes or so he reached his hand down and pulled her up. "He said it was ten or eleven miles so we can make that in an hour or two," Charlie said as Angela pointed to her left and Charlie could see the creek several hundred yards down the hill. From their vantage point he could see the creek meandering like a cow path toward the southeast. Charlie looked for Bigby but saw no sign of him. He put Sandy into a quick trot. She could keep that pace all day without any problem. Angela weighed next to nothing, and Sandy barely noticed her on her back.

After an hour passed Angela's sharp eyes detected the town of Hays straight ahead about a thousand yards. From the looks of Bigby's horse he was far behind them, so Charlie turned Sandy down the hill toward the creek. It appeared to be an easier road for her to travel than the one they were on.

"Any sign of Bigby behind us?" he asked the girl and Angela turned as far as she could to look.

"Nope. I don't see him."

Charlie asked Sandy for an easy lope, and they were at the outskirts of town in only a few minutes. It was a fair-sized town with several businesses and quite a few people were either walking or riding about. Before Charlie could ask someone for directions to the marshal's office it came into view. He dismounted, helped Angela down from the tall horse and tied Sandy to a railing. The two young people walked to the door and Charlie opened it for Angela to step in first. It was dark in the marshal's office but when his eyes adjusted Charlie saw a man smoking a cigar behind a desk.

"What do you two kids want?" the man asked gruffly. "The sweets are located in the general store if that's what you're lookin' for."

Charlie didn't appreciate his comment. "I like candy as much as the next person, but I can see you're wearin' a marshal's badge so you're who we're lookin' for." The marshal impatiently tapped a pencil on a stack of papers as he surveyed the pair from behind his desk.

"Are you here to confess to some awful crime?" the marshal asked. "Did you steal some new potatoes out of farmer Johnson's tater patch? Maybe you've already been to the general store and took some licorice from old George. That's a two-person job. One to distract old George and one to take the candy from the jar on his counter." Charlie and Angela gave each other a bewildered look.

"We ain't thieves," Charlie answered.

"Well, what are you then? A couple of runaways?" the marshal asked. Again, the pair looked at each other.

"I am. He's not," Angela stated, and the marshal looked at them with increasing impatience.

"Now look here, I'm a busy man and I ain't got time for riddles. You got two minutes to tell me what it is you want and then you have to get out of here and leave me be."

Angela stepped forward two steps and turned, facing away from the marshal. She reached behind her head and unbuttoned the top two buttons of her dress. She pulled the material apart and the marshal could tell she needed him to see it without her saying a word. He got up from his squeaky chair and approached her with caution, keeping his eyes on her bare back.

"Step over here into the light, young lady," he instructed as he took her gently by the shoulders and walked her backward a few steps toward the window. The marshal pushed the girl's long hair aside and saw a series of bruises and whelps on her back and winced at the sight. "I won't ask you to show me but are there more of these farther down your back?" Angela nodded. The marshal looked at Charlie. "You didn't do this did you boy?" Charlie also turned around, took his suspenders from his shoulders and unbuttoned his shirt in the front and let it fall to expose his own awful scars. The marshal swore when he saw Charlie's back and Angela snuck a peak as well and caught her breath. "Who did this to you young people?"

"Mine came from my dear old Pappy," Charlie said. He looked at Angela to let her know he wanted her to tell her own story.

"Mr. Marshall. Have you ever heard of Bigby's home for orphan girls?" she began.

"My name is Harrington. Marshal Carl Harrington. I've been by there once to deliver their check from the territory for runnin' the place. I had to be close to there for another reason, so I told the postmaster here in town I'd just take it to 'em." Marshal Harrington suddenly realized the girl could be implying she had received her stripes there. "Are you tryin' to tell me that CoraLu and Elmer Bigby did this to you?" Angela nodded. She shocked Charlie by turning her back to him, implying he help her button her dress. Charlie was glad it was so dark in the marshal's office so they couldn't see him blushing.

"They beat all us girls," Angela calmly said. "Sometimes they lock the youngest girls in a closet for two or three days without anything to eat or drink."

"Is that a fact?" Harrington asked. His anger was building in him.

"They make us work all the time making things they can sell. If we don't keep up, we get in all kinds of trouble. Sometimes we don't get fed if we don't make enough clothes." The marshal went to his desk and picked up the papers he had been working on and dumped them in a drawer.

"Come with me," he commanded. "When's the last time you two had somethin' decent to eat?"

"We had a fine meal of prairie chicken last night," Charlie said.

The marshal herded them toward the door. "I'm gonna go and check a couple of things. I'm treatin' you two to whatever you want to eat at the best restaurant in town unless you just want to eat at the Mexican place on the outskirts of town." Once the couple were seated and waited on, the marshal turned and headed out the door and down the street. Charlie watched him walk past the window of the restaurant and he noticed a few things about the man. The marshal was shorter than Charlie. He was wearing black trousers, a black vest and a black jacket. He had grizzled features including a salt and pepper beard. His eyes were dark and piercing. He looked like a man who could explode without much provocation. Angela and Charlie ordered hot cakes with butter and molasses, scrambled eggs and ham with a glass of milk for each of them.

Marshal Harrington was a man on a mission, and he walked quickly up to the clerk at the general store. He was after answers, and he was the type of man who could detect a lie from anyone, especially if he pressed them hard and fast.

"Well, howdy Marshal," the clerk named George greeted him. "What can I do for you?"

Harrington leaned over the counter and stared menacingly at the clerk. "Do the Bigby's come into town for material and needles and thread and such very often?" he demanded. George was surprised at the question but could tell the marshal was in a no-nonsense mood.

"Sure, they do. Sure, they do. They're some of my best customers," he answered nervously.

"What about finished product? What can you tell me about that?" George had a bewildered look on his face.

"I ain't followin' you, Marshal. What do you mean by finished product?"

"I mean like dresses and shirts and such," the marshal explained. "Do you ever buy any goods from them?" The clerk was beginning to perspire.

"I buy some but not too much," he explained. "Maybe the dress store buys some. Maybe they ship them by the post office or the freight office." His voice became higher as he did everything he could to get the marshal off his back.

"So, you're tellin' me that it didn't make you the least bit curious why they were buyin' so much stuff to make clothes and then sellin' 'em back to you?" The marshal was becoming more agitated each moment. "I'm waitin' for an answer George!"

"I, I guess I just figured they were keeping those little girls busy and teaching them how to sew is all," George stammered. "I didn't see no harm in it." Harrington slammed his open hand down on the counter and it echoed throughout the store, startling the other customers.

"You didn't see no harm in it!" Harrington shouted as he turned and stormed out the door. He headed for the dress store next. It was owned by a widow named Eugenia Standish. He slowed his walk because he didn't want to treat her like he just treated George. He recognized his need to calm down, but he wasn't the calming down sort. Eugenia had a little bell that tinkled when the door was opened either when a customer entered the store or was leaving the store.

"Good morning, Marshal," she greeted him. "This is a nice surprise. How are you on this beautiful morning?"

"I've honestly been better, Ms. Standish." She wagged her finger at him.

"How many times must I remind you to call me Eugenia?" she said. Harrington was doing his best to control his temper.

"Eugenia, we need to set aside the pleasantries. I need to

know if you buy dresses and shirts and such from CoraLu or Elmer Bigby."

"You're certainly in a poor mood, Marshal. Of course, I buy goods from the Bigby's every time they come to town. I can't make things as fast as they can and they're mighty reasonable, too." That statement did nothing to help the marshal's mood.

"I swear. Did it ever occur to you the reason they can turn out so many pieces of clothing is because they make the little girls in their care work like a bunch of slaves? There's a young lady only twelve years old over at the restaurant eating breakfast and she just showed me the whip marks on her back she got from either Elmer or his sister. She got whipped because she wasn't working fast enough making clothes for you to sell in your shop!" Eugenia was in tears.

"I had no idea that was going on, Marshal. I swear to you I didn't know!" Harrington had heard enough, and he turned to go.

"I'm fixin' to put them out of business. You'll have to make your own clothes from now on or get somebody else to do it. Them little girls ain't gonna do this no more!" He shut the door harder than he should have and the bell was still ringing as he got back to the restaurant. "Bring me a cup of black coffee, Seth," he bellowed. "I need it five minutes ago." The old waiter on duty hurried to fill his request. Charlie and Angela paused their breakfast to look wide-eyed at him. Harrington took two big swallows of the hot beverage, and it calmed him down some. The young people were afraid to speak. "How's your breakfast? Is it good?" They nodded in unison.

Harrington drank his coffee in silence and watched the two young people finish their meal. Angela and Charlie exchanged glances at each other, not knowing what to do or say.

"I thought I knew the people in this town," Harrington at last broke the silence. "It turns out they're money grubbers only interested in filthy lucre. The owner of the general store didn't seem it fit to tell me the Bigby's were buyin' more cloth than anybody else by a far sight and the owner of the dress store was more than happy to buy all the dresses and blouses and shirts and such as they were willing to sell her. I'm about to put the brakes on both their businesses." He paused in his rant to drain the last drops of his cup, and he waved the waiter away when he tried to refill it. "Young lady, I hate to ask this of you, but I need you to come back to the orphanage with me and convince the other girls I'm just there to help them and that's all. I need you to get them to tell me their stories so I can build a case against CoraLu and Elmer Bigby and put them in jail for a long time. Is there any older girls that could take charge for a while out there?" Angela nodded.

"Mary is eighteen years old and she kind of takes charge of us and tries to protect us from getting whipped. She has a fifteen-year-old sister that lives there named Dixie. Mary is old enough to leave on her own, but she won't go because of her sister."

"I can appreciate that," Harrington nodded. "It occurs to me I don't even know your names. You first darlin' and then you," he pointed in Charlie's direction.

"I'm Angela. I don't know my last name." That surprised Harrington and Charlie.

"My name is Charlie Mabry," Charlie said in turn.

"All right. I assume you've got your own horse Charlie." Charlie nodded. "I'll get a gentle horse for you to ride, Angela."

"I'll double up with Charlie," Angela said. "His horse Sandy is used to me." The marshal was fine with that arrangement.

"Seth, slap a piece of sausage on a biscuit for me will ya'. I'm in a hurry. Don't worry about wrappin' it up. I'll eat it on the way to the livery stable." The food came within a minute, and the marshal paid the bill and walked quickly out the door with the two youngsters close behind. Even though the marshal was short of stature they found it hard to keep up with him. "Do me a favor and go to the livery stable and tell the man in charge to get my gelding ready. Not the stud horse, the gelding. I'm going to get a rifle and some cartridges and lock my office and I'll be right there. The wrath of the Lord is about to reign down on Elmer and CoraLu Bigby!"

On the way out of town Charlie explained to the marshal

that they had seen Elmer out looking for Angela. Charlie said he thought the man was headed for town.

"He'll be following the creek. We'll waylay him there and take him back to the home. I want to see him and his sister squirm together."

It wasn't long before they saw a lone rider coming toward them along the creek road.

"Keep hidden behind me Angela," Charlie instructed. "It'll make it easier for the marshal."

"This is my good fortune, Marshal," Elmer said as he approached them. "I was just coming into town to see you. It seems I've got a runaway." He squinted his eyes when he recognized Charlie. "Hey, I know you. You're the kid I told how to get to town. You made it there I see." Harrington drew his pistol and pointed it at Bigby.

"Throw down your rifle, Elmer. Get rid of any other weapon you might have on you, too." Elmer complied with the order. "My eyes ain't as good as they used to be, but I can see somethin' else in your coat pocket. Throw it down too." Bigby dug in his coat and pulled out a double shot Derringer and tossed it away as well. "Last chance. If you're holdin' out on me and I find out about it I'm gonna just shoot you."

"That's all there is. I swear on my mother's grave," Bigby pleaded.

"Turn that bag of bones around and let's go see your dear sister," Harrington ordered, and it was then that Elmer noticed Angela behind Charlie.

"There you are my sweet child. We've been worried sick over you."

Angela stuck out her tongue at Elmer. "I ain't your sweet child Elmer Bigby and you're in a lot of trouble."

Harrington chuckled. "She's as right as rain, Elmer. You and CoraLu have got a lot of explainin' to do. You just ride in front of me where I can see you. If you try to run, I'll shoot you in the back."

Harrington must have made a believer out of Elmer because he behaved himself all the way back to the orphanage and he never said a word. As they crested one final hill the house came into view. It was a two-story structure with a big front porch. There was a white picket fence surrounding the yard and Charlie saw as they grew closer that it needed to be whitewashed. There was a big tree in the yard with a swing hanging from a low branch. On one side was a series of outbuildings. There was a smokehouse and next to it was a large barn with a corral attached to the east side. When they got within one hundred yards of the house the front door flew open and girls of all sizes and ages came rushing out, squealing and waving their hands when they saw Angela waving at them from behind Charlie. The boy took Angela's hand and helped her down from Sandy and she ran into the welcoming arms of her friends. The girls made a circle around Angela and danced around her. In the middle of the celebration one of the girls who appeared to be younger than Angela looked up at Harrington who was still mounted on his horse.

"You some kinda' law?" she asked, staring at Harrington's badge.

"I'm the marshal over in Hays. Where's CoraLu Bigby?"

"She's in the house with Dora," the same girl explained. "Want me to go get her?"

As soon as she asked the question the screened door of the house opened, and CoraLu Bigby roughly pulled a girl about Angela's age behind her. When the girl cleared the threshold, CoraLu gave her a swat on the rump with a long wooden spoon. CoraLu hadn't noticed their visitors at first.

"Didn't see you standing there Marshal," she said. "I see you found our little lost lamb. She's missed several days of chores. What am I going to do with you child?"

Harrington dismounted. "It was Charlie here that found her. He brought her into town, and we've had us a nice long chat. Have you taken supper yet? We're a might hungry."

CoraLu didn't look very happy when the marshal shared the

information about Angela with her. She looked at her brother, but he wasn't any help.

"We were just preparing the evening meal. We'd be most pleased if you shared it with us. The girls don't get much company," CoraLu said. "Girls, get three more places ready at the table."

"Charlie, do you mind putting the horses away? I've got some choice words for these two."

"Yes sir, marshal," Charlie said.

"I'll help you," Angela said as she broke away from the other girls who looked disappointed that she wasn't coming in the house right away. "We won't be long."

Charlie took the reins of Sandy and the Marshal's horse, and Angela led Elmer's old horse toward the barn. There was still an hour before sunset so the light inside the barn was still good. Charlie removed the saddles from all three animals and Angela got a stool to stand on so she could help brush them and cool them down. It only took a few minutes and when they were done Charlie turned to head for the house.

"Don't go yet Charlie. Please," Angela pleaded. "There's something you need to see up in the hay loft." Charlie looked up. There was a built-in ladder to the loft about midway in the barn.

"What is it you want me to see?" he asked. "Can't it wait?" Angela shook her head.

"I've been wanting you to see it all day. It won't take that long. Just go up and take a look around and see what you think about it," she said. "It's important."

Charlie was skeptical but walked over to the ladder. The first step was far off the ground so he leaped up and caught one of the rungs above it and pulled himself up until he could get his boot on the lowest rung. He climbed up ten of the wooden rungs to get to the floor of the loft and he pulled himself up. To his left was the last of the hay supply for the year. To his right were the outside double doors of the loft through which the spring hay could be fed. Leaning against the east wall next to the double doors was an old mattress, and he assumed it was stuffed with straw or hay. That seemed kind of strange to him. He stood at the end of the mattress and pulled it over and when it hit the floor it made a loud thump and loose hay and dust flew everywhere. Charlie turned his head and closed his eyes. Before looking down at it he waved the dust away from his face. Unlike the other side of the mattress the side that was turned up was stained but he couldn't see why. He walked the few paces to the loft doors and opened one to let in more light. When he walked back over to it, he saw several burgundy-colored splotches on the light blue and white material, and he knelt on his haunches to get a better look. Some of the stains were splattered while others were large, and they were concentrated more in the middle. Charlie got down on his knees and used a fingernail to scratch at one of the large stains and then he smelled it. He still wasn't convinced so he got down on his knees and bent over to put his nose within an inch of the same stain. It was the sickly metallic smell of blood that became even a greater mystery.

Charlie had been concentrating on the mattress so much that he forgot about the rest of the loft. Several candles were placed on the boards which held the outer planks in place. He wondered why anyone would light candles in a barn loft. Was someone living up here? That didn't explain the blood, though. One thing he knew for certain was that it wasn't a safe thing to do. He wiped the blood specks from his finger on his trouser leg and stood back up to survey the rest of the loft. Two things caught his eye simultaneously. Across the loft to the other side was a support beam that came up from the ground of the barn and was one of several which held the roof in place. It was round, and on the side facing him Charlie saw something even more curious. At about eye level there were uneven burgundy marks in the wood. There were four tally marks up and down with a slash through them which extended from top left to bottom right. There was one more tally mark underneath the others, and it was also straight up and down. Six. Charlie got close to the marks and leaned over to smell them, but he already knew what he would find. These marks also smelled like blood.

His focus shifted to his left where two portions of rope hung from the rafters of the loft. Each had been cut, and they were almost equal length. He instinctively knew all these things were related but he had no idea how. Blood on the mattress, six bloody tally marks on the beam, two ropes which had been cut. The only other thing he could see besides a pair of pitchforks was a short three-legged stool in the corner of the loft on the other side of the double doors. He liked trying to solve puzzles, but this one was very confusing. Charlie didn't want to give up and have to ask the girl for help yet. There was one other clue he hadn't considered, and that clue was Angela. What was her part in this mystery? Why did she want him to see it?

"Looks like you're just about to run out of hay up here," Charlie began. "Does Elmer cut his own?" There was no answer for a few seconds, and he thought perhaps Angela had left him and gone back to the house.

"Elmer has somebody he gets the hay from," she said. "He might bring it by any day now."

Charlie had figured that was the case. Elmer didn't look like the type who would be very good at manual labor. "Who does it come from?" he asked.

"A man named Whitaker," came the response from below. "He has a ranch north of here somewhere." Angela paused a bit before continuing. "He brings it in a big wagon with his three sons."

For some reason Charlie thought this line of questioning was important, so he persisted. "I reckon old Elmer uses the money he gets from workin' you girls to pay for it. It must take a powerful lot of dresses and such to pay for a loft full of hay." Again, there was silence for a while before Angela answered.

"That ain't how he pays for it."

Charlie thought it was strange to be carrying on a conversation with Angela down below and him in the loft above. "I believe I heard the marshal sayin' somethin' about a payment of some kind from the territory for him and his sister to run this home for you girls. I guess he pays for it that way." He had to wait several more seconds for Angela to respond.

"That ain't how he pays for it either."

Charlie's confusion became greater after each query. He had one more question for Angela before he was going to give up and simply ask her what it all meant. "How many years has this Whitaker fella' been bringing hay here?" This time there was more hesitation before the answer came from below.

"Six."

Charlie didn't believe the tally marks on the beam were from counting the number of years hay had been delivered. Why would they be in blood? There was something much more sinister afoot here. He was young but he was wise beyond his years due to his circumstances. The drovers on the horse drive were like many men. They liked to brag about things men did, things Charlie didn't fully understand about women. Wharton was the worst of the lot for that sort of talk. Charlie recalled an incident where Wharton told of a young girl he had supposedly molested and laughed about the amount of blood which poured out of her.

"How old is the oldest girl that lives here, Angela?" he wanted to know.

"Eighteen," came the short answer.

"One more question. How old did you say you were?"

"Twelve."

That made the oldest girl twelve years old when the Whitakers first started supplying hay. It was Angela's age. Charlie made his way to the ladder and turned around so he could come down facing it. He jumped from the last rung to the dirt floor which was partially covered with hay that had fallen through the cracks of the loft. He turned to face the girl and Angela's expression told him she hoped he had solved the mystery without her having to explain it.

"You ran away because you didn't want to be the next tally

mark on the post," Charlie said bluntly and Angela flung herself in his arms, surprising him. With her head buried in his chest she nodded. Charlie patted her back. He held her away at arm's length and used his thumbs to wipe away the tears from her cheeks. "Let's go and get the marshal. He needs to see this but when he figures it out, I sure am afraid of what he might do. What about the ropes? I couldn't figure them out."

"Two of the girls hanged themselves," Angela explained through her tears. "Another girl ran away, and Elmer must have found her and buried her because he left with a clean shovel and came back with a dirty one. My friend Dora ain't never said a word since it happened to her. Mary was the first and she's old enough to leave but she stays because of her sister. Dixie's only fifteen. That makes all six."

Charlie was almost too embarrassed to go on, but he felt the need to get some completion from this story. "Them men molested all six of those girls, one every year, and used their own blood to make the tally marks on the post. Ain't that so?" Angela nodded again. "Let's go on up to the house."

The duo walked side-by-side from the barn to the porch where Harrington was berating Elmer and CoraLu. The girls had been relegated to the house, but the marshal was swearing at the brother and sister so loudly it could be heard from quite a distance. Two of the smaller girls were listening from around the house but when they saw Charlie and Angela they ran as fast as they could toward the back. Charlie waited until he and Angela had climbed the steps to address Harrington.

"Get that girl in the house where she belongs!" the marshal shouted. "She's too young to hear some of the words I've got to say to these two." Harrington was as angry as he'd ever been, and he needed to vent that anger. "Well, spit it out! What do you want?"

"We've got somethin' we have to show you out in the barn," Charlie said while watching how CoraLu and Elmer reacted. They had a grave look of concern on their faces. "I think you might want to tie them up before you come with us." The marshal looked perturbed.

"Tie 'em up! I've got a good mad on and you want me to tie them up and come with you? Can't it wait?"

Charlie tried to stay calm to make up for the marshal's anger. "If you think you're mad now wait till you see what's out there." The marshal stared at the boy. He could see Charlie's sincerity in his eyes.

"Well, don't just stand there. Go and fetch me a rope!" Charlie complied and the marshal tied the pair as if they were murderous men instead of middle-aged siblings. Once he had completed his task he followed the two youngsters to the barn.

"It'll be dark soon, so we need to hurry," Charlie said. "You have to go up to the loft." The marshal looked at the ladder with the first rung so high off the ground.

"Give me a leg up," Harrington said. "I ain't as young as I used to be." Charlie did as he was told, and the marshal made his way quickly to the loft floor. "All right. What am I supposed to be looking for?"

"I can't tell you," Charlie responded. "It's important that you figure it out yourself. You're a lawman, ain't you? That's what you do, ain't it?"

"I'm in no mood to be sassed, kid. If I don't figure it out by the time it gets too dark to see I expect some answers.

"See all them candles up there? You could light one to see better," Charlie informed him. Harrington looked around and saw them. His first thought was why would anyone put candles in a hay loft. He thought he might as well take advantage of the extra light source. His eyes weren't as strong as they were a few years ago. He struck a match on the wood beside the longest candle, lit it and then he spit on the match so it wouldn't cause the whole barn to go up in flames. The flame didn't offer a lot of light since the sun hadn't set yet but this time of the year the sun seemed to go down quickly. He would soon need it, especially if the riddle took too long to solve.

The mattress was close to where he had gotten the candle, so he examined it first. Candles and an old mattress in a hay loft? He imagined someone had been sleeping up here but there were multiple stains on the mattress. He got down on one knee and held the candle close to it and took careful note of what the stains consisted of. He had seen enough blood stains in his career as a marshal to know that was what he was looking at. Harrington got back on both his feet and took in the rest of the loft. Two ropes hung from a rafter just a couple of feet apart from each other. He walked over to them and held the candle close to see the ropes had been cut. Then he saw the six tally marks made with blood.

"Charlie, if you've got this mystery figured out, I'd sure like to hear it," he called down. "Why don't you come on up here? Leave the girl down there." Charlie obeyed and was up the ladder in only a few seconds. "Here's what I see. Two cut ropes, six tally marks made with blood, a mattress with blood stains on it, and a whole bunch of candles. Is this some sort of devil worship or something? I know the Bible talks about the number six-six-six but there's only one six up here. That girl knows somethin' don't she?"

"There's a couple of things you didn't mention, marshal," Charlie began. There's a three-legged stool in the corner over there. The hay supply is next to nothin' so they're gonna need more soon." Harrington looked at both things as Charlie talked about them.

"My patience is runnin' thin, boy, so why don't you just give it to me straight up?" Charlie wanted to argue but he felt that wasn't wise.

"Okay. Here it is. The Bigby's get their hay delivered every spring from a rancher named Whitaker and his three grown sons. He don't take payment from gold or silver or folding money. He takes it from somewhere else for the last six years." Harrington had a blank look on his face.

"Somewhere else? What do you mean by that? I don't follow."

Charlie fidgeted on his feet. "He takes his payment in flesh," he managed, and Harrington's face lit up as he comprehended the situation.

"You mean this Whitaker feller and his three boys pick out a girl and rape her out here in the loft?" Charlie nodded. "They use the blood from each girl to make their mark?" Charlie nodded again. Harrington's blood pressure was reaching a dangerous point. "What about the two ropes that somebody cut?"

"Two of the girls hung theirselves. Another one run off into the prairie and Angela swears Elmer found her body and buried her. The blonde girl with the short hair ain't spoken a word since it happened to her last year. The oldest girl here is eighteen and she was the first six years ago and her sister is fifteen." Charlie stopped before driving home his final point. "Angela run off 'cause she was gonna be next."

"My Lord," the marshal muttered.

"And Whitaker could deliver the spring hay any day now," Charlie added.

"My Lord," Harrington repeated, and he walked briskly toward the ladder with Charlie on his heels. The marshal descended the rungs of the ladder and took Angela by the arm and headed out the main barn door. Charlie had to jump from the third rung from the bottom and trotted to keep pace. It was clear the marshal had bad intentions toward Elmer Bigby. They reached the porch and by the expressions on the Bigby's faces they were completely afraid of what might befall them. "Untie 'em Charlie." Once Charlie had freed the couple, Harrington pulled Elmer up, turned him to where his back was against the railing of the porch and hit him so hard in the jaw that Elmer fell backward over the railing. Rather than leap over the railing after him, Harrington walked quickly around the steps and into the bushes where Elmer had fallen. He then began beating him mercilessly. "You knew what was going on out there in the hay loft!" he screamed. "You let it happen! Did you do it to save some money? Is that why you done it?" He punched Elmer Bigby repeatedly in the belly and the face until Elmer collapsed on the ground.

He turned his wrath upon CoraLu. "How much did you know about all this? Don't you realize you caused three young girls to give up their lives? I ain't never raised a hand against a woman but I can't promise I won't do that for you!" CoraLu began to scream and sob simultaneously at the thought she might receive a beating like her brother had gotten.

Harrington turned his back on her and walked halfway across the porch before turning to Charlie. "Throw a bucket of water on that wretch and ask him if he knows when the hay is comin'." Charlie obeyed and threw the entire contents of a large bucket in the face of Elmer Bigby. Elmer sat up straight, coughing and strangling on the huge amount of water.

"The marshal wants to know if you have an idea when the hay delivery is gonna happen!" Charlie demanded. "If I was you, I'd tell the truth, or you may get your brains beat in some more."

It took Elmer several seconds to even be able to speak. "I don't know," he sputtered. "They just show up out of the blue." Charlie squatted down in front of him.

"Which direction do they come from?" Elmer pointed to a ridge about a quarter of a mile to the east from the house. It was barely visible in the dusk. "Always?" Charlie persisted. "Do they always come from that direction?" Elmer nodded. Charlie looked up to where the marshal stood listening on the porch. Harrington swore under his breath.

"We've got ourselves into a fine mess Charlie," he said. "We could load up the wagon yonder and haul all them girls to town but what do I do with them once we get there? Before we found out about this Whitaker feller, I was thinkin' about taking the Bigby's to town and leaving you here to watch over these gals. I was hoping to come back with some help." He became lost with his own thoughts and paced some more up and down the porch. "I'm pretty sure them boys ain't going to just let me arrest them when they get here. They're gonna put up a fight and things could get dangerous. One against four ain't good odds. They're liable to shoot me and then they'll shoot you and then they can do whatever they want."

"Two against four," Charlie simply said.

The marshal shook his head. "No, no, no. I can't put you in harm's way like that. You're just a kid. You don't know anything about bein' in a gunfight. On the other hand, I've been in more scrapes than I'd like to remember."

"You just said that if they shoot you, they're gonna shoot me," Charlie reasoned. "I might as well be with you when the shootin' starts. I ain't exactly afraid of much."

Harrington admired the boy's sand. "Well, let's go eat somethin' and we'll reason it out after that. They ain't comin' tonight."

The girls had prepared a good supper and after the meal the marshal instructed some of the older girls to get CoraLu and Elmer in the house for the night. He motioned Charlie to follow him out to the porch where he poured some tobacco into smoking paper, licked one edge so it would stick together, rolled it and lit it. He took a big drag from the cigarette and blew the smoke into the night air. It was gratifying to hear the girls working to clear the dishes and get them washed. They giggled at something every now and then and Charlie thought they made a good family. They had just inherited poor adults to watch over them.

"Listen to me close Charlie. Real close," the marshal said pointing the index finger of his right hand at Charlie. He had the boy's attention. "I reckon we have to stand and fight but I hate to put you in danger. I believe I'll send you up to that ridge in the morning and you can watch for the Whitaker's and then ride back here with the news if you see them. After that, if we're gonna survive this you have to do exactly what I say. Do you understand me?" Charlie nodded. "Repeat back to me what I just said."

"I have to do exactly what you say," Charlie said.

"Good. I don't always have time to lay out a plan, but I've been doin' some plannin' the last hour or so. When you come back from the ridge, I want you to get on this side of the fence with me. Have that cannon you carry leanin' kind of out of sight to somebody on the other side of the fence. I'm hopin' they see us and wonder what we're doin' here. I need them to come up to the fence as close as possible to the water trough. I'll make sure they can see my badge and when they ask what we're doin' here I'll tell them the truth. We returned a runaway back to the orphanage. I'm probably going to tell them right then and there that I know what's been goin' on for the last six years and that I'm puttin' them under arrest. When they won't be taken, I'll shoot the first one of 'em who draws a gun. I don't care if he draws it nice and slow to make a point. If I let him do that, they'll have the advantage. They've already got the advantage in numbers. If one or more of the others draw on us after that feel free to open up on them with that howitzer. What you have to remember is that if we don't shoot them, they're gonna shoot us. The sons will probably be on horseback so you can't concern yourself with maybe shootin' an innocent horse in the process of shootin' them other men. Be sure and wear your belly gun in case there's more shootin' and you don't have time to reload your shotgun. Believe me when I tell you it's gonna be quick." After a slight hesitation he added "I can't believe I'm goin' to war with a kid."

While the marshal had been talking, Charlie had been peering out to the water tank outside the fence. He was trying to visualize what might take place if the fight ever happened. "Are you with me so far?" Harrington asked. Charlie nodded nervously. "I'm assumin' you ain't never shot nobody before." Charlie shook his head this time. "Well, you're about to grow up mighty fast."

"I killed my Pa with a frying pan," Charlie announced. "I ain't never shot nobody though."

Harrington knew how to motivate the boy. "You just remember Charlie what them men have already done six times. The girls they abused were a lot like you. They didn't deserve it and neither did you. They couldn't defend themselves and they still can't. That's up to me and you. Don't flinch when the time comes. Just watch them and blow whoever pulls to hell. I know I can count on you."

That took a lot of the dread away from Charlie. Now he had a mission. Punish the abusers.

"We need to get some sleep," the marshal said. "Claim yourself a spot here in the front room. All the girls sleep upstairs. CoraLu and Elmer can sleep tied up in a corner. I'll want you on that ridge at daybreak and I need you to be as out of sight as possible."

Chapter 16

Charlie did not sleep much that night. The possible excitement of the coming day kept him awake but the marshal certainly didn't have any trouble sleeping. He snored so loudly that Mary, the oldest of the girls, came down the stairs to see what or who was making all the noise. Charlie saw her and waved weakly and received a shy smile in turn. When she had satisfied her curiosity she turned and quietly made her way back up to bed. Charlie had thought for a moment she might come downstairs to talk with him since they were both awake. She was older than him, but he felt they shared a common bond. They both suffered from abuse even if they were in different forms.

The marshal removed the rope from the Bigby siblings at first light. Elmer had pleaded with him, promising they would not run. CoraLu was in tears from being bound all night and thanked Harrington over and over as she ran to the outhouse. Charlie was eager to get to his assigned post and wolfed down his breakfast of eggs and biscuits with molasses.

"What are you gonna do as soon as you see something?" the marshal asked.

"Come right back as fast as I can get here," Charlie replied as he walked out the door to fetch Sandy. One of the girls filled a canteen for him and brought a cheese sandwich for his lunch. Once Sandy was saddled, Charlie pointed her in the direction of a small grove of persimmon trees at the crest of the hill overlooking the road the Whitakers would be using. The few trees offered some shade for him and his horse but also allowed him to hide Sandy from view. The terrain sloped away from him slightly and he could see for nearly a mile down the road. A large hay wagon would be unmistakable from a long distance, so it wasn't as important to stay vigilant. However, he wanted to guard against falling asleep after a restless night. He knew that would be disastrous.

Charlie was a growing boy, so he ate his sandwich long before the sun was high in the sky. He didn't own a pocket watch, but he guessed it was somewhere around ten o'clock in the morning. He had just finished the last bite, wishing he had another sandwich when he noticed Sandy turn her head to the east. He had been sitting in the shade in the middle of the trees and now he stood. Charlie strained his eyes to see what had caught Sandy's attention and his heart began to race. Something would appear for a moment and then disappear again behind a mound of earth. His eyes played tricks on him from this distance, but Charlie kept peering in that direction until at last his patience was rewarded. All he could see at first appeared to be a moving haystack, but he was certain this was what he had been waiting for. The wagon had come from the north and then about three quarters of a mile away the road curved to the west toward him. Riders came into view beside the wagon with hay piled so high it made the boy wonder how it stayed on. Two large draft horses pulled the wagon and as it got a bit closer Charlie could see there were two riders on the seat and there were three mounted horsemen walking slowly beside it.

Charlie untied Sandy and climbed into the saddle. Something was bothersome with the two figures on the wagon, and he wanted to make certain he gave the marshal an accurate report. It seemed to take the wagon forever to get within one quarter of a mile and at that point Charlie had seen enough. He turned Sandy back toward the house which was only half a mile away. A couple of the younger girls had been watching for him and when they saw him, they ran inside to alert the marshal who appeared at the door a few seconds later. Harrington was walking toward the fence as Charlie tied Sandy closer to the barn, so she wasn't as likely to be hurt by a stray bullet. He ran as fast as he could to give his report as the girl named Dixie brought his shotgun out to him. He climbed over the wooden fence and was embarrassed he had forgotten it. She handed it to him and then ran back to the house without saying a word.

"Are they comin'?" the marshal asked, and Charlie nodded his head. "How many are there?"

"Three men on horseback but we've got ourselves a problem marshal." Harrington waited patiently for the boy to explain. "There's two people on the wagon. One is an old man, and the other is a kid. He looks to be about Angela's age." This took the marshal by surprise.

"Miserable, wicked wretches," he muttered as Charlie propped his shotgun against the fence as he had been instructed. "The kid must be Whitaker's grandson, and his Pa is on one of the horses. That just beats all. They're bringin' a kid for his first experience with a girl. Well, they'll take Angela or any of the other girls for that matter over my dead body." He spit angrily on the ground. "That kind of changes my plans. You can't shoot the old man with your eight-gauge 'cause you might hit the kid and as far as we know he ain't done nothing wrong yet. You'll have to leave old man Whitaker to me if it comes to that. Remember, I'm shootin' the first man who pulls and then you let loose with your shotgun if anybody on your side of the wagon tries anything. Don't flinch, son. It's the only way we walk away from this fight. If somehow they choose to fight another day they'll have us over a barrel. It needs to end right here and right now." Charlie picked up the heavy shotgun and placed the barrel through the top rail and the one below it. It was a menacing weapon even though it was being wielded by someone so young.

The wagon crested the hill by the trees Charlie had hidden in and moved slowly forward. Marshal Harrington made certain his badge was on full display even though it would take the men a few more minutes to get close enough to make out anything about the two. As the hay wagon and crew got within fifty yards they could see the marshal's badge. They spread out a bit with one man on horseback to the right of the wagon as Charlie and the marshal viewed them and two to the left. Harrington saw that Charlie had been correct. The boy beside the old man appeared to be twelve or thirteen years old and wore a round hat that made him look even younger. He was certainly too young to be involved in a situation like this, but Charlie reminded himself he was only two or three years older than the kid.

"What brings you out to these parts, marshal," old man Whitaker asked. "I don't recall ever seeing you around." Harrington looked at one man and then another, wary of the first move.

"To be right honest about it I've only been here once," he explained. "I thought I should pay a visit since it's under my jurisdiction." The old man had white hair under his black hat, and his beard was also snowy. He looked the part of a kindly old grandfather.

"No need for you to bother, Marshal. We take real good care of this place, don't we boys?" The three men on horseback laughed at the off-handed joke. Marshal Carl Harrington was not amused.

"You like jokes don't you boys?" he began. "I don't find any of this very funny at all." Whitaker stared at him from the wagon seat.

"I don't know what you're talkin' about Marshal. Maybe you should just come right out and say what's on your mind," the old man said. "We're just here to deliver hay for the year."

Harrington was careful not to lock eyes with the old man as he spoke. He continued scanning back and forth, watching for the first move to be made. "I'm sure that's what you're here to do. I ain't got no doubt about that. It's how you demand payment that's got me all knotted up inside. Most criminal types don't go around leavin' clues for the law to find but you boys weren't worried about that at all, was you?" The demeanor of the men changed dramatically as the marshal spoke. "One of the girls asked this boy here by my side to go up into the loft to check things out. Once he did that it didn't take him long to see what was happening up there and then I looked and came to the same conclusion. I've seen lots of things as a lawman that makes my blood curdle but when I saw them six tally marks on the post and found out what they meant it made me as mad as I believe I've ever been." The two brothers on Charlie's side looked at each other as the marshal finished his assessment and Charlie was certain they would be the first ones to pull their pistols, but they simply sat and listened.

"We don't know nothin' about any tally marks on a post," Whitaker lied.

The marshal continued hammering his point. "I don't suppose you know anything about the two ropes beside that post either do you? Or how about the blood-stained mattress and all the candles?"

Whitaker shook his head with conviction. "We don't know nothin' about any of that either,' he said. "Why would there be candles in a hay loft?"

"Well, you ain't nothin' but a black liar, sir!" Harrington said with a raised voice, and it was all Whitaker could do to control his anger. "Let me tell you what I believe is going on here and I won't sugarcoat it one little bit. Every year for the last six years you men deliver the hay in the spring, and you somehow convinced or threatened Bigby to let you have a different little girl to molest as payment. Naturally she would bleed, and you took her blood and made a new tally mark on that post. I'm sure you fellas was real proud of your accomplishment. Maybe you don't know it, but the two ropes were where two of the girls hung themselves. Another girl ran off and died out on the prairie somewhere. Bigby found her and buried her so you're all responsible for the deaths of three little girls and for that I'm gonna take you to town and put you in front of the judge to see what he can charge you with." Charlie and the marshal hadn't talked about this turn of events.

"You'd think after all my years of bein' a lawman I'd remember some of the things he could charge you with,"

Harrington continued. "Rape is the most serious accusation. Rape of a minor is a whole lot worse. Let's see, there's child endangerment, sodomy and assault. I'm pretty certain there's gonna be a long list." As the marshal spoke, he began to notice the man on his right becoming very agitated. He appeared to be the oldest of the three young men.

"Which one of you is this boy's pa?" Harrington asked. The man on the other side of old man Whitaker spoke up.

"That would be me," he flatly stated.

"I see," the marshal said. "I reckon you brought your boy to teach him how to be a pervert like his old man, his grandfather and his uncles." That statement almost caused the boy's father to draw first.

"Marshal, I don't think you really want to tussle with us," old man Whitaker spoke up again. "We're four hard men facing one hard man and a boy that looks like he's about to piss his pants." His sons laughed, gaining a little confidence.

"Let me ask you three sons a question," Harrington said. "Did your Pa ever beat you?" None of the three younger men responded. "Come on. I want an answer."

The trio looked at one another and the one on Charlie's far left finally answered. "Pa never did anythin' to us we didn't deserve." The three sons nodded their agreement.

"That's right and I wailed the tar out of you when you did deserve it," the grizzled old man said proudly.

"If this was a more polite conversation, I'd ask Charlie here to take his shirt off so you could see his back. What his Pa done to him was shameful. He's got more scars than you could count. He's been through an awful lot. He killed his Pa with a skillet, so I don't think this stage is too big for him to handle. Besides all that, the shotgun he's got pointed at you two on our left could blow you clean in half." Harrington paused to let that last statement sink in. "Here's my offer. That hay's still important for this place to survive so you'll unload it in the loft. We'll watch over you to make sure you don't try anything. Then we'll load you up and take you and the

Bigby's in their wagon and all the girls in this hay wagon once it's empty and we'll all go to Hays together and I'll let the judge sort everything out. I thought about leaving the girls here with a couple of the older ones in charge but men from your ranch are bound to come lookin' for you and that could be bad for these young ladies, so why don't you throw down your guns and turn that wagon toward the barn and let's get that hay unloaded."

Whitaker sat fuming on the seat of the wagon. "What happens to my grandson?" he asked.

"I ain't got that far, to be honest. I wasn't expectin' him. We'll put him up in a hotel while you stand trial, I reckon." Charlie sensed the corner had been turned and there was no going back.

Whitaker slowly set the brake of the wagon and dropped the reins to the floor. "We can't let you do that, Marshal. If we go to trial, they're liable to hang us or put us in jail for a mighty long time and I won't survive that. I'm not willin' to let anything happen to me or my boys over some girls their families threw out like slop. They ain't worth it. We're better than they are."

The marshal's instincts were right. It was the man on his right who attempted to draw first. His nerves or fears or anger made him awkward, and Harrington drew his pistol and shot him in the chest above the heart, and the force of the bullet knocked him from his horse. The two men on Charlie's side were smoother drawing their pistols but the boy was ready for them. He already had the shotgun trained on the father of the boy in the wagon and when Charlie fired the right barrel of the shotgun the pellets hit him in the chest, neck and face. The noise from the big gun caused the other brother's horse to rear up and he shot wildly in Charlie's direction. Charlie felt a sting in his left shoulder just before he fired the shotgun again. Some of the pellets hit the man's horse in the head but they also blew him out of his saddle and onto the ground. Old man Whitaker yelled at his grandson to get down on the floor of the wagon as he drew his pistol and that gave Harrington a chance to put a bullet in his chest.

The horse Charlie had shot turned and trampled his rider and then ran off shaking his head violently. The boy on the wagon began screaming in a high-pitched voice. He shook his grandfather and then jumped off and ran to his father who was dead. He buried his face on the bloodied chest and wept uncontrollably.

"You need to sit down Charlie," the marshal ordered. "You did fine, son. You did real fine." Charlie's left shoulder began to ache as he sat down with his back to the fence. He looked at it and blood was spreading all over his shirt, down the sleeve and soaking the entire left side of the dark blue material. The sting he had felt was a bullet which had hit him just below the collar bone. He used his right hand to reach across to his left shoulder and felt the collar bone. Then he took his left hand and crossed over to the collar bone on the right side and they felt different. He remembered when he was only five or six years old and was sitting on a horse on the farm and his father stuck the horse in the withers with a sharpened stick he had been whittling on. The horse bucked Charlie off, and it broke his collar bone. James had to take his brother to town again to have the doctor treat him.

The marshal looked over his shoulder as he crouched down to examine Charlie. The girls came boiling out of the house to come out and see what had happened. "Mary, you and some of the older girls help Charlie into the house and then boil some water. I'm pretty sure that bullet is still in him. There ain't no exit wound. I've got to check on these bodies." The girls obeyed and helped Charlie to his feet. Harrington checked the two men on Charlie's side, and they were both dead. He checked old man Whitaker and found him dead as well. He walked in front of the draft horses and just as he got to the one on the right the man arched his back and blood gurgled from his mouth and he then drew his last breath.

The young boy was lying on the ground with his head on his father's chest and he was crying with huge sobs. His tears mingled with the blood on his father's shirt. Now that the confrontation was over the reality of what came next hit the marshal. In a day, maybe two, men from the ranch would come looking for their boss.

Harrington knew he had to get everyone out of the house and at least on the way back to town before they arrived. There were four dead men to deal with plus this young boy weeping at his feet. Then there was the problem with Charlie's wound. It had probably hit the bone and stopped there, and it would be difficult to remove. He didn't have the skill necessary to take it out, but Charlie appeared to be a bleeder and had lost a large quantity of blood. The boy was in dire need of a real doctor, but he was twenty miles away from one. The last problem was the hay on the wagon. He didn't care whether it was unloaded properly but he did need to get it off the wagon so it could transport everyone to town with one trip. He couldn't leave the girls here alone and he had to take CoraLu and Elmer Bigby to jail.

"Why are you here boy?" he asked the youngster who wiped the tears from his face with his sleeve.

"You killed my Pa. You killed my grandpa. You killed my uncles."

Harrington looked down on him with pity. "I sure didn't make any plans for you bein' here," he said. "That's just the way it is, son. You try to plan for everything that could possibly happen and then when the time comes something new comes along. I've seen it happen many times. You didn't answer my question. Why are you here?"

The boy sat and stared at the body of his father. He reached around his father's neck and untied his kerchief so he could blow his nose before he answered. "They just said somethin' about makin' a man out of me on this little trip. They talked all the way here about how good a girl felt, and they were gonna show me once we got here. I didn't exactly know what they were talking about." He paused long enough to look over his shoulder at his grandfather dead on the wagon seat. My Ma sure didn't want me to go. She and my Pa got into a big fight about it and Pa put her in her place. She cried for two whole days and nights before we finally left."

"What do you mean about your Pa puttin' your Ma in her place?"

The boy looked up at Harrington through his misty eyes. "He hit her and knocked some sense into her," he said. "My grandpa did that to my grandma for a long time. He told me that finally one day she stopped sassin' him. I reckon that's just what you have to do." Harrington listened in disbelief.

"No. No, it ain't. You listen to me boy and you listen good. Your grandpa and your Pa and your uncles brought you here to watch them do what they've been doing for six years and that is to rape a little girl as payment for that wagon load of hay and maybe they were gonna encourage you to take part and hope to make you like them. Maybe your Ma suspected what they were coming here to do and she didn't want you to be a pervert like him. Sorry to be so blunt but that's the straight of it. If I would have had more men and more time, I would have taken them alive so they could stand trial for what they done and the judge could've sentenced them all to hang." He visualized that for a moment. "That's a hangin' I would have truly enjoyed." He started to walk toward the house, and he motioned for the boy to come with him. "I need to check on Charlie and you don't need to be out here by yourself, and I can't take the chance of you runnin' off to tell the folks back at your ranch what happened here."

The boy got up silently and walked beside the marshal with his head down. They marched up the stairs and followed the blood trail into the kitchen where Charlie lay on the table. The boy had lost consciousness, but the girls had managed to stop the bleeding.

"Marshal! Marshal, I can help! I can truly help!" CoraLu cried. "You're worried about getting that bullet out of his shoulder, but I believe I can get it out." She stared wide-eyed at Carl. "Maybe if I help you could put in a good word with the judge for me." Harrington stared back at her.

"I should have known you wasn't gonna help him out of the goodness of your heart," he replied. He felt Charlie's wounded shoulder. "His collar bone is busted. Can you set that too?" She came alongside him and examined the shoulder area as well.

"It appears to be a good, clean break. I believe I can push

them two pieces together good enough until we can get him in to see a real doctor. That bullet has to come out first. He might not survive the trip to town." Harrington felt he had no choice but to trust her.

"Go ahead and get at it but I warn you if you do somethin' to that boy to hurt him to spite me, I'll shoot you right in the head." He turned to see Elmer in the doorway to the kitchen. "I'm gonna help your sister all I can," he began. "You take this boy out and find two pitchforks and unload that wagon. Then I want you to find somethin' to wrap them bodies up with and load them onto the wagon. I don't care how you do it just line them up toward the front. Can any of you girls take a saddle off a horse?" Three older girls raised their hands. "Good. I need you to take those men's horses out to the barn, take their saddles off and put them in the corral." It was at that point he experienced panic. "Oh, God. I forgot about the one horse that took some buckshot to the head and run off. It's probably headed back to the ranch right now." He started for the front door. "You all need to get busy! I've got to go and take care of that animal before it gets too far."

Once outside the marshal remembered Sandy was still saddled and tied toward the barn. He grabbed the reins and spurred her into a full gallop toward the road where he hoped he could find what he was looking for, but his prey had a ten-minute head start. He was impressed by Sandy's speed and willingness to answer the call for more. Another ten minutes passed before he found the horse who was on his front knees rubbing the dirt frantically with his head, trying to relieve the sting of the buckshot pellets. When he saw Harrington, he jumped up and tried to continue running north but the marshal cut him off and herded him south and west over a ridge before pulling his pistol and shooting him dead. The buzzards would give his position away in a day or two but at least the horse wouldn't make it back to the ranch in an hour to set off the alarm.

Harrington looked all around to make certain no one had heard the shot and turned Sandy back toward the house. She didn't even appear to be winded, but he was reluctant to push her any longer today, so he put her into an easy lope. When he got back to the barn, the girls were finishing their assigned chores, and he left Sandy with them to tend to.

"Once we're done here, we can help get the hay off the wagon, Marshal," one of them said. Harrington tipped his hat to them.

"Much obliged ladies." He trotted back toward the house where he found CoraLu laboring over Charlie. She had made a one-inch incision all around the bullet wound and two of the girls were trying to keep the skin spread apart with butter knives while CoraLu fished for the bullet with a piece of wire which had a loop on the end.

"I don't have the right kind of tools for a job like this," she complained. "It's stuck in the bone all right. I was hoping to fit this loop over the bullet to at least jar it loose so I could get it out somehow." Harrington's heart sank at the prospect of Charlie possibly losing his life.

"A couple of you girls that ain't helping in here go on out and help kick the hay out of that wagon. The rest of you can start gettin' some food scraped together for the trip to town. I'll be out directly to help get those bodies stored in there. Bring some grain and hay and water to the horses on the hitch, too." He pulled his watch out of his pocket. Three o'clock. "If we can get all this done before dark we'll leave tonight. Gather up some blankets, too. It gets cool this time of year out on the prairie."

Everyone jumped to their jobs as soon as they felt he had dismissed them. He hoped they weren't performing at their best because they were afraid of what he might do to them if they failed. He would make sure later to compliment them on their hard work. He returned his focus to Charlie. "That ain't gonna work CoraLu and you know it. Maybe you'll get lucky, and you can keep tryin' until I tell you to stop but then I need you to stitch him up as fast as you can so we can get out of here as quick as possible."

The next hour was full of frenzied work, but no one complained, and no one shirked their duty. "I need somebody to go tell CoraLu to stitch Charlie up. We'll leave as soon as she's done." Four girls of varying ages ran at the same time for the house. CoraLu already had needle and thread ready before she opened Charlie's shoulder, so it was no chore for a seamstress to close the wound. In fifteen minutes, they had everything loaded and began their journey to Hays. They had put a little hay back on the wagon to make a bed for Charlie and with everyone else on board it made quite a load. The marshal encouraged the boy named Roland to sit on the seat next to him. He didn't feel it was healthy to have him ride in the back where he could see the wrapped-up bodies of his kin. The rest of the wagon was filled with four dead men, the brother and sister, Charlie and twelve girls ranging in age from eighteen down to eight. Sandy and the marshal's horse were tied to the back of the wagon and followed along.

"What about the horses back in the corral?" Angela asked. "You're not just going to leave them there to starve to death, are you?" Harrington smiled at Angela's tender heart.

"When we get to town, I'll send somebody to turn 'em loose," he explained. "They'll be fine until then." That satisfied her. "We should be able to make five or six miles before it gets too dark to travel any more. We'll make camp, get a fire going and eat whatever you brought for us. That's the only meal we'll have until we get to town. Then we'll start again at first light. That way we can make it to Hays by middle of the afternoon."

When they stopped to make camp, Harrington allowed CoraLu and Elmer to have their hands free to eat some bread and butter but then promptly tied them to a tree. He didn't trust them not to run off while he sat up with Charlie. He didn't care for how shallow the boys breathing was, and he fretted about it without knowing what to do to help him. They hadn't even got Charlie out of the wagon for fear of hurting him worse. They just threw more blankets on him to keep him from catching a chill. As Carl sat with a blanket draped over his shoulder, Angela sat down close enough to him to share it.

"I'm scared, marshal," she said as she leaned her head on him. "Is Charlie going to be alright?"

Harrington struggled with what to say to her. The two of them had become close friends. "It's all in God's hands now, Angela," he began. "We just have to trust He'll do what's best for Charlie even if it don't make a durned bit of sense to us here below." In the silence that followed the marshal had a thought. "Do you know how to ride a horse, Angela?" Even in the dark he could see her big, brown eyes looking right back at him.

"I don't know how to ride fast but I know how to ride at a trot," she said. "Why do you want to know that?" Harrington looked back at Charlie and worried he might not survive without help soon.

"You've been mighty brave through this whole ordeal, Angela. I'm gonna ask you to be brave one more time when the sun comes up."

"I'd do anything for Charlie," she said innocently. "What do you want me to do?"

"Sandy is already used to you. I'll saddle her up first thing in the morning and I need you to get to town as fast as you can on her and get the doctor and tell him it's a matter of life and death that he meet us on the road that runs by the creek. Tell him Charlie has a bullet stuck in his shoulder and that he has a broken collar bone. Can you do that?" Angela nodded. "That'll save us some precious time. Every second might be important."

Thirty minutes before sunrise Harrington saddled Sandy. Angela was ready and he cupped his hands to give her a leg up.

"Can I get started, Marshal? I know it's still dark, but I can walk Sandy until it gets to where I can see where I'm going. I can hear the stream so I can follow it." Harrington patted her leg.

"You bet you can get started. You're a brave young lady and I'm awful proud of you." She smiled down at him and turned Sandy toward the sound of the creek. "The Lord bless you and keep you, sweetheart!" he called after her and she waved her hand without looking back at him. This activity stirred the others in the camp.

"Where's Angela going on Charlie's horse?" one of the girls asked. Harrington was making his way to the draft horses to get them hitched.

"She's going for the doctor. Once she finds him, he can meet us as we're making our way and I figure that will save at least an hour or two for Charlie." He checked on the boy one more time and then busied himself with the horses. "He's gonna need all the help he can get."

Chapter 17

Sandy didn't seem to mind who was riding her. She was a well-behaved horse, and Angela became used to her quickly. Angela's eyes adapted to the semi-darkness, and she coaxed Sandy gently into a trot. When the sun enlightened the crude road Angela became acutely aware of the urgency of the situation and she decided to experiment with trying to get Sandy to go faster. She held the reins tightly with her left hand and the saddle horn with her right. She hadn't noticed the two large Navy pistols in their saddle holsters draped over the saddle horn before but in the early light she could see them. She also had wondered what her legs were touching because they weren't touching Sandy. On her left was the huge shotgun in its scabbard and on her right was the old carbine Charlie carried in another scabbard. He was certainly prepared for anything or anyone.

Angela gently kicked Sandy with her heels, but the horse did not respond. "Come on, Sandy. Come on, girl," she coaxed but Sandy kept trotting along. She tried clicking her tongue but that didn't work either, so she kicked harder and used her voice at the same time and Sandy lurched forward into a lope which nearly unseated the girl. When Angela righted herself, it didn't take long to get used to the gait and she patted Sandy on the neck to thank her for not throwing her on the ground.

After a few hours the town came into view and when she entered the town, she asked the first person she saw on the street where the doctor's office was. She didn't know how to tie Sandy to the railing, but she trusted her not to go too far. Angela didn't bother to knock and once she was inside, she saw a kindly looking older gentleman sitting at a desk with books and papers piled everywhere on it.

"Good morning, young lady," he said as he removed his spectacles. "What can I do for you?"

"Doctor, my friend Charlie needs help. He's been shot and the bullet is stuck in his shoulder. His collar bone is broke, too." The doctor stood up and immediately began preparing his bag with the needed tools.

"Good heavens! Well, he's obviously not with you so where is he?" he asked.

"He's with the marshal and they're on their way to town but the big hay wagon they're in is awful slow. The marshal thought I could make it to town and bring you down the creek road to meet them a lot faster than they could get here."

The doctor was satisfied that his bag was ready. "Time's a wastin' girl," he said as he took Angela by the arm. As they passed through the door the doctor noticed Charlie's horse. "I see you're well mounted. Bring her down to the livery stable and we'll get my buggy and be on our way. It's just at the end of the street. You'll see it."

With help from the livery owner the buggy was ready in no time, and the doctor put his fine horse into a quick trot. Sandy struggled for a bit to find the correct gait but soon matched the speed. By noon the wagon came into view and when Angela waved at it the doctor was surprised at how many hands waved back. Harrington was happy to see him and the doctor pulled his buggy up beside the hay wagon.

"Hello, Doc!" the marshal greeted him.

"Mornin' Carl. Say, it looks like you've been out harvesting young ladies. Where's my patient?" He grabbed his medical bag and got out of the buggy and headed to the back of the wagon. "Well, I guess that's a fool question. Of course he'd be back here." Some of the girls had to help him into the tall wagon but once there he worked quickly. "Build me a fire would you Carl and then boil some water. If you don't have a pot, I believe there's one in my buggy." He pulled back the dressing CoraLu had placed on Charlie's shoulder and smelled it. Good. There was no sign of gangrene yet. "My God CoraLu! Are you the one who butchered this boy or is this Carl's handiwork?" CoraLu's back straightened.

"I did the best I could with what I had and that ain't saying much!"

Everyone could see the concern on the doctor's face. "Come on over here and help me, CoraLu," he instructed. He laid out his surgical tools and told her what each one was and told her to pass whatever he asked for quickly. "Just bring me the water, Carl. These instruments were sterilized after I used them last so they'll have to do. This boy can't wait."

All were mesmerized with the doctor's speed and skill. He cut away the thread that held the wound together and then used spreaders to separate the flesh. He inserted some sort of device he called a probe and once he found the bullet he was able to grasp it with another instrument and had it out within minutes. He dropped the bullet into Harrington's hand. The collar bone fit back together easily, and he stabilized it. "I'll show you how to properly sew a wound," he said as he prepared needle and suture. "It ain't like sewin' a garment, you see. It needs to be like this." He skillfully closed the wound and bit off the suture close to the end and tied it off.

Harrington was still concerned. "He looks mighty pale, doc." The doctor nodded his head in agreement.

"Too pale. He needs nourishment. He needs some good broth for now when we get him back to my office. The trick'll be to get him to wake up so he can take it. I'm headin' back to town to get some broth heated and we'll put him to bed." Before he was helped from the wagon he looked back toward Angela. "I'll bet anything this young lady here can get him to wake up. Keep the same speed, Carl. We don't want to jostle him any more than we have to." He was still spry for an older man and before long he had turned his buggy around and headed it back to Hays. Harrington was impressed that the doctor never once asked about all the variety of people in the wagon, dead or alive. He was too busy doing what needed to be done.

It seemed to take forever to get to town but finally they were able to get Charlie settled in a bed and Angela went to work begging Charlie to wake up so he could get some broth in his belly. She wasn't successful but all it took was a kiss to his forehead from the pretty eighteen-year-old named Mary to make him stir. Angela was jealous but she got over it when she saw some color come back to Charlie's face after partaking of some of the chicken broth the doctor had ready for him.

Harrington pulled the doctor aside once Charlie had awakened. He seemed to be out of trouble for now. "Doc I could sure use some help." As he listed all the things he had to do he would stick one of his fingers out as if he was counting. "I have got to get CoraLu and Elmer down to jail first. Then I've got four dead bodies, so I have to get the undertaker busy with them. I also got to figure out what to do with that lone boy in my group. His Pa and grandpa are two of the dead men. Then there's the girls to deal with. You got any suggestions for me about what to do with all them kids?"

"When things calm down, I'd sure be interested to hear this whole story but for now I think we need to get the parson over at the church involved with the children. Maybe he'll know what to do or who to rope in for help."

That alone gave the marshal instant relief. "You're a lifesaver, Doc. I'll take CoraLu and Elmer to jail and then see the parson. I don't know what we can do with twelve girls and one boy, but we've got to do somethin'".

"I wish I could help you, but I need to stay with this boy," the doctor said. "He's lucky to be alive with all the blood he's lost."

"Doc, that kid has been through more hell than both of us put together. He'll make it." As Harrington made for the door and opened it, he turned back for one more thing. "You've seen his back. You know what I mean when I tell you that he'll make it."

Chapter 18

"I want to go home," Roland informed the marshal when Harrington stepped outside the doctor's office. A small group of people had gathered around the large wagon to look at the girls who sat quietly in it. Most of the girls couldn't remember the last time they had seen a town of any kind, and they stared back wide-eyed. The marshal put his hand around the boy's shoulder and guided him up to the seat.

"A lot has to happen before I can take you back so that probably won't be until tomorrow," he explained. "We're going down to the church to talk to the parson about caring for all of you for a little while. Maybe he can get some of the church goers in this town to feed you. I have to see about your Pa and your grandpa and uncles and get them tidied up. If we don't get to leave tomorrow to take you to your kin, I'll need to send somebody to tend their horses back at the farm. I don't want to turn them loose yet. They'd just go back to the ranch and start a ruckus. Everything just needs to fall into place so we can leave tomorrow morning. That would be the best thing." He drove the wagon toward the inviting church building at the end of the main street.

The parson proved to be invaluable. Not only did he open the church sanctuary to the girls to live in for the time being, but he took the boy into his own home, and his wife did everything she could to comfort him. Once that was settled Harrington took the horses and wagon to the livery to get the horses taken care of, including Sandy and his own mount. Then it was on to the undertaker who had been watching him like a vulture as the marshal made his rounds.

"Oliver, I've got four dead bodies in that wagon over yonder. I reckon I should have brought them here first before the team got unhitched but it's been a long day and I ain't thinkin' straight."

"Don't worry, Marshal. Me and my boy will take care of them," the undertaker said. "What kind of funeral do you want for them?"

Harrington shook his head. "Just straighten 'em up some and put 'em in boxes. I'm sure the rest of the family will want to claim the bodies when they find out what happened. I hope to take care of that matter tomorrow. If the family that's left won't foot the bill, I'll make sure the city pays for them as long as it ain't too expensive. They weren't worth spendin' too much on." The businesslike man never said anything more. He simply motioned his boy to follow him as they walked toward the stable. That was the only thing Carl liked about the man. He didn't ask any questions, and he didn't try to negotiate.

Evey hour he made his rounds of all his new charges. Each time he checked on Charlie there would be another one or two of the girls there to watch over him. Charlie would only respond to Mary stroking his face and kissing his forehead so when the doctor wanted Charlie to eat something he just sent for the pretty blonde girl. If Angela was present when Mary came into the office she stomped out and sat on a bench on the boardwalk outside the office until Mary went back to see about the other girls. The older girl would come out of the office door and smile at Angela as if to let the younger girl know she had performed her important duty. Angela waited until Mary turned to walk away before she stuck her tongue out at her. That made her feel better and she could go sit with Charlie again.

After Harrington was satisfied that Charlie was making some progress, he would move on to the church to check on the girls. They were no trouble at all, and the older girls watched over the younger ones. They had grown up in such a hostile environment, this place seemed like heaven, and they were content. At last, he would check quickly on CoraLu and Elmer in the jail. He arranged to have food brought to them and the good people in town were more than happy to provide for the children. The greatest amount of support came from Eugenia Standish and George, the owner of the general store. Carl thought perhaps they were making up for their past indiscretions concerning the girls and all the work they had done to keep a steady cash flow for their stores. Harrington finally allowed himself to get something to eat and he walked past the church about a hundred yards where a small Mexican café stood by itself. The food was to his liking and so was one of the senoritas who waited tables but even she couldn't get him to stop thinking about everything he had to do starting early in the morning. He helped her with her English, and she helped him with his Spanish most meals but this time she just watched him eat as she stared at him with her big, brown eyes. He often wondered what the townspeople would think of him if he ever married this beautiful Mexican girl.

He made one last check of Charlie before going back to the office to try and get a little rest. He was met with the whining of CoraLu and Elmer.

"We've been talking Marshall," CoraLu began. "We know you'll have to take that boy back to his home and break the news to his mother and whoever else is left after you and Charlie killed all those men. Who's going to take care of us while you're gone? What happens if they take the news badly and end up shooting you dead and you never come back? What happens to us then?" Harrington sighed and leaned against the bars of her cell.

"Good God almighty," he said. "It'd sure make it simpler if I just opened up your cells, told you to head for the door and then I could just shoot both of you in the back. That'd make my life a whole lot easier. On top of that it would be a pleasurable experience. I'll just get the keys." He turned to retrieve the keys from outside the cells.

"She didn't mean nothing by that, Marshal!" Elmer quickly added. "We just ain't never been in no cell before and we're just worried is all."

Carl stopped to look at him in his separate cell. "I'd be worried too but you might want to get used to it," he said. "Now, I'm gonna try and get some sleep. If either one of you vex me anymore, you're gonna regret it so just shut up and close your eyes and mouths. I'm taking Roland back to his family's ranch tomorrow and if everything goes according to plan, I'll be back late tomorrow night. Somebody from the café will bring you somethin' to eat. If you want anything besides bread and water, you'll behave yourselves." He laid down on his side on his cot but had to put a pillow over his head to drown out the wailing of CoraLu Bigby.

Chapter 19

The marshal was troubled through the night by thoughts of what the Whitaker family might say when he informed them of the demise of four of their menfolk. It did no good to consider what he would say if he was in their shoes because he knew what those men were and despised them for it. He recalled being a witness in many trials where friends and families of heinous murderers defended them to the end and blamed him for hangings and jail sentences when he was simply upholding the law he had sworn to defend. He wondered what kind of man Roland might become now that he had been spared from the exposure of evil. Maybe he would be able to recognize the hand of the devil and run from it or perhaps he would live the rest of his life being resentful toward the marshal. Carl might have another person to be wary of for the rest of his tenure as a lawman for when the boy grew to be a man he could seek revenge.

He woke up when the rest of the town began to stir. He gathered some provisions for the trip and walked across the street to the doctor's office to check on Charlie. The doctor was asleep in a chair by the boy's bed and Carl didn't bother waking him. Charlie was breathing evenly and as Carl felt his forehead, he could not detect any fever so that was a relief. He crept out quietly so they could continue to rest and crossed the street again to the small parsonage and knocked on the door. He heard light footsteps coming to the door before the knob turned. The door opened and the parson's pretty wife smiled at him.

"Come in marshal and have a bite of breakfast before you

leave," she said cheerfully. "Roland is already stuffing himself. He can certainly put away food, but I like to see that." The smell of bacon, eggs and biscuits was too good to turn down.

"I don't want to put you out, ma'am but it sure smells fine," he said.

"Nonsense. Come on in. Lawrence is already at the church checking on the girls. When the two of you leave, I'll go over and look after breakfast for them. My, what a joy they are!"

The marshal followed her to the kitchen table where Roland sat finishing his meal. He glanced up for a brief second and neither one had a word for the other. The woman put a plate of food in front of the marshal and then poured a cup of hot coffee for him.

"Much obliged, Muriel," Carl said as he stuffed the napkin in his shirt and spread it out. "This ought to keep us for a while. What do you think, Roland?" The boy wiped his mouth after taking a last sip of buttermilk.

"May I be excused? I'd like to go over to the church and say goodbye to the girls if that would be okay with you." Muriel smiled at his politeness.

"I think that would be nice. You're excused."

"We'll be on our way as soon as I finish breakfast," Carl called after the boy as he sped out the door. He looked into the eyes of Muriel before he began to eat. "I reckon he's got a right to hate me. I kind of wish things would have been a little different out there but I had to play the hand I was dealt."

"I won't bother you with asking questions, Marshal," Muriel said. "I'm sure you did what you had to. How was your young friend this morning?"

The food was delicious, and Muriel also placed some honey on the table. "Him and the doc were both asleep, so I didn't wake them up. I figure rest is pretty good medicine right now. He didn't have a fever."

Muriel had packed a lunch for him and the boy. Carl finished his food, thanked his host and went to check on the girls. When he walked through the front doors of the church, he saw some of the older girls brushing the hair of the younger ones. A pair of elderly ladies were busily passing out homemade muffins and there was jelly and milk on a table by the altar for the girls to serve themselves. They all greeted him, and he waved and smiled at them. They were adapting quite well to their temporary environment. The parson appeared from a room behind the altar and smiled at Carl.

"Good morning, Marshal," he said. "The congregation is all pitching in to provide for these young ladies you brought us."

"I can see that," Carl answered. "They're a pretty rough bunch so I hope they didn't cause you any problems." The angelic faces just smiled up at him.

"Not one problem at all," the parson replied. "I don't want you to concern yourself about their welfare. You just go and do what needs to be done. They're welcome for as long as they need to be here." Roland sat with Angela and three other girls, and they were smiling and giggling. Carl thought that was ironic. Angela was going to be the next victim of the Whitaker clan and that might have included Roland in some way. That thought alone gave Carl some sense of vindication for what he had done. He shook hands with the parson.

"Son let's be on our way. It's gonna be a long day so we may as well get started." Roland stood up and awkwardly hugged the girls he had been talking to and waved at all the others. Carl also waved to the girls and he and the boy walked the short distance to the livery where the draft horses had already been hitched to the wagon for them. His own horse was also tied to the back of the wagon. He thanked the owner for his kindness, and they pulled out of town.

Carl thought they could make the twenty-seven-mile trip in nine hours if everything went well. They sat in silence for the first three hours, and Carl was grateful at first but didn't think it was a good idea not to speak at all for the entire trip. He didn't want to talk about what had happened the day before so he watched for anything that would start a polite conversation. Finally, he saw five deer drinking in the creek and he pointed them out to Roland just before they sprinted off.

"I counted five. How about you?" he asked. The boy continued to stare straight ahead. "Tell me about your ranch, Roland. Do you have a horse of your own? How about pets? You got any of them? You could tell me about your ma and your grandma."

Roland didn't answer right away. "Are we going to stop where the girls live and pick up my uncles' horses?" he asked. Carl nodded.

"We'll do that and feed the other farm animals right quick. It won't take but just a few minutes." They arrived at the farm at around two o'clock and Carl was pleased with their progress. The pile of hay from the wagon had been blown about and other wild animals had come for a free meal. "You want to help me out and toss some feed out for the chickens while I tie the horses to the wagon and feed the bigger animals a little bit?" Roland didn't answer the question, but he performed the small chore and waited for Carl to finish. Carl completed his task but before he walked out of the barn he turned and looked at the ladder that led to the loft. "Roland come in here to the barn a minute."

Roland came in and stood in front of the marshal. "I've got something to show you up there in the loft." He looked over to the ladder. "I'll give you a leg up. That first step is mighty high. I need to find a box to stand on or somthin' for me to get started up."

Roland started for the ladder. "I can do it myself. I don't need no help." He jumped up twice before he finally grasped the last rung, and he struggled to pull himself up, but he was at last able to get one of his feet on the lowest rung and he started climbing. Carl couldn't find anything to help him, so he did what Roland had done and struggled even harder to get his foot up. He ran a splinter into the skin below his index finger on his right hand. He looked at it and swore at the pain before using his teeth to grasp the end of the splinter and pulling it out. He got to the top and Roland hadn't moved more than three feet from the top of the ladder.

Carl put his hand on Roland's back and gently coaxed him forward towards the old straw stuffed mattress first. "I reckon you can't hate me any more than you already do so I'm just gonna tell this to you straight," he began. "Did your Pa or your grandpa or your uncles ever tell you how they got paid to bring hay to this farm every spring for the last six years?"

"They talked all the way here but none of it made any sense to me. They sure seemed excited to get here," Roland said.

"I'm sure they were," Carl said. "I don't know if they had been bringing hay before six years ago and got paid in paper or coin but at some point, they decided to demand payment from CoraLu and Elmer Bigby to give them one of the girls to molest." Carl paused for a moment. "Do you know what that word means?" Roland was staring at the stained mattress.

"Hurt?" Roland answered.

Carl was already regretting bringing Roland up here to talk to him. "It ain't my place to tell you about the birds and the bees. Maybe somebody else in your family has already talked to you about that. Have they?" Roland shook his head. "I was afraid of that," Carl said. "Tell me this. Do you know the difference between a boy and a girl?"

"There's just me back home at the ranch. My uncles weren't married so there weren't any other kids." Roland thought for a moment. "I know I like talking to the girls from the farm. They were nice."

"You and the girls were gettin' along just fine back at the church, weren't you?" Roland nodded. "You wouldn't want anything bad to happen to them now, would you?" Roland shook his head. "Well, your Pa, your grandpa and your uncles were fixin' to do lots of bad things to Angela, and they were gonna make you watch and maybe join in. You wouldn't like that would you?"

"What kind of bad things?" Roland asked.

Carl exhaled. He was struggling to explain it to the innocent boy. "This ain't gonna make a durned bit of sense but maybe you can ask your Ma or grandma about it later. The first time a girl has relations with a fella she bleeds." Roland had a blank look on his face. "From down below!" The marshal grabbed his crotch. "That's where the difference between a male and a female is. For the last six years your kin has been molesting a young girl making her bleed and then taking some of that blood and marking that post over there with a tally mark. That's why there's blood on the mattress. They do the bad things on it." It was clear Roland didn't understand but the marshal continued. "The two ropes is where two of the girls couldn't stand the shame and they hung themselves and had to be cut down. The stool they used to stand on is in the corner over there. One of the other girls ran off and got lost and died out on the prairie. The girl they call Dora hasn't said a word since it happened to her. Mary and Dixie somehow managed not to lose their minds after it was done to them. I know this is a lot of information for you to chew on, but I thought it was important that you know what kind of fate Angela was gonna suffer if they'd have gotten to her." Roland stood at attention silently. "I couldn't allow that to happen."

The boy took one more look around before he walked to the ladder and descended. The marshal followed close behind. They started the last seven miles of their journey in silence again before Roland spoke at last.

"I wouldn't want anything to happen to Angela either," he said as he continued looking straight ahead. "I'd have hated myself forever if I had anything to do with that."

Carl had compassion for the boy. "This sort of thing has to stop somewhere. Maybe it stops with you," he said.

Somewhere between two and three hours from the farm a group of buildings formed a nice sized complex at the bottom of a hill. Two women were hanging out laundry and saw the wagon approaching. Roland was excited and began waving at them. "Is it alright if I jump off and run to them, marshal? That's my Ma and grandma." Carl made a motion with his hand for Roland to proceed, and the boy landed with a thud from the seat of the tall wagon. Carl wondered what the boy might tell the pair of ladies before he could reach the ranch. He watched the boy intently and could tell by the reactions of the two women that Roland had told them the fate of the men in the family. He reminded himself he had to go and take his medicine. When he finally pulled up, he set the brake and climbed down. Once on the ground he removed his hat and walked toward them.

"Mrs. Whitaker," he began. "Sorry. I reckon you're both Mrs. Whitaker." It wasn't the ideal way to start the conversation. He turned his attention to the older woman. "I hate to be the bearer of bad news, but your husband and three sons were killed yesterday morning." He turned to the younger woman. "I'm sorry about your husband."

Both women had a hand over their mouths and tears formed in their eyes. They made their way to each other and embraced before crying on each other's shoulders.

"Roland told us," the older woman said. She dabbed at her eyes with a kerchief she kept in her bosom. "Did you do the killin' marshal?"

Carl nodded. "It was me and a kid who found one of the girls on the prairie and brought her to town and she told us what had been going on at the farm for the last six years. We went back with her and confronted your menfolk when they showed up and wouldn't turn themselves in. My young friend took a bullet in the shoulder, and he also got his collarbone busted but I believe he's gonna be alright."

"Why don't you come in and we'll get a cup of coffee for you? You've had a long trip from Hays," the older lady said. Carl was shocked that the pair was taking the horrible news so well. The marshal followed them into the larger of two houses. He presumed the big house belonged to the patriarch and matriarch of the family and the smaller house belonged to Roland and his mother. The marshal took a seat where he was directed, and the younger Whitaker widow brought cup and saucer to him.

"I figured I owed it to you two ladies to explain everything while I brought Roland back to you," he started but the elder widow held her hand up to stop him.

"Marshal, I believe we know what they were doing to get themselves shot. You know how men love to talk and brag about themselves. My husband also talked in his sleep." She stopped and looked at the boy. "Roland, there's a new foal out in the barn. Why don't you go see it? It was born to that tall mare you like. We've been expecting it for weeks and it's finally here. Go see it and come up with a name for it." Roland knew he was being dismissed from the conversation, but he went without argument. His grandmother listened for his footsteps down the stairs of the porch before continuing. "Marshal, I'm so ashamed of what my husband and sons got themselves into. It had to do with those girls at the orphanage, didn't it?"

"Yes ma'am," Carl replied. "Excuse me ladies but I don't even know your names."

"Poor manners on my part," the wife of the old man said. "I'm Corrine and that's my daughter-in-law Amanda. We honestly tried to think of a way to get word to you about what we suspected was going on there, but my husband always sent someone along with us on the rare occasion we got to go to town. They watched us like a hawk." Corrine braced herself before asking the next question. "Just say it out, marshal. Tell us what they did to make you kill them."

Carl took a sip of his coffee and sat the cup and saucer on a small, low table in front of him. "Over the last six years your men have been trading a wagon load of hay to the farm every spring and taking payment by molesting a young girl each year. Three of the girls lost their lives because of this thing happening. Two hung themselves in the hay loft and one ran off and died out on the prairie somewhere. I have CoraLu and Elmer Bigby in jail in town right now. They'll stand trial for all kinds of charges. I expect CoraLu will die in prison, but they may hang Elmer. I know we have to use a duly designated hangman for the job, but I sure wouldn't mind springin' the trap on him myself."

Amanda wept when she heard that three girls had lost their lives.

"Did he molest the girls too Marshal?" Corrine asked.

"No, but they both beat the girls if they didn't do what they were told. They had them making clothes for the dress shop and other places and the girls had a quota to meet. It didn't matter how young the girl was she would still get a beating. I saw the marks on the backs of a couple of them. They also locked some of them in a closet for a couple of days until the girls soiled themselves. I nearly beat Elmer half to death when we figured out what had been going on in the hay loft. They were both guilty by lettin' that happen."

"I'm sure our menfolk threatened them into that decision," Corrine said. "They were good at threatening and beating people up to get what they wanted."

"Including us," Amanda added, and Harrington noticed a bruise on her cheek which had nearly healed.

"I assume the bodies are all in Hays?" Corrine asked.

"Yes ma'am. I figured you'd want to come in and claim them and bury them somewhere here on your property."

Corrine looked out the window toward the wagon. "I see you brought your own horse to go back. You're probably in a hurry."

Carl picked up his cup and took another sip of hot coffee. It had been good to calm his nerves. "Yes, I need to just turn around and head back. I want to check on my young friend and all them young gals. The parson and his wife took care of Roland last night and they opened up the church to give the girls somewhere to stay until we can figure out what to do with them. By the way, Roland seems to be a fine boy."

"We're very proud of him," Amanda stated. "My husband and I got into a heated argument when he insisted on taking

Roland with them on this hay delivery. I didn't want him to…" her voice trailed off.

"We didn't want him to end up like his grandpa, Pa and uncles," Corrine finished the thought.

"I probably overstepped my bounds but when we stopped at the farm to get the two horses and feed the farm animals, I took him up to the hay loft and showed him some things. He's probably gonna have some questions for you about the difference between girls and boys," Harrington explained.

"What was up there?" Amanda asked, and Carl immediately regretted mentioning it.

"A bloody mattress, some candles, part of the two ropes the girls used to hang themselves, a stool they probably stood on before they kicked it away and six tally marks on a post. The marks were made from the blood of each girl they took up there."

The two ladies each covered their mouths at the same time to stifle a scream. Corrine stood up and took her coffee cup to the window and looked out. Roland was in front of the barn petting his dog and talking to the ranch foreman. Both were smiling and she thought that was a good sign for Roland.

"I think it was very wise to show Roland the hay loft Marshal," she said. "He won't harbor any ill feelings toward you or anyone else in authority now that he's seen what his kinfolk were responsible for. I wish I could have prevented this from happening somehow. I feel guilty that life was lost because of my husband and sons. You didn't take them away from me. They were gone long before you confronted them." She stared out the window a little longer. "What will become of the rest of the girls?"

Harrington had lots of time to think about that on the way to the ranch. "I honestly don't know. It would be good news for me if I got back to Hays and all the girls got adopted. I have to consider other possibilities for them, though. They haven't been gettin' the education they need so I guess the best thing for them would be to move back to the orphanage with somebody that could teach them how to read, write and do arithmetic and such.

I would want somebody who wouldn't be a slave driver and force them to work."

"Do you know someone like that, Marshal," Amanda asked. Harrington shook his head.

"No, I don't. I'll have to post it around town. Maybe there's somebody right under my nose who would be the perfect fit. Maybe somebody knows somebody." Carl was anxious to get back to town, but he felt he owed it to these women to answer all their questions.

"Marshal, how old is the boy who was shot?" Corrine asked.

It occurred to Carl he had never heard of Charlie's age. "I don't rightly know. He might be sixteen or seventeen. His soul is a lot older than that though. I was awful proud of how he handled everything. He ain't got nobody except a sister and her family west of here and a brother who has a family of his own in Springfield back in Missouri. I believe I'll encourage him to stay around Hays."

"We'll stop in and see him when we come to town to claim our own," Corrine decided. "Roland might want to come along to visit him and the girls. Would you stay and eat with us, Marshal?"

Carl got up and took a last sip of his coffee. "I thank you, but I'm needed back there. Would it be too much to ask for a sandwich or something I could eat on the way?" Amanda got up from her seat quickly.

"I'll see to it," she said as she headed toward the kitchen. "I'll pack a few pieces of fried chicken from earlier and some fresh bread." That sounded wonderful to the marshal. Harrington walked over to the window beside Corrine.

"Are you ladies gonna be alright? I don't see any other men besides your foreman."

"My husband and sons took care of most everything. They ran off all the other help one way or another. Miguel is the only one who had the thick skin to stay. I believe he can recruit other men to help on the ranch now that he alone is working the place. We'll be alright," she said confidently.

Amanda came back with food wrapped in butcher paper and handed it to Harrington.

"Much obliged," he said. "When you come to town look me up and I'll introduce you to Charlie and help you with any legal matters you might need to take care of." He walked out the door and down the front steps and waved at Roland who waved back. "I hope to see you again soon young man. All them girls will be happy to see you too." Harrington released his horse from the wagon and got up into the saddle without spilling his meal, tipped his hat to the women and began the trip home.

Chapter 20

Harrington arrived back at Hays a little after seven o'clock p.m. He went directly to the doctor's office to check on Charlie and found him sitting up sipping broth from a cup. Charlie grinned at him as he walked through the door.

"I have to say it does me good to see you awake and doing so good boy," he said with a smile. "How are you feelin'? You look like you're gettin' some color back in your cheeks."

"My shoulder burns some and I'm afraid to move because of my broke collar bone," Charlie reported. "The doc had to practically lift me up so I could sit for a while instead of lay on my back." The marshal looked around the office.

"Where is Doc?" he asked. "Is he in the back room?"

Charlie took another long sip of his broth. "I don't rightly know Marshal. Some lady with an apron on came over here about an hour ago and said something to him and he told me he had to see about somebody. That's all I know." Harrington didn't care for mysteries, especially after a long day.

"An apron you say? That's mighty curious. I'd better go and check on the girls. It could be that one of them is sick. I'll see you again before you bed down for the night."

"You don't have to keep fussin' over me like an old mother hen," Charlie said. He was quite happy someone cared enough about him to fuss over him.

"You need to shut up and drink your broth," the marshal said as he left the office. A light was on at the jail, so he turned slightly to the left to check it rather than turning slightly to the right to go to the church. The door was unlocked, and he entered the office area which contained his desk, a small table and his uncomfortable cot. The door to the cells was also ajar and the keys were off the nail, so he made his way inside cautiously. The doctor was sitting on a wooden stool, and he was bent over CoraLu Bigby listening to her heart. He turned when he heard someone enter.

"Hello Carl," he greeted the marshal. "You made good time. We've got a situation here."

"What kind of a situation Doc? What's wrong with her?"

"She's dyin'! That's what the situation is and it's your fault Marshal!" Elmer accused.

Harrington took a step toward Elmer, and the beak-nosed man took a step backward. "I've had a long day Bigby. I don't need any sass from you. Do I need to remind you that you wouldn't be in the predicament you're in if it hadn't been for what the two of you done." That shut Elmer up for the time being and Carl turned his attention back to Doc. "I saw Charlie and he said a girl with an apron came and got you, but he didn't know where you were going. I saw the light on out in the office from across the street."

"That girl with the apron works at the restaurant. You'd know that if you ever went in there, but you prefer the Mexican place on the outskirts of town. She's the one who's been bringing meals to these miserable wretches. When she brought their supper, she noticed CoraLu wasn't moving so she came and got me." The doctor put his stethoscope back in his medical bag. "It's not good Carl. I can tell you it's not good at all. Her heart doesn't sound right. I think maybe part of her heart just shut down."

"You mean like a heart attack?" Carl asked.

"That's exactly what I mean. We need to get some men and a stretcher from my office and move her over there so I can keep an eye on her." The doctor was never one to waste time so as soon as he walked out the jailhouse door, he grabbed the first two men walking by and ordered them to help. Within minutes they had

160

CoraLu in the only other patient bed in his office and he went back to work.

Carl felt helpless but then remembered he hadn't checked on the girls yet, so he made his way to the church. As he entered the building, he saw Muriel sitting on a tall stool toward the altar. She was facing the girls, reading a story to them. Beside her was a chalkboard with the letters of the alphabet listed on it and it was clear she had been taking the opportunity for some teaching moments. The marshal thought how perfect she would be for the girls at the farm, but she already served an important function at the church with her husband. She finally looked up and saw Carl standing just inside the doorway.

"Come in, Marshall. We're almost finished with our story for the evening," she said. He let her continue and observed the beautiful little girls listening raptly to the kind woman. True to her word she finished a minute later with a flourish. "Alright girls, go and say goodnight to the marshal. It's time to start preparing for bed."

The girls streamed to Harrington, and he hugged the first two to reach him. "Good night, ladies," he said, causing them to smile. "I have some good news for you. Your friend Roland should be in town in a day or two and he'll want to come and say howdy."

"Did you stop and feed our animals, Marshal?" one of the youngest girls asked.

"I sure did. They were all just fine when I got there. I'll be sure and send someone out every other day or so to check on 'em and feed 'em." That made all the girls happy to hear it. "Now do what this nice lady tells you and settle down so you can get some sleep."

"We got to see Charlie today," Angela reported. "He's sitting up to eat now."

"I was just there, and I saw that very thing. He's gonna be up and around before you know it." He looked in Muriel's direction. "Could I have a word with your husband, ma'am?" he asked.

"Certainly, Marshal. He's out back of the parsonage cutting some firewood before it gets too dark."

Harrington tipped his cap to all of them and walked back out the doorway. He made the short walk to see the parson who was giving up for the day due to the impending darkness.

"You're back," Lawrence said. "You've made a long round trip of it. How did the family take the awful news?"

"Well, they had their suspicions of the menfolk for some time, so it wasn't that much of a surprise to find out they'd been caught and punished for their transgressions," Carl said. "It's hard to explain but they seemed to me to be relieved. Roland told me his Pa punched his Ma in the face when they got in a fight over whether or not Roland was going to go with them to the farm. He also told me his grandpa beat his grandma pretty regular. It seems to run in the family. I just hope that stops the evil and Roland can be a normal young man."

"Mary showed me the whip marks on several of the girls. Were those men the ones who did the whipping?" Lawrence asked.

"The ones who did the whipping were CoraLu and Elmer. The Whitaker men did a whole heap worse. I'll have to tell you that story another time. One of the reasons I'm here is about CoraLu. She had a heart attack or somethin' in jail. Doc has her in his office right now working on her. The other reason is that I wanted to let you know that in the next day or two the Whitaker widows and Roland will be coming to town to claim the bodies. I'd appreciate it if you'd give them a word of encouragement. They seem fine but I sure liked both of them and want them to be taken care of."

"I'll certainly do that, Marshal," the parson reassured him. "I'll wash up a bit and go over to the doctor's office to see what I can do. She may want to confess her sins before it's too late."

"She's got plenty to confess to," Harrington replied. "I appreciate everything you and Muriel are doing. It takes a load off me."

Lawrence put his hand on the marshal's shoulder. "Those girls are just a pure joy. They are very interested in learning everything they can. I tell them a Bible story after breakfast and then Muriel gives them a taste of school and a story after supper. I've never seen such a well-behaved bunch." He patted Carl's shoulder three times as he walked over to the wash basin and splashed his face and washed his hands before moving quickly across the street to continue doing his service. Carl thought to himself how fortunate the town was to have Lawrence and Muriel in Hays. They were young and he hoped they would make this their home for many years.

He wasn't hungry so he decided to go back to his office and as he started, he noticed a lone man standing by the door. As he got closer, he recognized Judge Jacob Treadway as the man waiting for him.

"You're a hard man to corral, Carl," he said with a broad grin on his face. Harrington reached out to shake the judge's hand.

"I've been mighty busy the last couple of days, that's a fact. What can I do for you? Are you bored out of your mind with nothin' to do or are you just that dedicated to your craft?" Carl teased.

"I arrived at noon and came straight here to check to see how things were going, and the door was locked. A pretty young thing came over with some food and opened the office for me. I was surprised to see a man and woman incarcerated in your fine facility. What's their story?"

Carl unlocked the door and walked in first to light a lantern and the judge walked in when the light illuminated the room.

"How's my sister? How's CoraLu, Marshal?" Elmer asked with a hint of dread in his voice.

"Doc's working on her. When I know something then you'll know something. Stop your frettin' and I'll make all three of us some coffee." Carl closed the door to the cells so he and the judge could speak freely. He busied himself by throwing out the old coffee, rinsing the pot and then preparing more.

"What seems to be the problem with his sister?" Judge Treadway asked.

"Doc thinks it's her heart. The little gal who let you in earlier in the day brought over some supper and found her passed out on the bed. She had the good sense to get the doc right away and he was checking on her when I got back."

"Got back from where?" Treadway persisted.

Harrington stopped and gathered his thoughts before answering. "I don't know how much I should tell you, Judge," he began. "I don't want to say anything that's gonna hurt the case I have against them." Without any doubt the marshal had the judge's full attention.

"Just start out by saying 'in my opinion'. I don't believe I've ever seen an old war horse like you get so shook up. It must be serious."

Harrington stoked the fire in the pot-bellied stove so the coffee could boil. He prepared three cups so he could pour as soon as it was ready. "Alright then," he started, "in my opinion that man in there and his sister were running what appeared to be a legal orphanage for little girls about twenty miles east of here. They were collecting money for taking care of them from some organization or another of the government of the Territory of Kansas. They were also working those little girls' fingers to the bone making clothes they could turn around and sell in town for extra profit. If the girls didn't meet their quota or do anything else they thought was wrong they would beat the girls or lock them in a dark closet for a couple of days until they soiled themselves."

Judge Treadway listened with interest to the story. "The law isn't very clear on what constitutes child abuse, but I can tell you without reservation I won't condone it. We could add child endangerment to the list of offenses and maybe get them a little time in territorial prison but that's about all. Can you see the whip marks on the girls?"

Carl checked the coffee pot, but it wasn't anywhere near ready yet. "Those are just the minor offenses, Judge. A young boy named Charlie Mabry found one of the girls who had run away from the orphanage. He brought her into town, and she showed me her whip marks. The three of us went back to confront CoraLu and Elmer but the same girl took Charlie out to the barn and showed him the hay loft that was the sight of the worst kind of evil I believe I've ever dealt with. For the last six years a rancher named Whitaker along with his three sons would bring hay from the spring harvest to the orphanage, but they took their payment in trade for one of the little girls. They molested them up in the loft Judge. There was a mattress in the loft covered in blood and they would take the blood of each little girl and make a tally on a support beam in the loft. Two of the girls they abused hung themselves and the cut ropes are still hangin' up there not far from that beam. Another girl ran out onto the prairie and died there. It was enough to make my skin crawl. All this is just my opinion, you understand."

The judge sat with his mouth open as he listened. Carl poured hot coffee into the three cups, handed one to the judge, placed another on his desk and carried the third cup into Elmer and shut the door again when he finished.

"In your opinion, did the brother and sister know what was going on in the loft?"

"They didn't take payment in coin or folding money so in my opinion they sure did know," Harrington replied with contempt.

All the judge could do was shake his head and take a sip of coffee. "God in heaven," he said under his breath. "We need to catch those men and charge them with raping a minor. Six minors! That would be enough to hang them."

Carl suddenly felt very weary and sat down behind his desk across from Judge Treadway. "They just happen to be across the street, but you'd have a hard time hanging them unless you want to hang dead men." The judge squinted at Carl as he waited for an explanation. "While we was there the Whitakers delivered a load of spring hay again and me and that kid Charlie confronted 'em and I was determined to shoot the first one that pulled and when that happened it was like the worst cow town shootout on a Saturday night. We killed all four of them, but the boy got shot in the shoulder and nearly died before we could get him to the doc. He's over in the doc's office right now recovering."

The judge was dumbfounded. "How old is this young man?" he asked.

"I reckon he's fifteen or sixteen. I need to ask him sometime. He's got quite a story to tell, too."

"Let me get this straight, Carl. You and a fifteen- or sixteen-year-old kid faced off with four grown men?"

"Well, Charlie was armed with an eight-gauge shotgun so that increased his chances. He took out two and I took out two." Carl sipped his own cup of coffee. "He's a good boy. I was mighty proud of him. Ask him sometime to show you his back. He's had a rough go of it."

"Is there anything else I need to know about this case, Carl?"

"There is one more thing. The Whitaker men brought a boy of about twelve years of age with them. The only reason I can see that they would do that knowing what they had in mind was to give him his first taste of their kind of sickness. All this is in my own opinion, of course. We kicked the hay out of the wagon, and I used it to bring the dead bodies of them four men, the grandson, CoraLu and Elmer and all the little girls plus Charlie to town. The girls are being taken care of by our good parson and his wife in the church. The dead men are in the undertaker's office, and I took the grandson back to his mother and grandmother this morning."

"You are to be commended, Carl. How did the women take the news?"

"After talkin' to them it made me see they had been beat by their men and they seemed to know something was goin' on at the orphanage. They were shocked at the news of what the truth as I see it was." Carl sipped at his coffee once more. "I forgot one thing, Judge. It was Charlie who figured out what was going on up in that loft. The girl he found running away just told him to go up and look around in the loft. He's quite a young fella'".

The door to the jailhouse opened and the doctor entered. "Hello, Jacob," he said to the judge. Carl filled a fourth cup with coffee and handed it to Doc as he pulled up another chair.

"It appears you come in bearin' bad news," the marshal said. "Is CoraLu still among the living?"

Doc sipped his coffee and turned the cup in his hands. "You won't have to worry about prosecuting her, Carl. I couldn't do anything about her heart. Did she show any signs of sickness last night?"

Harrington shook his head. "She was all upset and wailed most of the night. I just figured she hated being in jail. She didn't say anything to me about feeling sickly."

The doctor heaved a big sigh. "I guess I'd better break the news to her brother." He stood up and groaned before moving toward the door that separated the office from the cells. As he entered, Elmer stood up with a concerned look on his face.

"Is CoraLu gonna be alright, Doc?" he simply asked.

"Well, I'm sorry Elmer, but CoraLu didn't make it. She was too far gone when I got to her. I'm not certain I could have done anything for her even if I had known she had a bad heart."

Elmer looked as if he would break into tears, and he turned his back on the doctor in case he did. "I'm all alone now, Doc. What's going to happen to me? Will they hang me?" The fact that he was already thinking about his own well-being spoke volumes to the doctor.

"I suppose that depends on the lawyers, jury and judge. I'm a doctor. I don't know anything about the law."

Judge Treadway did not reveal himself to Elmer. He waited for the doctor to come back out and motioned for him to shut the door behind him.

"Six people could have been tried in this case and now five of them are deceased," the judge said. "I'll go over to the church tomorrow and talk to some of those girls to get their story and I want to see those whip marks. If what you told me is true Marshal, it seems to me that he's liable in part for the deaths of those three girls you told me about. If we can prove or get him to admit that he knowingly allowed a different girl each year to be molested by those four perverts, plus the fact they whipped the other girls for no good reason, worked them like slaves to make money for themselves, and locked some of the girls in a dark closet for two whole days, then we should be able to get a conviction. If that happens, I'll recommend the death penalty, and he'll hang right here in town."

"The Whitaker widows will be in town sometime in the next couple of days in case you need to talk to them," Carl mentioned. The judge nodded his agreement.

"They'll be needing to get their menfolk in the ground back on their ranch. We won't start the trial until they get that done," the judge reasoned. "How long is the trip from here?"

"I make it to be twenty-seven miles to their ranch. The orphanage is only twenty miles," Carl answered.

"I wish somebody would tell me what's going on around here," the doctor complained. "I suppose I can ask Charlie. He can't go anywhere."

Chapter 21

Harrington had almost given up on the Whitaker ladies to make it to town the next day. It was four o'clock and there was no sign of them. He just got his watch back in his pocket from checking it when a buckboard driven by Amanda Whitaker pulled into town right in front of his office. Her mother-in-law sat beside her and the marshal walked up to the buckboard to assist Amanda first as she was nearest the boardwalk and then Corinne slid over, and he assisted her as well. Roland jumped off the back.

"I didn't know if you were going to make it today or not," he stated. "I can escort you to the hotel and help you with your bags. Maybe you'd want to freshen up a bit?"

"All in good time, Marshal. We wanted to see you, the young man named Charlie, our men and the girls and we've already found you."

"Where are the girls, Marshal?" Roland asked. He turned to his mother. "Is it alright if I go and see my friends, Ma?" His mother smiled at him.

"I suppose that would be fine." The boy looked at the marshal for help in finding them.

"They're all still at the church. That's where you'll find them. No need to knock on the door. It's always open to everybody." Armed with that information, Roland sped off.

Since they were close to the doctor's office, that became their first stop. The doctor had Charlie up walking around when their visitors arrived. He guided the boy to a straight-backed chair before he greeted the ladies. The marshal introduced them as the widows of old man Whitaker and one of his sons. Charlie felt like he was backed into a corner and had no way of escaping. He was very nervous and didn't know what to say to them. Corinne immediately put him at ease.

"You're making great progress, young man," she began. "I'm sorry you got hurt."

"I'm sorry about your hurt too, ma'am," Charlie replied.

Corinne simply smiled at the perfect response. "I don't want you to blame yourself for anything that happened, just like I don't want the marshal to blame himself. It was all my husband and sons' doing. If they hadn't been in the wrong none of this would have ever happened. We still have Roland, and I will do everything I can to steer him down the right path. I just hope it's not too late."

"He's a good kid," Charlie said, and Corinne thought that was a funny statement coming from someone so young himself. She patted him on the hand and told him to do what the doctor told him so he could get better as soon as possible. Charlie thanked them and smiled as they were escorted out the door by Marshal Harrington. They were on their way to the undertaker's office.

It had always made the doctor uneasy that the undertaker was only three businesses down from his own. He wasn't the only one. Several people receiving treatment from him complained about it and remarked that if something went horribly wrong, they were at least close to who would be taking care of them next. The undertaker came to greet the women as soon as they entered his establishment. He led them to a back room where the bodies of the Whitaker men lay in four open pine boxes. Amanda gasped upon seeing her husband lying dead, but Corrine couldn't shed any tears. One of her first thoughts was a selfish one. Her husband could no longer beat her for any reason deserved or not. She moved her jaw around and found it to still be sore from a vicious blow he had delivered only three days ago. She couldn't remember the reason for his wrath. Maybe that was because it was something petty or maybe she was getting older and more forgetful or maybe it happened so often it was difficult to keep things straight. Undertaker Josiah Hilton allowed the ladies to mourn for a bit but there was business to be transacted.

"I can sell you four better coffins if you like," he said. "I didn't want to presume that you might want something nicer, so I began with these simple pine boxes."

The women were still lamenting their loss and didn't even look at him while he was speaking. "These will be fine, thank you. We will be spending the evening in town and would appreciate your help loading them first thing in the morning." Hilton bowed slightly to her. "I'll take the bill today if you have it prepared." He scurried off to retrieve it.

The marshal had been standing away to allow the women to grieve but he now moved to Corrine's side and whispered, "I'm sorry again for my part in all this." She indicated for him to follow her away from her daughter-in-law who still bent over her husband's body. She wept quietly and stared into his face. Corrine spoke softly.

"Please don't fret, Marshal. You were only doing your duty. My husband never beat his boys, but it never stopped him from beating me. My son Boyd who was married to Amanda there was the same type of man. He never beat Roland, but Amanda and I had to comfort each other many, many times. I have to try as hard as I know how to stop this from happening to Roland and when he becomes a father someday maybe he'll be a good man to his children and his wife. If he turns out alright, it won't be because of his male kin. You will get part of the credit for showing him what they were like and maybe he'll run from their ways."

Harrington didn't know what to say so he bowed his head and looked at the floor.

"I'd like to go and meet the girls now, Marshal," Corrine said. "I need something to brighten my day a little." She reached out her hand to her daughter-in-law and Carl held the door open for them as they made their way out to the street and started walking toward the church. The sounds of children playing and laughing, including Roland, met their ears as they approached. They were playing some game in which the person who was 'it' had to close their eyes tight and guess what someone else placed in their opened hands. The girls had made Roland promise not to put any type of crawling creature in their hands.

"Roland aren't you going to introduce your new friends to us?" his mother asked.

"I don't remember everybody's name, Ma," he explained. "This is Angela, this is Dora, this is Mary and her sister Dixie. I'll have to work on learning the rest of their names." He pointed at each girl as he spoke their name. To the girls he said, "This is my Ma and my grandma." The girls weren't used to seeing people where they lived so they were excited about meeting Roland's mother and grandmother. A pleasant woman with the children approached the two ladies.

"Hello. I'm Muriel, the parson's wife. It's a pleasure to meet you."

"Muriel, this is Corrine Whitaker and her daughter-in-law Amanda Whitaker," the marshal said.

"We're pleased to meet you," Corrine began. "These girls seem to be doing well."

Muriel turned to look at the children as they played. "They seem to be happy despite their circumstances. The presence of Roland has brightened their day even more."

"What will become of them?" Amanda asked.

Muriel let out a sigh. "I wish I could tell you. My hope for them is that someone will adopt each and every one of them. Tomorrow is Sunday and I will be certain to make sure the children all wash behind their ears to make good impressions to anyone who might be considering adoption. I want you to meet my husband. I'll go and fetch him." Muriel went inside the church and after just a couple of minutes she returned with the parson. "This is my husband, Lawrence." The ladies introduced themselves.

"First of all, let me say how sorry I am for your loss,"

Lawrence began. "If there is anything we can do for you or anything you need we'll do our best to supply it."

Corrine smiled at him. "You both are so kind. I believe we have everything we need for now. We'll be leaving with our menfolk in the morning. Muriel told us she hoped the girls would be adopted. Parson, what happens if people don't adopt them. I think the odds of having all twelve find new homes at the same time are rather slim."

"I'm working on that possibility. To make things even more challenging we have two sets of sisters, and I would insist on them staying together. My wife and I can be very persuasive," he said with a wry smile.

"It's none of my business but the tall blonde girl named Mary appears to be seventeen or eighteen. Would it be possible she could take over the orphanage? I believe the girls would be very happy if she would be willing to take on the job."

The parson appreciated the woman's interest in the girls. "We have considered that. Mary has been at the orphanage for six years and CoraLu and Elmer Bigby made no attempt at providing an education for the girls. I'm afraid Mary wouldn't be qualified to teach them. What we really need is to locate a retired teacher or someone like that who would be willing to move in and become somewhat of a headmistress at the orphanage." Lawrence hesitated for a moment before continuing. "I am angry and disappointed at the way the two of them treated these girls. I am fighting the urge to go over to the jailhouse and give them both a piece of my mind."

Carl shifted his weight from foot to foot. "You can't give CoraLu a piece of your mind anymore, Lawrence. She passed on just a little while ago. Doc thinks she had a heart attack."

The parson looked at Carl, a look that showed his shock at the news. "Oh, my goodness," is all he could say for a few moments. "She was awful close to her brother, Marshal. How did he take the news?"

"Why is it everybody knows about these people except me?

I think he's in shock, to tell you the truth. I can't spend a whole lot of time worrying about how he feels. The judge wants to begin proceedings with his trial. With all the evidence against him it should be an easy case to get a conviction on a bunch of charges."

"What will become of him, Marshall?" Muriel wondered. "Might he be hung for his wrongdoing?"

"I truly couldn't say," Carl said. "I'll give my testimony, and Charlie will give his. I'm gonna do my best to keep any of the girls from having to deal with testifying. They've been through enough. I know the judge, though, and he'll do whatever it takes to get a full conviction and the worst penalty possible for Elmer."

Amanda stole another glance at Roland and the girls as they laughed and played. Then she looked at her mother-in-law who smiled at her knowingly. They would have much to talk about when they were alone.

Chapter 22

Corrine and Amanda later sat in the hotel café and waited for their supper. They had left the church, and Corrine withdrew enough funds from the bank to pay the undertaker for his services. They returned to his office to settle their account and rented a room where they napped for the better part of an hour. It was close enough to supper time to go downstairs, find a table and place their order.

"What's on your mind, daughter?" Corrine asked.

Amanda stirred some cream into her cup of piping hot coffee. She did not make eye contact with her mother-in-law. "I taught school for two years in the Oklahoma Territory before I married your son. I don't deny that I have been thinking about what the parson said about finding a retired teacher for the orphanage. I always longed to teach children. I've been giving Roland his education for his whole life. Do you think I've done well by him?"

Corrine loved her daughter-in-law. She was a ray of sunshine in her dark and dreary world. "Roland is a very bright boy, and you have cultivated his desire to learn despite the male adults in his world making fun of him. You've taken him through the sixth grade."

"I have all the teaching books to help him all the way through secondary school. What would you think if I took on the task of being headmistress of the orphanage? Roland could have a dozen friends when he hasn't had anyone his entire life. I could help teach the girls along with him." Amanda looked at Corrine to see if she could read what she was thinking. "I could promise to let Roland come and visit often. I don't want to take him out of your life completely."

Corrine listened carefully. "As soon as the parson mentioned a retired teacher, I could see you were interested. Let me be the devil's advocate. Roland is a growing boy, and he will soon be feeling the urges all young men feel except he will be among twelve girls of various ages. What happens if he becomes like my husband or my sons? What will you do then?"

"I would bring him back to the ranch," Amanda answered.

"If he were to suffer from the same lust, what would keep him from running away and going back to the orphanage?" Corrine pressed.

"I would enlist Mary and some of the older girls to help me watch him like a hawk. It seems odd to talk about worrying about such things from my own flesh and blood," Amanda said. "I know it's selfish of me to want this for me and Roland, but it would also benefit lots of young ladies. I'm trying to consider the greater good."

Corrine considered Amanda's argument. "When I got married, I thought we would stay in Ohio and work the family farm there, but my husband had other ideas. He wanted to have a large ranch and the only way we could manage that was to move west to the wilderness to purchase cheap land. He forced me to leave my mother, father and siblings and wouldn't allow me to go east to visit. I couldn't even go to either of my parents' funerals. We fought the Indians over the years. We suffered drought in the summer and horrible snow and cold in the winter. Seven miles away from me doesn't seem like that much if you were to take on this responsibility and if you don't come to see me, I'll come to see you. Being around all those young girls would be good for me. We need to get back to the ranch tomorrow to bury our dead, but we can inform the marshal of your intention if you're serious."

A smile came to Amanda's face. "I think we should also tell the parson and his wife. They are trying to recruit couples to adopt at least some of the girls. Maybe this news will change their mind."

Chapter 23

The judge was determined to bring Elmer Bigby to trial quickly. He allowed Elmer to attend a graveside service for his sister the day after she died before he was taken back to jail and two days after that the trial began. There would be no district attorney or defense lawyer facing off against each other because neither existed. The judge would try the case himself in the town church house and when the time came for it to start, the church was packed with all kinds of spectators. Wild stories had circulated until none of them were true. Charlie, Carl, along with Mary, her sister Dixie and Angela were the only ones in the makeshift courtroom who knew the whole truth. Everyone else followed their human nature and speculated on what the truth was.

Judge Treadway banged his gavel on the makeshift bench to bring the court to order. "I don't want any public demonstrations one way or the other in this case. I'm not afraid to clear everybody out of here if I need to so just keep that in mind. Elmer Bigby, you are the defendant in this case. The first charge against you is as follows; fifteen counts of child abuse which include whipping of the children in your care, working them to the point of exhaustion, and locking a number of the girls in a closet for up to forty-eight hours at a time. The second charge is even more serious; six counts of child endangerment. This charge is being brought against you for engaging in conduct that places a child at risk from death, injury or physical or mental impairment. How do you plead?"

Elmer was already overwhelmed by the proceedings. "I don't understand the question, Judge."

Treadway was accustomed to dealing with people like Elmer Bigby. Most people were ignorant of the law, especially if they lived outside a town. "You've only got two choices, Elmer. You either say 'guilty' or 'not guilty' depending on how you feel about what you've done." Elmer was extremely confused and anxious, but it seemed he only had one choice.

"I reckon I'll have to plead not guilty, Judge," he said quietly.

Treadway made note of the plea. "Very well. You may also address me as Your Honor," he informed the defendant. "I am going to hear testimony from five people and after they are finished, I'll allow you to tell your side. I find it very upsetting that the two girls I will call to the stand don't know their last names. We will begin with Angela. Young lady come up here and raise your right hand and place your left hand on the Bible. Angela obeyed and almost forgot which was her right hand and which was her left. "Do you swear to tell the truth, the whole truth and nothing but the truth, so help you God?"

"Yes sir," was all that Angela could manage. Treadway motioned her to sit in a chair to his right.

"Since three of the four testimonies will come from very young people, I want to explain something to them all right now. Angela here has sworn to tell the truth. If we find out later that you didn't tell the truth, you can be charged with what is called perjury. That simply means that you lied under oath and that can be a very serious charge against you. Keep that in mind. Now, let's get started. Angela, how old are you? Do you even know?" Angela looked wide-eyed at the judge.

"I think I might be twelve, but I don't know for sure," she said in a stammering voice.

"I'd say from the looks of you that's a pretty good estimate. You ran away from the orphanage, didn't you Angela?" The young girl nodded nervously. "Do girls run away from there very often? Have you ever known anyone to run away?"

"I remember when I was little one of the girls ran away," she said, and the crowd giggled a bit since she was only twelve years old now.

The judge didn't appreciate the reaction from the crowd and banged his gavel once. "Order! I can tell right now you all are going to try my patience. What do you remember about this girl who ran away?"

"I was awful little, and it was several years ago so I don't remember a whole lot about that," she answered honestly. Treadway jotted down her response.

"You're doing fine, young lady. You're doing just fine," he said, trying to put her at ease. "But you ran away recently, didn't you?" Angela nodded her head. "Why did you run away? You must have known it was dangerous. Did you know where you were going?"

"No sir. I just knew I couldn't stay there."

"Why did you feel that you couldn't stay at the orphanage?" the judge pressed.

Angela squirmed in her seat a little bit. "Sometimes me and the other girls couldn't sleep so we talked about all kinds of things. Nobody would come right out and say what it was, but I sure didn't want those bad men to pick me to take to the loft. No sir."

"I see," the judge said. "So, you decided to run away to keep from getting chosen. Why did you worry so much about being picked?" Angela looked down at her feet. She was so short that her feet didn't touch the floor.

"I was of the right age." The crowd gasped and whispered in low tones.

Treadway gave another rap of the gavel for order. "What you're telling me is that a girl around twelve years of age was taken to the hay loft each spring by some bad men?" Angela once again nodded her head. "I see. Very good. Someone found you out on the prairie after you ran away. Can you point to the person who found you?" Angela pointed directly at Charlie and Judge Treadway wrote once again in his case notes. "I will let the record show that Angela pointed to a young man named Charlie Mabry. We'll get to his testimony in a while. What did you tell him?"

"I told him that I ran away from a home for girls and I had been gone for three days and then we seen Elmer out looking for me," she explained. "He was walking and leading his horse. He stopped once in a while to try and find tracks."

"I see. What happened then?"

Angela became more animated in her response. "Charlie went down by himself and talked to Mr. Bigby, but he didn't let on that he knew where I was. He got Elmer to tell him where the nearest town was and that was Hays. Charlie's real smart." Again, the crowd found that statement humorous but this time the judge didn't strike down with the gavel.

"That'll be enough of that," he warned. "What happened next, Angela?"

"We made it to town and talked to the marshal and the three of us come back the next day to the orphanage." Judge Treadway nodded his approval.

"You've done a fine job, young lady," he complimented. "That's all the testimony I'm going to require from you. You may go back to your seat in the crowd." Angela slipped out of the chair and made her way to the front row where Charlie saved a seat for her. The boy was feeling well but was quite pale from being in the doctor's office for so long. He had his arm in a sling to keep his collar bone stable. He barely felt the effects of being shot. It paid to be young and able to recover quickly.

"Charlie, you're next. Come on up here so I can swear you in. You saw what Angela did. Put your left hand on the good book, raise your right hand and answer this question. Do you swear to tell the truth, the whole truth and nothing but the truth, so help you God?"

Charlie's mouth was as dry as cotton. "Yes, sir, I do," he managed.

"State your name for the record," the judge ordered.

"Charles Mabry, but everybody just calls me Charlie."

"How old are you, Charlie?" the judge asked.

"My brother told me I was born in 1856," Charlie said. "The month was January. I don't know the day."

"Well, it's 1871 now so that makes you around fifteen and a half years old. My first question is this; what were you doing out on the prairie by yourself? Where's your family? Where did you come from?"

Charlie had no idea how detailed the judge wanted him to be. All he knew was that he was awfully afraid of the situation he found himself in. "I'm from Missouri, Your Honor, not too far from the Territory of Kansas and the Territory of Oklahoma. I've got an older brother who lives with his family in Springfield, Missouri. I have an older sister who lives with her family in Garden City, Kansas. My Ma and Pa are both dead. I was the only one left at home with my Pa and when he died, we lost the farm, so I had to go and find my brother. I lived with my brother and sister-in-law and nephew for a while until I caught on with a rancher who was drivin' a herd of horses to a fort in Colorado to sell to the army. When that job was finished, I went back to Garden City and stayed a while with my sister and her husband and my niece and nephew there. I decided to make my way back to Missouri 'cause I was happiest there. My brother and his family treated me real good. On my way back across the Kansas Territory I found Angela hiding in the bushes."

The judge had been listening intently and so did the crowd of people. "Weren't you a little afraid to be out on the prairie by yourself?

Charlie considered his response carefully. "Most of the time I'm a light sleeper so I figured I'd hear any trouble comin' my way. I was countin' on my horse to warn me in case I didn't hear anything." The crowd was amused by that answer, but Treadway did not reprimand them because he had to chuckle himself.

"Just out of curiosity, Charlie, what do you mean you're a light sleeper most of the time?" the judge asked. "What happens when you sleep soundly?"

Charlie thought of the warning about perjury. He was very afraid he could go to jail if he didn't tell the complete truth. "Bad dreams could come to me. Bad things can happen when you're sound asleep."

Judge Treadway found that to be an interesting way to describe it. He noticed Carl out of the corner of his eye fidgeting in his seat. "I'll remind you that you are under oath, young man. Do you suffer from nightmares?"

Charlie could feel his face redden. "Sometimes," was his simple and honest reply.

The judge was growing impatient. "Stop beating around the bush, Charlie. Tell the court why you have nightmares."

Charlie decided if he was ever going to get past this line of questioning, he would have to give the judge a straight answer. "I have nightmares because of something my Pa did to me when I was sound asleep." The court grew deathly quiet. Charlie looked down to the floor because he could feel all the eyes in the room were on him even more than they had been before.

"I woke up in the middle of the night with my Pa beating me with a whip he had made just for me. It had three tails. He hated me from the day I was born because my Ma died having me. He beat me every day he wasn't drunk. I've got the scars to prove it if you think I'm lyin'." Several of the ladies in the crowd dabbed at their eyes with their kerchiefs.

"I believe you, son," Treadway said. "I would like to see your back some day but now is not the time. Let's go back to after you talked to Elmer Bigby. Tell the court what happened after that."

"We made sure we stayed far enough away from him he couldn't see us before we cut back to the creek that flows into Hays. We followed it into town and found Marshal Harrington and he took me and Angela back to the orphanage. Angela showed him the whip marks on her back from where she said CoraLu or Elmer hit her. The marshal was awful mad when he checked the backs of some of the other girls and they had whip marks too. Even the littlest girls." The crowd mumbled amongst themselves, and Judge Treadway had to use the gavel once again. Elmer stared at a spot on the floor between his shoes.

"What did CoraLu and Elmer have to say about that when the marshal confronted them about it," the judge inquired.

Charlie remembered everything about that day, and he didn't recollect the brother and sister saying anything at that point. "I can honestly say I didn't hear them talking about that."

"I see," the judge said. "Where were you while the marshal was asking about the whip marks?" Charlie took a deep breath and let it out.

"Could I have a drink of water, Sir?" he asked. "This is kind of a long story, and I would sure appreciate it if I could have a bit." There was a pitcher of water and a glass on the judge's desk. He poured until the glass was half full and he handed it to the boy. Charlie gulped the water down and passed it back to the judge. "I'm mighty grateful. My throat was just all kinds of dry." The judge nodded and smiled and made a hand motion to Charlie to indicate he could proceed with his testimony.

"I wasn't with the marshal because Angela had asked me to go to the barn with her, so I did. When we got to the barn, she told me I should go up to the loft and look around to see what I thought. She didn't want to go with me. I thought it was a strange thing to be askin' me to do but there was somethin' in the way she just kept lookin' up at the loft that made me agree to go and look. I went up the ladder and my eyes had to get used to it being a little dark and dusty. I opened one of the loft doors to let some more light in. I remember seeing two things that I thought was awful curious, but I don't remember which one I saw first."

"I wouldn't worry about the order, Charlie," Treadway reassured him. "You're doing fine. Please continue."

Charlie thought some more. "I reckon I saw the mattress first since it was the biggest thing up there. It was leaning against the wall close to the loft doors. I pulled it over so it would be flat on the floor and when I did that, I noticed it had a lot of stains on it. I scratched at one of the stains with my fingernail and when I smelled it, I could tell it smelled like iron. I knew it was blood. I've smelled blood plenty of times before. A lot of times it was my own." Somewhere in the crowd a woman made a sound as if she were about to swoon and the judge craned his neck to see who it was. After a moment he motioned Charlie to continue. "There were candles on one of the boards that was nailed on the inside. I thought that was mighty strange to have candles where there was a lot of dry wood and hay."

"That seems strange to me, too," the judge agreed. "Go on."

"Well, I got up from my knees and kept lookin' around. What I saw next is why I have nightmares sometimes. Across the floor a little ways was a big beam going straight up and down and was one of several holding the roof on. It had something on it so I went over to look at it a little closer, but it was just a mystery to me. There were four tally marks on the wood going straight up and down and then there was another tally mark that went from the top left of the other four marks and went down to the bottom right. Then there was one more tally mark underneath those five so that made a total of six. I sniffed at the post and I could smell the same smell that was on the mattress."

"You mean the tally marks were made from blood?" the judge asked, wide-eyed.

Charlie looked into the judge's eyes. "Yes sir. That's what I mean." This news caused the courtroom to burst into exclamations and talk back and forth, and Treadway had to pound the gavel numerous times to quiet everyone.

"Order! I will have order in this court!" he exclaimed. "Quiet down right this instant!" The crowd finally settled down. The judge was clearly flustered. "Alright Charlie. What else did you see in the hay loft?"

"Just to the left of where the tally marks were there was two pieces of rope hanging down from a cross beam. They'd been cut with a knife. In the corner of the loft was a three-legged stool. On the far side of the loft was a little bit of hay left and two pitchforks."

"Is that all?" the judge inquired.

"Yes sir," Charlie answered. "That's the last of it."

"After you took inventory of the loft what did you do next?" Treadway prodded.

"I went back down to ask Angela some questions. I asked her if Elmer and CoraLu cut their own hay and she said they didn't. She told me the hay was brought in the spring by a man named Whitaker and his three sons. I asked her if CoraLu and Elmer paid for the hay with the money they made off the work the girls done and she said no. I asked her if the money they got from the Territory for runnin' the orphanage paid for the hay and she said no again. Then I asked her how long the Whitakers had been delivering hay and she told me six years. My next question was how old the oldest girl in the home was and she told me that Mary over there is eighteen years old. I asked Angela how old she was and that was when she told me she was twelve. I put it all together and asked her if she ran away because she was afraid she was going to be next and she said yes." That information brought on another chorus of wails from the ladies in the crowd to cursing of Elmer from the men. It took Judge Treadway even longer to restore order this time as he pounded the gavel repeatedly until the crowd quieted. They were fearful that if they didn't obey the judge he would clear the room, and they wouldn't get to hear the rest of the story. For the first time, Carl feared there might be such an outpouring of anger that Elmer might even be lynched.

"You people are starting to make me angry!" he shouted at them. "I told you to shut up!" Treadway had to pour a short drink of water for himself and finish it off in one gulp. He could have used something much stronger. "Charlie, what about the two ropes?"

"Two of the girls hung themselves. Judge, do you remember Angela talkin' about one other girl that ran away from the home?" The judge nodded. "Angela wasn't for sure, but she believes Elmer went and found her on the prairie and buried her without bringing her back. One of the other girls named Dora hasn't spoke a word since it happened to her. Mary and her sister Dixie were the other two." There were more gasps and murmurs but this time they were more subdued after all the warnings the crowd had received.

"You are quite an extraordinary young man, Charlie," the judge observed. "Let me see if I can summarize what you've told the court. The six tally marks were made with the blood of six twelve-year-old girls to pay for the delivery each year of a load of hay and CoraLu and Elmer Bigby knew about it and agreed to it. The perpetrators were this Whitaker fellow and his three adult sons. Does that sum it up?"

Charlie had a look of concern on his face. "I reckon they knew about it Your Honor but maybe they couldn't do anything to stop it." The judge was busily writing notes but finally looked up at Charlie.

"They should have never agreed to it in the first place. It was a vile act. Why aren't the Whitakers in jail Marshal?" Treadway already knew the answer.

Carl stood up when he was addressed. "They're all dead Your Honor. If I could make a request of the court I believe Charlie's been through enough. I'll testify about them when it's my turn."

"The court is in agreement with you, Marshal," the judge said.

"Your Honor, while I'm at it, due to her tender age I would also like to ask the court not to call Dixie. I believe her sister Mary can handle it a little better and their testimony is liable to be about the same." Treadway scratched his chin whiskers and looked at Carl for a good, long while.

"Normally I wouldn't honor that request, but I don't want to cause her any more distress. I will do everything in my power not to have her testify. Thank you, Marshal."

"Charlie, you can step down and take your seat. The court calls Mary next." The pretty blonde girl stood up just as Charlie was sitting down and they glanced briefly at one another. Judge Treadway swore her in and had her take a seat beside him in the witness chair. "Miss, I know this is going to bring back some awful memories. I also know it's going to be hard to tell in front of all these noisy folks. However, it's only proper that the defendant hears all the testimony against him." He turned his attention to the crowd once again. "I'm on my last nerve with you people. This is possibly going to be hard to hear so just imagine how hard it is for her to tell it. You make me call you down one more time and I will clear the court except for me, Mary, Elmer and the marshal as a witness. That won't hurt the trial one bit. Mark my words," he said as he shook the gavel at the audience. He turned his attention back to Mary and wanted to be kind and compassionate but needed to hear the truth. "Mary, do you know your age?"

Mary looked at the judge with her light blue eyes. "I'm eighteen years old, Your Honor," she stated.

"How did you come to be at the orphanage, young lady?"

"Me and my sister Dixie were taken when Indians raided our farm. Our parents were killed. It was a terrible thing to see. The army trailed us and rescued us three days later. They didn't know what to do with us and Elmer Bigby just happened to be at their fort doing some kind of business when we were brought in. The army let him take us to the orphanage him and CoraLu ran together."

"I see. Do you know how old you were when you first arrived at the orphanage?" Treadway asked as he busily wrote on his paper.

Mary had to think about that question for a bit. "I'm not certain, Your Honor. I may have been ten years old, which would have made my sister seven."

"What was the place like when you first got there?" Mary had a perplexed look on her face as if she didn't understand the question. "How many girls lived there? Did you have to work immediately?"

"Oh. I think there were six girls when we got there so we made eight. CoraLu taught us how to sew but we didn't have to make anything at first," Mary said. "Sometimes we would hear CoraLu and Elmer arguing about money. It seemed like they weren't making enough or something like that. Us girls talked about maybe they got paid depending on how many girls lived with them."

"Did you feel like you were mistreated at first? What about food to eat? Did you ever go hungry?"

"Things were pretty good when we got there. We only had meat on Sunday and maybe leftover meat on Monday or Tuesday if there was any. Me and my sister never complained. We had a roof over our heads and food to eat, even if it wasn't so great."

"When did things change for you girls?" Treadway asked.

Mary looked at him with her ice blue eyes. She blinked once. "Probably about when I turned twelve."

The judge smiled reassuringly. "I know this is the hard part for you to tell but it's important to the trial that you give us the most complete picture of what happened at that point in your life. In fact, it's important to all the girls that you provide the best testimony you can." He looked at the pitcher of water and the glass. "Would you like a drink, Mary?"

She nodded nervously and the judge poured the water for her. Instead of handing the glass back to him, she held it with both hands and cradled it in her lap. "Thank you, Your Honor. You're very kind."

"Please proceed when you're ready. Take your time."

"I remember one morning CoraLu Bigby took the buckboard and left and didn't get back until the next day around the middle of the day. She had a whole wagon load of supplies and most of it was bolts of different colored material and that was a mystery to us girls. The next day she told us we were going to start making dresses and men's and boy's shirts and we had to finish so many a day or we would get punished."

"Interesting. What kind of punishment did she administer?"

"At first it was just a rap on the wrist with a stick," Mary continued. "When she got really mad at us, she had a homemade paddle she would use on our rumps. She expected too much from us, and it didn't take long for her to make a whip out of a stick, a nail and an old piece of leather. That's when she would lay into our backs with our clothes on and later, we had to bare our backs so she wouldn't tear our dresses. I tried to get her and Elmer to whip me instead of my little sister. Sometimes it worked and sometimes it didn't.

"Help me understand something, Mary. At what age could a girl leave the home?"

"Eighteen, Your Honor," Mary stated.

Treadway felt he knew the answer to his question before he asked it. "Why are you still at the orphanage?"

Mary couldn't believe he would ask such a foolish thing. "I am waiting for my sister to turn eighteen. Then we'll both leave as fast as we can." The judge nodded knowingly as if he understood her reasoning.

"Thank you, Mary. I had to ask that question. What else happened when you became twelve years old."

Mary gathered her thoughts. "Like I said before, sometimes CoraLu and Elmer would argue about money. I remember one night they were yelling at each other about the hay supply for the year. They had bought some more animals, and they needed hay for food and bedding. They had a pretty good business going for themselves with the clothes we were making. I wondered why they didn't pay for the hay with that money, but I sure wasn't going to ask them. I didn't want to get in trouble. I remember it was a sunny day in the spring when the hay wagon got to the barn. It was brought by an older man and his three sons. I found out their names later. They were the Whitakers."

Mary had to stop for just a moment. She dreaded telling the rest of her story. The judge gave her all the time she needed.

"Me and another girl had to go to the barn to do our chores. I saw the older Mr. Whitaker talking to Elmer and CoraLu, but they were too far away for me to hear anything. I seem to remember CoraLu having a shocked look on her face while they were talking. Everything was fine for a while. Before I knew it, CoraLu was at the barn door calling for my friend to come help her do something, I don't remember what. I watched them leave and after I turned to finish doing my chores, I heard someone behind me and then a big hand covered my mouth and one of the sons carried me to the loft ladder where he handed me off to another one of the sons. I remember they were all laughing and they had a scary look in their eyes like they were wild or something. I tried to fight them but as we got higher on the ladder, I was afraid I would fall. When they got me in the loft, they threw me on a dirty mattress filled with straw and started tearing my clothes off." Mary stopped and looked pleadingly at the judge. She didn't want to tell the rest of the story. "Do I have to go on?"

The judge looked at her and shook his head gently. "Let me help you, Mary. They molested you, didn't they?" She nodded and tears ran down her cheeks. The makeshift courtroom was eerily quiet as the crowd listened to the horror. "Do you understand the meaning of that word?" Mary nodded. "By molest I mean rape. Did they rape you, Mary?" She gasped and wept but was able to nod her head again. "Two last questions and you can be done. The first question is this. Did they make a tally mark on that support post in the loft when they were done?" Mary was trying not to cry out loud and she was able to nod once again. "The last question is this. Where did they get the blood to make that tally?" Mary looked at him with surprise and shame on her face. She pointed to the spot, and the judge put his hand on her shoulder. "That's fine. You've done well, Mary, and I thank you and the court thanks you. You may step down."

Mary felt dirty and ashamed at what had taken place then and she had to relive it today. She sat between her sister Dixie and Angela and finally the tears flowed uncontrollably. Muriel was sitting behind the girls, and she offered a hankie to Mary. After a few seconds it became apparent that Mary wasn't going to get over her crying spell anytime soon, so Muriel got up, walked around the people in her row and took her by the hand and led her out of the church. Once they were outside, Muriel took Mary in her arms and just let her cry. She wished she could take the hurt away.

"Everything is about to change for the better, Mary," she assured the young girl. "I know it won't change the past but let's believe there is going to be a brighter future for all of you girls." Dixie couldn't let her sister suffer alone so she got up from her seat and went outside and joined the pair and all three wept.

Back in the church the judge shot an accusing look at Elmer Bigby who stared at a spot on the wall behind the judge. "Marshal, are you ready to testify now?"

The marshal got to his feet and strode to the witness chair. "I sure am, Judge. Swear me in and let's get started." Treadway complied and Carl sat down.

"First of all, do you want to add to any of the testimony we've already heard?" the judge asked.

Carl considered that for a moment. He knew Angela's story and he also knew Charlie's. Mary's testimony was the first time he had heard the details of how the Whitakers bargained for one of the girls instead of receiving a cash payment. He was ready to crucify Elmer in any way he could without fabricating anything. "No, Your Honor. I believe they covered everything for their part of the story. Charlie had asked me to look at the loft by myself to see if I came to the same conclusion he did. To be honest, he did a better job at figuring everything out than I did and what he described is exactly how it looked."

"Alright. Tell me all the events that happened after you discovered the secrets of the loft. Take your time and don't leave anything out," the judge instructed.

"Yes, Your Honor. I ain't proud of what I did to Elmer when I came back to the porch from the barn. I knocked him over the porch railing, and I really wanted to hang him on the spot. CoraLu too but I stopped short of that. My choices were pretty poor. I thought about using the Bigby's buckboard to get the twelve girls and CoraLu and Elmer out of there and head for town. The ground was soft from the spring rains so we would have been easy to track and out in the open if the Whitaker boys would have come after us. I considered sending Angela to town to get help since she already knew the way. I couldn't go myself and leave Charlie alone with everybody. I didn't want to think about what might happen if the Whitakers came while I was gone. My one other choice was to send Charlie for help but that would have put me at the mercy of the Whitaker clan. I finally just made up my mind to make a stand with me and Charlie against them four."

"Marshal, I generally agree with your decisions, but I must question this one. I know you think highly of the young man, but did you really believe he was up to the task? He could have very easily been killed rather than wounded."

Carl looked Charlie in the eye. "I really hated puttin' him in that position, Your Honor. I tell you the truth. If he hadn't been armed with a shotgun, I would have probably loaded up everybody and took our chances with runnin'. If he would have got killed, I don't know what I would have done."

"Did you consider holing up in the house instead of confronting them when they were all on horseback or on the hay wagon?" Treadway reasoned.

"Yes, sir, I did. Once they knew they'd been found out the four of them would have gotten mighty desperate. These were evil men. They might have burned us out and killed all of us. I had to weigh all these options in my head, and a standoff was the best I could come up with. I kind of hoped they would turn around and go home and then we could make a run for it."

"Tell the court about the events of that day, Marshal," the judge ordered.

"Yes sir. Charlie went up on a ridge that had a few trees for cover so he could be my lookout. I told him to just come straight to the house when he spotted anything coming down the road. He was only gone a couple of hours before he came and said the wagon was comin'. He surprised me by sayin' there was a kid on the wagon seat next to old man Whitaker. There was also three men on horseback. I like to try to be prepared for anything and I had gone through all the different things that might come our way, but I sure hadn't planned on that kid."

"Why do you think they brought this boy?" the judge asked.

"I never asked them but if I was guessin' I'd say they wanted to show him what they thought would make him into a man," Carl replied. Treadway shook his head slightly as he continued to write. He motioned the marshal to continue. "I told Charlie that the first man to pull his gun was gonna' get shot. It didn't matter if he pulled real slow like because once the gun is out that man has the advantage over us. There was one man on a horse on my right side and two men on horses on Charlie's side and the old man and boy were in the middle on the wagon. Charlie had his scattergun resting on the top rail of the fence that surrounded the yard. I just had my pistols, but I was ready."

Carl took a moment to gather his thoughts about what happened during the parlay with the Whitakers. "I tried to reason with them. The hay needed to be unloaded for the use on the farm, so I told them to get to it while I watched over them and then we'd every one of us go to town together. I didn't figure they'd care for that idea, and they didn't. I remember Whitaker making a threat about it being four against one man and a scared boy, but they shortchanged Charlie. The man on my side finally broke and he made a poor attempt at drawing his weapon and I shot him dead. The men on Charlie's side drew and he blew one of them to hell and the noise from that cannon spooked the other son's horse and it reared up on him. He got off a shot just as Charlie fired his other barrel and he fell to the ground dead, but his bullet found Charlie's shoulder. The old man took just a second to pay attention to his grandson's safety and that gave me time to shoot him."

Everyone in the makeshift courtroom listened raptly as Carl described the grisly scene. Judge Treadway caught up on his note taking for a few quiet seconds. "Is there anything else about the gunfight you'd like to tell the court?"

"The boy jumped down from the wagon and hurried over to where his Pa was layin' dead and cried over him. I don't blame him. It was a lot to take in. I went to check on the man I had shot first and he took his last gurglin' breath just before I could deliver the kill shot," Carl explained.

"I assume you turned your attention to your young accomplice?" Treadway asked.

The marshal was taken aback by the statement. "Accomplice? That makes us sound like criminals, Judge. He's my partner." Charlie smiled at what he considered a compliment.

"I stand corrected," the judge said. "I apologize to the both of you. What happened next, Marshal?"

Carl took a deep breath and let it out. "We got him into the house, and he was bleedin' like a stuck pig. CoraLu claimed she could help gettin' the bullet out, so I let her. I told her if she could take care of him, I'd mention it at her trial and it might be a credit toward her account. I told Elmer to take some of the girls and start kickin' the hay out of the wagon and on to the ground. We needed the wagon, and we didn't have time to store the hay. The horse belonging to the last man Charlie shot had been wounded in the head and had run off. I didn't want it to get back to the Whitaker ranch because it might set off an alarm with any other men on the place and they'd come runnin'. I found it and put it out of it's misery and went back to the house."

The judge held up his hand for Carl to halt for a minute. "It should be told to the court that CoraLu is not on trial because she died while in custody here in the marshal's jail." This caused another round of murmuring which the judge halted with just a steely glare. "Continue."

"I'll give credit where credit's due. CoraLu made a good try at gettin' that bullet out but it was lodged in the bone, and we didn't have the right tools to pull it. His collar bone was also busted. I'm not sure how that happened. The doc thinks the bullet hit Charlie's collar bone and broke it and ricocheted into his shoulder bone."

"Is that true, Doc?" Treadway asked Doctor Teague who was sitting behind the young people in the front row.

"Well, Judge that's just me speculating. To find out for sure I would have had to make the incision a lot longer and I didn't see any need to put the young man through any more than he'd already had to endure," the doctor explained.

"Agreed," the judge said. "Go ahead with your testimony, Marshal. What happened when you gave up trying to remove the bullet?"

"I told some of the girls to gather up enough store for us to make it town and the rest of us helped Charlie outside and finished up taking the hay out of the wagon and loading the four dead bodies in the front of the wagon just behind the seat. We got Charlie on board plus all twelve girls, CoraLu and Elmer and the Whitaker grandson named Roland and then we headed toward Hays. It was too late to make the whole trip, so we made camp and the next morning I charged Angela with riding Charlie's horse on ahead to town and get the doc. I was honestly afraid he might bleed to death before we made the whole trip. She did a good job and came back with him and saved us a lot of travelin' time and Doc was able to get the bullet out and stop the bleedin'. Then we finished the trip to town." Carl stopped and looked at the judge. "That's about it, I reckon."

"You can step down now, Marshal. The court thanks you for your service and your testimony." Carl had been sitting too long and when he stood up a few bones cracked causing some light laughter from the crowd of people. Carl swore at them under his breath, but the judge's keen ears caught every foul word. "That'll be enough, Marshal. Take a seat or if you need to, stand over by a wall." Carl chose to stand.

"That leaves us with one more testimony and that will come from the defendant. "Elmer Bigby, take the stand," the judge ordered. Elmer already looked like a defeated soul. His shoulders were slumped, and he looked like he bore all the cares of the world on his back. He sat down carefully in the wooden chair and made the mistake of making eye contact with several people in the crowd and they stared back at him with hatred.

"Elmer Bigby, do you swear to tell the truth, the whole truth, and nothing but the truth so help you God?" the judge asked as Elmer raised his right hand and placed his left hand on the Holy Bible.

"I do, Your Honor," Elmer said but it sounded like the words had come from someone else.

"Elmer, I want you to look at me." Judge Treadway waited patiently while Elmer slowly turned his head and met his gaze. "This is your chance to defend yourself. It's your last chance to defend yourself. There won't be any appeal to a higher court or anything like that, so I suggest you make the most of it." Elmer nodded weakly to let the judge know that he understood. It occurred to him there was no hope. No hope at all. The judge had already demonstrated his disdain for everything that had happened, and Elmer was the last to lay the blame on. CoraLu was dead and so were all the Whitaker men. The testimony from the marshal and the young people were like nails in his coffin.

"Are you alright, Elmer? Do you need a glass of water?" the judge inquired. Elmer nodded weakly again, and Treadway provided him with a drink.

"I'm much obliged for that, Your Honor," he managed.

"Let's get on with it then. I'm going to ask you some specific questions and I want you to think about your answer before you give it but remember you're under oath," the judge explained. "How long have you and your late sister had that home for girls?"

Elmer's mind was in a fog, and he found it hard to concentrate. "Near as I can figure, we've had it for about twelve years."

"I see. What were things like when you first started it?"

Elmer thought back on happier times and even smiled a bit. "Neither me or my sister ever married and at first the girls were kind of like the children we never had. The Territory paid us to make a home for them, so everything was nice at first."

"How much did the Territory pay?" the judge wanted to know.

Elmer shook his head. "I don't know. CoraLu took care of the books and then teaching the girls how to cook and sew and such. I was the one who did all the outside work. It was enough money to keep us supplied with food and provisions. You have to believe me when I tell you that we wanted to get our girls ready for them to find a man to settle down with when they come of age. That's the truth."

Treadway listened intently to Elmer's explanation. "That's a noble thing you two started. What happened to make it all change?"

Elmer had to stop and calculate his dates correctly. "I had gone to the Whitakers and bargained for a small hay crop each year for several years. Every time they made their delivery, I would notice them looking at the girls, but they never tried anything or said anything to me about doing somethin' bad. Once in a while they would say something to one of the girls like 'Howdy cutie' or words like that." Elmer stopped.

"Something caused them to change. What was it?" the judge asked patiently.

Elmer glanced at the judge before he continued. "They changed after the girl named Mary had been at the home for a couple of years. They sure noticed her. She was the prettiest of the lot."

That statement irritated Judge Treadway. "My God, Elmer! You make it sound like they were like so many cattle in a corral!" Elmer regretted the way he had described Mary and sought to make amends.

"I apologize. What I meant to say was she was the prettiest girl amongst all the other girls, and they liked her the most because of her looks." Mary, Dixie and Muriel had come back inside and were standing by the door. Mary blushed a crimson red at the way she was being talked about, and she wished she could bolt from the courtroom again. The judge noticed that as well.

"Mary, if you wish, you may be excused from this testimony," Treadway said to her. Mary shook her head and looked straight at him.

"No, Your Honor," she said with conviction. "I'm determined to see this thing through and bring an end to it." The judge smiled at her with admiration.

"As you wish. Elmer, you may proceed with your testimony."

"It was the spring of her second year at the home and old man Whitaker came to the house and said he and his boys wanted to renegotiate their payment for the hay. I told him we couldn't afford any raise in his rates and that he'd just have to cut back on what he put in the hayloft for us. He told me he had no intention of cutting back on our supply but instead he wanted to put all the hay on his big wagon in the loft for us and that they wanted me to keep our money and that they wanted a small favor in return for the fodder."

"Go ahead, Elmer. Tell the court what they proposed."

"He told me they wanted Mary for a couple of hours as their payment. He told me nobody had to know about it, not even me. He told me to stay in the house with my sister and the other girls and to keep them away from the barn for a while. I didn't even tell my sister about what was going on. We sang songs with the girls and told loud stories for a couple of hours so we wouldn't hear the screams. After a long time, one of the sons came to the front door and told me to bring a blanket for Mary. I picked one up and started out the door when CoraLu asked me what was going on. I told her to move the children to the back of the house until I told her different and I went out to the barn to get Mary. Her clothes were nearly gone from her body, and she was bleeding down her leg. She also had blood coming out of a cut on her cheek and one on her lip. She was in really bad shock, and I wrapped her in the blanket and had to finally carry her into the house. I knew I couldn't keep it from my sister, so I called her and had her take care of Mary's wounds."

"How did that make you feel when you went to the loft to check on your hay supply?" the judge asked. "Was there a tally mark on the support post? Was there a stain on the mattress? Where did that mattress come from?"

"I threw up in the hay loft, Your Honor. I reckon they brought the mattress with them. It didn't belong to us."

"You didn't answer all my questions, Elmer. Was there a stain on the mattress and was there a tally on the post?"

There were tears in Elmer's eyes as he nodded to the judge.

"I want to hear you say it! Was there a stain on the mattress and was there a bloody tally on the support post?"

"Yes, sir," Elmer finally managed. "There was both."

Judge Treadway had to pour himself a drink of water and halt the proceedings while he calmed himself. His anger had gotten the best of him for a moment.

"Knowing what they did to this poor girl, why did you let it continue for years after that? Was the hay that important to you? Did you like saving the money that it would have cost to purchase it?"

Elmer looked like a poor, frightened animal to the people watching the trial. "I tried to find somebody else to supply us, but nobody had enough to spare. Old man Whitaker threatened me from the second year on. I had already committed the sin that caused our fall."

"I don't wish to hear about all five of the other occurrences. There are two that I do want to hear about. The first one concerns the young girl who ran away and was never brought back to the orphanage. Tell the court about her. Did she run away before or after the Whitakers molested her?"

"It was after, Your Honor," Elmer replied.

"Well, get on with it then."

"I took a pan of water to the barn to let her clean up and I also took some fresh clothes for her to change. She didn't want to come back with me to the house after the Whitakers left and I finished my chores, so I left her in the barn for a while. My sister told me I should go back and check on her after some time had gone by and when I went out there, she was gone. I hitched up the wagon and went after her. I didn't find her until after dark. It looked like she had stepped wrong in the dark and fell and hit her head on a rock. She was dead when I found her and as it happened, there was a shovel in the wagon, so I dug a grave for her out on the prairie."

Judge Treadway removed his spectacles and took out a pocketknife to sharpen his pencil. He took time to settle his nerves before he asked about one of the girls who hanged herself. In one way he wanted the trial to be over but in another way, he wanted Elmer to squirm in the witness chair.

"Let's move on to the second girl who hung herself," he began. "How could you be so stupid as to let that happen twice? Didn't you learn anything from the first one?"

"I watched her as close as I could!" Elmer defended himself. "A man has to sleep sometime!"

"So, she snuck out to the barn when you were asleep? Where did the girls get the rope?"

"I don't know the answer to that, Judge. Maybe the Whitakers left rope for both the girls."

It was all Treadway could do to control himself. "You're blaming dead men for leaving a way for two girls to do away with themselves? That's pretty convenient for you, isn't it Elmer? They're not around to defend themselves. I'll tell you what makes me wonder. It makes me wonder why those two girls took their own lives in the very spot where the crime took place." He stopped to ponder it for a moment. "I suppose desperation causes people to do a lot of things we don't understand."

Treadway made some final entries in his notebook. He finished and closed it gently. "Elmer Bigby, stand up and face me." Elmer complied. "These things you're on trial for weren't mistakes, they were atrocities that caused three young girls to take their own lives. We didn't even mention one of the other girls who has never spoken a word since that day when it happened to her. I don't know if she ever will." The judge stopped for a moment and stared at Elmer. "Child endangerment can take on many forms. The least of those forms would get you a jail sentence but in this case, it caused death. If the Whitakers were still alive, I would sentence them to hang for what they did. Every one of them. I wouldn't have given CoraLu the death penalty simply because she was a woman. I find you guilty of all six counts of child endangerment which ended in tragic death on three counts. I sentence you to hang by the neck until you are dead. May God have mercy on your soul, Elmer Bigby. The sentence will be carried out in two days at seven o'clock in the morning. Court dismissed." The judge hammered the gavel once and Carl jumped up to rush Elmer back to the jail. He was afraid of what the crowd might do to the condemned man and several hateful accusations rained down on him.

Chapter 24

The impending hanging caused great revelry in town. Carl had anticipated that and had recruited a pair of trustworthy men to deputize who were to handle minor infractions over the next two evenings. Anything serious would fall to Carl's responsibility. The new deputies were zealous in their appointed jobs, and they soon had all the other cells full of drunk or disorderly men and Carl had to weed out the least of the offenders to keep things manageable in his jail. The three men who were left made so much noise Elmer couldn't sleep. He laid on his bunk and tried to remember happier times. He was disappointed because there weren't that many happy times to recall. He missed his sister. CoraLu was the one person he was always able to talk to about anything that was troubling him. He wished he had been the one who died of a heart attack because CoraLu wouldn't have been hung, and she could have at least had a life in prison.

The three cell mates were released early the next morning, and Elmer was able to get some rest after their departure. When his lunch was brought to him, the marshal asked him what he wanted for his last supper on earth.

"If it can be found in town, I'll have it made for you," Carl told him. "Some people in your circumstance find comfort in eating their favorite meal the night before. Elmer had always heard that was a tradition, but he never dreamed it would befall him.

"I reckon a juicy steak with some mashed taters and brown gravy would be just fine," Elmer replied. "Maybe a slice of apple pie for my last dessert."

"That's easy enough. The town should be settled down some tonight so I'll try and keep the cells empty so you can rest. I can't guarantee anything, though," the marshal said.

"For some reason, I'm scared of going to sleep and having you wake me up just in time to go meet my Maker," Elmer shared. "That would be an awful thing."

"Do you want me to fetch the parson for you to talk to tonight? He'd probably be willing to take supper with you. He's a good man."

Elmer shook his head as he stared at the floor between his feet. "I never set foot in a church my whole life. I reckon it's too late to worry about that now."

"Suit yourself. I'm obligated to ask," Carl said. "I'll go and put your order in for supper, so it'll be here in good time tonight."

Morning came and Elmer had fallen asleep just as he feared. The marshal woke him up by noisily unlocking the cell door and Elmer sat up quickly when he heard it. He had been dreaming of sitting at the kitchen table with his sister back at the orphanage and they had been sipping coffee and eating sugar cookies.

"It's time, Elmer," the marshal simply said. "Back up to the bars and let me put the irons on you." Elmer complied. There was no use in trying to escape his fate. He felt helpless and hopeless as the marshal directed him out the door of the jail. They turned to their right as soon as they got outside, and it was a short walk to an alley where the gallows waited. Several dozen people had gathered to witness his demise and Charlie and Dr. Teague stood side by side near the stairs of the gallows. Hays was a centrally located town in the Territory, and many condemned criminals met their end here. They employed a permanent hangman, and he now waited for Elmer at the top of the platform. Carl escorted Elmer as far as the steps and then motioned him to make the climb himself. Elmer thought he might pass out before he got to the rope. His knees were weak, and his heart was beating rapidly. The hangman directed him to the trap door and placed the rope expertly over his head and rested the knot over his left shoulder.

"Any last words?" the hangman asked. Elmer was unable to speak, and a black hood was placed quickly over his head. His last thought was that this whole thing was going too fast and then the trap was sprung, and he fell to his death.

Charlie flinched when the trap door swung downward and from his vantage point, he could see Elmer's body turning and twitching for just a few seconds before he was still. It was a terrible thing to witness and as much as he despised the man it was still difficult. Doc Teague waited for the body to be let down to the ground before he examined Elmer for any sign of life. He took his hand to feel for a pulse and used his stethoscope to listen for a heartbeat before he looked at Carl and gave a slight nod to indicate Elmer was deceased. The undertaker then took over to prepare the body for burial and it was at that moment that Charlie thought of something they had forgotten.

"We didn't think to find out from Elmer where the money for the orphanage was hid," Charlie said to Carl and Dr. Teague. "I'll bet there's all kinds of money the girls could use when they go back." Neither of the older men had considered the money.

"Maybe one of the girls will know where it is," Doc said.

"If they don't, we'll have to go out there and turn the place inside out to find it. Charlie's right. That money could go a long ways to helping get that place started up again and do it right this time," Carl added. "They need a fresh start."

"Who's going to run the place?" Charlie asked.

Carl clapped Charlie on his good shoulder. "I don't know. Sometimes good things happen when you don't expect it. I'm still hopin' to find a retired teacher who'd want to take the job. We'll just have to wait and see what happens."

Chapter 25

Three days after Elmer met his Maker, Corrine, Amanda and Roland Whitaker made the trip back to Hays to finalize some business with their attorney and banker. Before they could even tie their team up at the livery stable Roland had already leaped out of the buckboard and ran to the church yard where some of the girls were playing. They were all excited to see one another. Charlie was at the stable doing some light work because he was going stir crazy at the doctor's office. The bed he had been occupying since he got to town was needed by another patient so he asked old Ben, the stable owner, if he could sleep on the hay in the barn. Ben did him one better and let him sleep on a cot in the tack room. He liked the boy and enjoyed his company.

"Howdy ladies," Charlie greeted. "I'll take care of your team for you."

Corrine was concerned about Charlie getting hurt unhitching the team. "Are you sure you're up to that, Charlie? Are you already healed enough?"

Charlie had already started the job of removing pins to free the two horses from the wagon. "Don't worry. I won't try to get their harnesses off by myself. The doc says I'm nearly all the way better, but he doesn't want me to take any chances." Corrine was satisfied.

"Alright Charlie. Amanda dear, we have much to accomplish in the next few days. Let's go and secure a room at the hotel and then see if the marshal will join us for lunch so we can get his opinion about your plan." Charlie didn't mean to eavesdrop, but he overheard that part of the conversation, and he wondered what the plan might be. He knew what he hoped it would be.

"I was hoping to ask the minister if he would join us," Amanda replied. "What do you think?"

"Let's start with the marshal. He seems to be a reasonable man, and he cares for the welfare of the children. He'll be a strong ally for us."

When they met Carl, they didn't let him in on what they were thinking. He accepted the lunch invitation but was secretly disappointed because he had wanted to go and have lunch at the Mexican establishment so he could see his pretty Ariana. She wasn't expecting him so she wouldn't be disappointed. Carl found them already seated in the main restaurant in town and joined the two ladies.

"Thank you for accepting our invitation, Marshal," Corrine began. "I hope we didn't interfere with any plans you might have had." Carl didn't want to admit anything, so he simply shook his head. "Let me begin by asking if anything has changed with the girls. Has anyone come forward to begin adoption proceedings? Has anyone inquired about taking on the job of headmistress for the orphanage? I noticed a flyer on your posting board by your office door advertising the need for someone." Their waiter came and took their order before Carl could respond.

"As of yesterday, nobody had asked about adopting any of the girls. I can tell you that's been mighty disappointing. Those are some of the finest young ladies I think anybody could want." Carl took a sip of his coffee. "I'm wonderin' if maybe the facts that came out at the trial kept people away from them. That would irritate me because it wasn't their fault. I could see not taking the older girls after what they've been through but some of those little ones are cuter than bugs. As far as findin' somebody to take over the home, I ain't heard anything either. We'd have to go and ask the Parson or his wife. The girls have sure taken a shine to them. I believe they'd take all of 'em if they could but you may or may not have noticed that Muriel is pregnant."

"Well, Marshal, my daughter-in-law would like very much to discuss a possible solution with you. Isn't that right Amanda?"

The younger woman smiled. "Marshal Harrington, I was a schoolteacher for a while before I met my husband. I have been teaching Roland at home because his father and grandfather didn't think he needed any more school. They were angry with me when they found out what I was doing but I put my foot down and continued because I love to teach, and I know the value of education. My understanding is that the girls are way behind in their studies. I'm worried about what they will do when they leave the home if they can't read properly or perform basic mathematics problems." Carl listened hopefully as Amanda spoke.

"Am I understandin' you to say you'd like to take the job of being the headmistress at the home for those girls?" he asked. Amanda nodded excitedly.

"I feel like I am much more qualified to do the job than the previous people who were there. My proposal is to move into the house with Roland and start helping the girls to grow into young ladies. I have no idea about how the orphanage is funded or anything like that. I wouldn't be doing the job to make money. I'd be doing it because it's what I love to do. My mother-in-law made me swear to have Roland visit her often." The women stared at Carl and waited patiently for his answer. Luckily for him, the food arrived but it had become secondary in importance. He began to think about the implications of Amanda accepting the position.

"I just told Doc and Charlie the other day that good things can happen out of the clear blue sky. I ain't much for believing in miracles or such as that and I've never been a prayin' sort, either, but this is some of the best news I've ever heard of. I admit I don't go to church but once every two or three months and that may be generous. I went this last week to sit with the girls, though and the Parson preached a mighty good sermon about the Hebrews crossing the dry Jordan River to go into the Promised Land to take it over after they come up out of slavery in Egypt. The priests carrying the Ark were told to carry a stone each out of the river that God had dried up and make an altar out of it so that people from then on could see it and remember what had happened. He called it a spiritual marker and asked the congregation if they had any spiritual markers we could remember. This will sure be one for me for the rest of my days." He wasn't used to talking for so long at a time, so he paused to take a couple of bites of his meal.

"Let me tell you what I know about the orphanage, good and bad. The Territory pays a monthly amount for the upkeep, and I believe your salary is included with that. That wasn't good enough for Elmer and CoraLu Bigby, though. They made the girls sew clothes to sell to the local dressmaker and then that merchant would just tack on a percentage for her profit. Old George at the general store sold lots of cloth material and thread and needles and such to CoraLu so he was happy, too. That activity would have to stop. I won't allow it."

"I've been thinking about that too, Marshal. I wouldn't make them do slave labor like it sounds to me they were doing. What if the girls could do some sewing for their own profit? I could keep their record of earnings separate and save it for when they graduate, so to speak." Carl liked everything she was saying. "They would get some education from me plus they could save for their future lives away from the home and I promise I would care for them and never punish them like we understand happened."

"Let's talk about another problem and I don't mean to be disrespectful. Roland is a growing boy whose grandfather, father and uncles did unspeakable things to underage girls. I'd be lying if I said it didn't bring up some concerns with me having him live with all these girls who already like him a whole lot. Have you thought about that?" he asked.

"I understand your concerns, Marshal. I suppose every mother would say what I'm about to say but I believe he is different from what the men in his life were like," she explained. "I know boys can change as they get older. All I can do is promise to watch him like a hawk and I'm hoping some of the girls who are older than him will watch him as well and report to me if he exhibits any bad traits. If that happens, I will send him to his grandmother and away from temptation."

Carl looked at Corrine to see if he could detect any misgivings she might have about Amanda's plans. He didn't see any.

"Charlie made a good point after Elmer was gone. He wondered where Elmer and CoraLu hid all their savings. I asked every single one of the girls if they had any idea and none of them were any help so it's there somewhere because there wasn't that much in the bank under their names. I believe there was eighty-two dollars and some change and if you get the job, you can open an account and deposit that or just take it to the house and squirrel it away somewhere for future use. Some of us are going to go the farm and search until we find it. God only knows what they did with it."

"We can help, Marshal. Roland is very good at finding anything I misplace," Corrine said.

"I can't tell you how happy this makes me," Carl stated. "We need to see the judge and have him approve it with whoever needs to know at the Territorial board. That'll take some time, but I don't think the parson and his wife would have any problems with taking care of all those gals. After we get done eatin' we should go to the church and tell them, but we shouldn't say anything to the girls to get their hopes up in case somethin' doesn't work out. Oh, but there's one more little thing we need to talk about."

"What would that be, Marshal," Amanda asked.

"Elmer did all the heavy lifting and work at the orphanage. Roland is only twelve. You could use someone who could do the bigger chores."

"Do you have someone in mind?" Corrine asked with raised eyebrows.

Carl smiled. "Maybe so," was all he said.

Lawrence and Muriel were thrilled at the news. The girls

were too busy playing tag with Roland to notice the adults speaking in a corner of the churchyard. Judge Treadway was almost as happy as the parson and his wife and he vowed to begin the proceedings the next day.

Harrington left the Whitaker women to continue all the other tasks they had to do, and he meandered down to the stable where he found Charlie awkwardly trying to operate a pitchfork to clean out some stables. Carl had spoken with Doc Teague, and the doctor assured the marshal that the boy was able to do almost anything he wanted but Charlie was afraid of hurting his collar bone again.

"Why don't you lay that fork down and sit with me a while," Carl suggested. "I've got somethin' to ask you." Charlie was curious and he discarded the pitchfork and sat on a wooden bench with the marshal. "What are you thinkin' about doin' when you get back to normal, Charlie?" he asked. Charlie hadn't allowed himself to think that far ahead but he supposed there were only two possibilities for him. He could either strike out on his own and try to figure out his future or he could go back to Missouri and live with or close to his brother and his family.

"I ain't exactly sure. My brother and sister-in-law took me in and treated me real good. I suppose I could go back there." Charlie considered his options. "I never had a chance to think about what I wanted to do when I got to be an adult. I liked being a drover. Maybe I could do that for a living." Carl listened to his young friend carefully.

"Let me run somethin' by you and see what you think," the marshal said, capturing the boy's attention. Amanda Whitaker, the younger of the Whitaker widows, is mighty interested in moving her and Roland to the orphanage and being the caretaker and teacher for the girls. She used to keep school before she got married to that miserable wretch of a husband of hers. The girls never got any book learnin' and she's got some other ideas to help the girls, especially when they get old enough to leave." The marshal paused to see how his words were affecting Charlie. The boy shifted his gaze from the marshal to the ground and then back up to the marshal again. "There are outdoor chores that her or the girls can't do so she needs a man to do them. We wondered if you might be interested in taking that job on. You could take Elmer's old room, and she'd take CoraLu's. What do you think about that?"

Charlie's heart pounded and his mind raced. "I don't know what to make of all this," he said honestly. "I sure do like it out there and I know how to do most things that need to be done on a farm."

"You don't have to make the decision just yet," Carl mentioned. "Why don't we make a trip out there and search for the money Elmer and CoraLu stashed away? The last time you were there you had too many other things on your mind. You can get more of a feel of the place and maybe that'll help you make up your mind. How about it?"

"When do we go?" was all Charlie said, and the marshal smiled.

"How about tomorrow morning around eight o'clock? We'll search in all the usual places and see what we can find," Carl suggested.

"What are the usual places, Marshal? I found some of my Pa's money under a loose floorboard."

"Well, some people hide their money in a mattress. Others hide it in a cookie jar or a sugar bowl. You're good at solving riddles, Charlie. We'll have a good time searching for hidden treasure."

Chapter 26

It felt good to be riding Sandy somewhere other than the corral. Charlie and the marshal cleared the outskirts of Hays and headed their mounts east to follow the creek. The sun was shining, there was little, or no wind and the sky was dotted with small, fluffy clouds. They conversed only slightly as they rode, and Charlie's mind was filled with the possibility of working at the orphanage and he truly hoped they could find a large stash of money to make things easier for Mrs. Whitaker, Roland and all the girls. They arrived as the sun was high in the sky.

"Why don't you go out and feed the animals," the marshal suggested. "They haven't been tended to for a couple of days. I'll go in and start pokin' around to see what I can see."

Charlie obeyed and the animals were glad to see him. They milled around him as he talked to them and fed each group in turn. Carl entered the house and immediately had a sense that something was amiss. He decided to start in the kitchen and look in the sugar bowl. With a house full of little girls that liked sweet things that seemed an unlikely place to store money, but he wanted to satisfy his curiosity. He could see the kitchen table as he walked out of the front room and the sugar bowl was lying on its side with the contents all over the big table. Young Eli Morris, the young man he had sent to the orphanage to feed the animals and check on things hadn't said anything about finding any sign of tampering. He was a trustworthy sort, so Carl felt whoever had been in the house was there only recently.

Carl didn't have any sense of an intruder still in the house, but he drew his pistol just in case. He would wait for Charlie to come in from the barn. In that way, he could go upstairs and check and if someone was up there and tried to get past him, Charlie would be downstairs to stop them in their tracks. The cookie jar lid was askew, so he checked it and found only a few stale cookies in the container. Carl suddenly remembered that Charlie wasn't wearing his belly gun for the ride here. He went to the porch and when he saw the boy coming, he whistled at him. Charlie stopped at the sound, and the marshal held his own pistol up and then pointed at Charlie and the boy understood what he meant. He took his holster from the saddle horn and placed it over his shoulder to secure it as he walked to the porch.

"We've already had somebody goin' through the house," Carl explained. "You stand at the kitchen door so you can see the front door and the back door, and I'll go upstairs. I may scare somebody your direction so be alert." There were two sets of stairs, one in the middle of the first floor and one in the back on the far side of the kitchen. Charlie could hear the marshal's footsteps upstairs, but his steps were the only ones. He looked at the overturned sugar jar and the sweet substance all over the table and floor. He observed the lid of the cookie jar being beside the jar. He heard the marshal coming down the back stairs much quicker than he had ascended the middle stairs.

"You didn't see anything out of the ordinary in the barn, did you?" the marshal asked.

"No, sir," Charlie responded. "They weren't worked up or anything. As far as I can remember they were all there."

Carl headed for the back door. "I'm going to go and check the other outbuildings. You go out front and see if you can find any tracks." Once again, Charlie obeyed and exited out the front door and walked to the gate leading out of the front yard. He checked the hitching post and found some tracks that had been made in the last day or two. He studied them for a few moments, making sure there was only one horse involved. He walked around the area to see if there were any other clues and couldn't find any. He walked around to the back of the house and spotted the marshal walking back from the smokehouse.

"Did you see anything, Charlie?" Harrington asked.

"There's one set of tracks out front and they look to be a day or two old," Charlie reported.

"Well, let's do some searchin' and when we're done and headed back to town we'll see if we can pick up the trail. I'll start in Elmer's room and move on to CoraLu's room. You say you found some of your Pa's money under a loose floorboard. Why don't you start by checking the floors, upstairs and downstairs? Then look in the cabinets. We'll both go upstairs and check all the girl's rooms after that."

Charlie began his task. "My bet is we'll find the money in the barn somewhere, but not in the hayloft. Or maybe he dug a hole somewhere and buried it."

"You're right. I forgot that was another way people hide their money," Carl said. "If it was me, I'd try and find a dry spot where nobody would think to look. Little girls can be pretty curious, so he'd want to take care where he stashed it. I thought this might be easy for some reason but now I ain't too sure."

The pair scoured the house with no luck. Charlie found some little treasures a few of the girls had hidden from the others. He supposed that was human nature, but he had never owned anything of value except for some arrowheads he had found on the family farm. They moved out to the yard and walked around looking for any bare ground. They branched outside the yard fence to look before moving to the barn.

"Why did you say Elmer wouldn't have hid the money in the hay loft?" Carl asked.

Charlie had already thought about that. "I think he felt guilty about what went on up there. He would have to go up to fork some hay down but I bet he did it as fast as he could so he could get down from there double quick."

"Well, that's the way I'd feel about it, that's for sure," Carl said. "If we don't find anything in the next half hour or so we should probably see about tracking whoever was here before it gets dark."

Charlie tried to reason things out. The girls didn't like Elmer so they wouldn't follow him out to the barn. It didn't make any sense to him that Elmer would have hidden any money in the house where he would have been paranoid about being found out. When he had been in the barn before, his focus was on the loft but now he was concentrating on everything on the ground floor. Elmer had reins and bridles and other items strewn everywhere that needed mending or some other type of repair. There was a workbench along the east wall, and it was clear to him that Elmer was a disorganized man. There was no order to anything and that didn't sit well with Charlie. He liked for things to be in their proper place. Staring at the same things repeatedly wasn't doing any good. He needed to see things from a different perspective. He needed to pay more attention to anything that was different or looked out of place.

Charlie was facing the workbench, and he turned around and looked directly behind him. There were three feed sacks stacked beside a pair of large wooden barrels. Charlie walked over to the barrels and studied them for a minute or two. There was something about them that wasn't right, but he couldn't put his finger on what that was. He stared at one and then he shifted his attention to the other and stared at it. At last, he detected a slight difference between the two barrels. One of them barely had any dust on the lid compared to the other. He tried to pry the lid off, but it was stubborn. On the workbench he found a small pry bar and he used it to open the barrel. Inside, there was a white flour sack, and he reached to remove it. The sack jingled a bit, and it was tied with some twine, and he fumbled with the knot until he at last untangled it. He opened the mouth of the sack and peered inside where paper money and coins filled around one half of it.

"Marshal, I found it," he said simply, and Harrington walked quickly from the opposite side of the barn. He peeked inside and then smiled at Charlie.

"That's some fine detective work, Son. This will go back with us, and we'll deposit it in the bank. How did you come to find it?"

Charlie pointed at the two barrels and picked up the lid he had pried off. "This one didn't have much dust on it like the other one did. I figured it was probably because it was gettin' used." Carl almost clapped Charlie on his bad shoulder but caught himself.

"I knew you were good at riddles. I don't reckon there's much reason to take the time to track whoever broke in. Maybe there was some money in the sugar jar or the cookie jar. We'll probably never know but this here appears to be a fair sum. We'll let the banker count it when we get to town. Let's head on back."

The pair returned to Hays just in time to catch the president of the bank before closing. He was perturbed at being asked to do a task normally performed by a teller, but he wanted to stay on Carl's good side and agreed to count the contents of the flour sack, make out a deposit slip and put the money into the orphanage's account. It amounted to three hundred and eighty-seven dollars which was a tidy sum in the marshal's estimation.

"Let's go to the saloon and celebrate," the marshal announced to his young friend.

"I can't go in there," Charlie replied. "I ain't old enough to drink in the saloon."

Carl gave Charlie a perplexed look. "What's the worst thing that can happen to you if we walk in there?"

Charlie didn't have to think long about that question. "I reckon they'd just throw me out," he said.

Harrington laughed. "Young man, you've been beaten, shot and had your collar bone broken. You've had lots worse things happen to you than gettin' thrown out of a saloon. Besides, you're with me. That ought to count for somethin'."

"Did I ever tell you about the time a fella on horseback run over me on purpose and knocked my shoulder out of place? The same shoulder I got shot in!"

"Don't you fret about going into the saloon. I'm only gonna buy you a sarsaparilla anyway. There'll be no hard drink for you, youngster. I'll drink a beer or two and then we'll go down to the Mexican place for supper."

Charlie thought it best not to say anything about the beautiful Mexican girl the marshal was interested in. He was looking forward to seeing her for the first time to see what all the fuss was about. The saloon was busy, but they found a lone table in the back and the marshal ordered their drinks. Charlie didn't know what to think about the bustling place. There were card games going on at several of the tables, smoke hung like a fog over the entire room and men were drinking in every corner of the establishment. A dozen or more conversations were taking place at the same time but somewhere to Charlie's left he thought he recognized a voice. It belonged to a man who had his back to Charlie, and he was talking to three other men.

"It didn't look like anybody had lived there for a while, so I waltzed right in and made myself at home. I helped myself to thirty dollars from the sugar bowl," the man bragged. Carl noticed Charlie concentrating on what the man was saying and listened as well.

"Where was this place? How far out of town was it," another man asked him.

"By my estimation it was about twenty miles east," the first man explained. "It was just an old two-story farmhouse out in the middle of nowhere. It looked to me like a big family had been living there but they weren't there anymore, but they left me a little present." The other men laughed at his joke. Carl had heard enough and got up out of his chair to cross to their table. He came up alongside the first man.

"Are you in the habit of just walkin' in where you please and steal what you want, Mister," Harrington began.

The bragger looked up at Harrington. "It ain't stealin' if there ain't nobody been living there for a while. They abandoned the place." Charlie had gotten up to stand by the marshal and get a good look at the man who was doing almost all the talking. The seated man looked up at Charlie when he noticed him and his expression turned into surprise. "I know you, kid. Your first name is Charlie. I remember that much. I figured maybe them Indians that stole our horses stole all of Dunham's horses too." Harrington was surprised at this turn of events, but he said nothing.

"Mr. Dunham bargained with them to go behind us and see if we were being followed. He told them to stop whoever it was," Charlie explained.

"Is that a fact?" the man asked. "They left us stranded but we killed one of them braves. We nearly died of the wet and the cold before we made it to a town."

"Who is this big mouth, Charlie?" the marshal asked.

Charlie continued to stare. "His name is Wharton. He's no good, Marshal. I rode with him on the horse drive I told you about. I caught him trying to steal Mr. Dunham's payroll and supply money. He got on his horse and ran right through me. It knocked my shoulder out of place, and I couldn't ride for a few days."

"Stand up Mr. Wharton," Harrington ordered. "How much of that thirty dollars you stole do you have left?"

"Steal? I didn't steal nothin'. The house was abandoned, and I helped myself."

"For your information, the house was only abandoned temporarily. The folks who live there are fixin' to go back soon. I asked you a question. How much of the stolen money do you have left?"

Wharton scooted his chair back along the wooden floor and began to stand and draw his pistol, but the marshal was ready for him and drew his own weapon and hit him between the eyes with the butt end of his pistol and Wharton dropped immediately. Carl rifled through Wharton's pockets and found a little over twenty dollars. He relieved the collapsed man of the money and stuck it in his vest pocket.

"A couple of you fellas get over here and haul this man to the jailhouse for me, will you?" Carl made a quick search for any other weapons and found nothing. "I'll be along in just a minute."

Two burly cowboys grabbed Wharton by his arms and dragged him unceremoniously across the floor, up one step and through the swinging double doors.

"What about you other men here at his table? What do you know about this Wharton?" Carl asked.

"We just met him an hour or so ago, Marshal. He bought us drinks and that's the honest truth," one of the men said.

"Did you see him with anybody else?" the marshal pressed.

"He was here when we came in, Marshal," another one of the men said. "He was here at the table by himself and at the time there wasn't another empty table in the whole place. He saw us and asked if we wanted to sit with him and that's when he bought the first round of drinks for us. We was fine with that."

Harrington felt they were telling the truth. "I can hold him for two days for petty theft, but I recovered what he had on him. After that I'll threaten to beat him within an inch of his life and tell him to vamoose." He didn't appear to be talking to anyone, but he was speaking to Charlie. "That's the best I can offer. I just met him, and I hate his guts."

"Some people grow on you after a while but he ain't one of those kinds of people," Charlie said. "He just gets worse as time goes along."

Chapter 27

Much happened over the next forty-eight hours. Marshal Harrington was obligated to let Wharton out of prison, but he wasn't obligated to be nice about it.

"You ain't welcome in this town. If you come back, I'll give you another rap on your skull or I may just shoot you. It will depend on my mood," the marshal threatened. "I can warn you that most of the time these days my moods are pretty sour so don't try me. When you leave you can go any direction except east. I don't want you anywhere near that orphanage again."

The judge had expedited Amanda to be the next headmistress of the orphanage and Charlie had decided to accept the offer to be the caretaker, at least for a while. He posted a letter to his brother in Missouri telling him his whereabouts. Amanda had been worried that Roland would balk at moving to the farm from their ranch, but he was excited about the opportunity. He wanted to be close to all his new friends. The girls helped Amanda with the purchase of supplies they would need for the move back. The parson and his good wife had tried to find homes for at least some of the girls but not one couple followed through on their initial interest in adoption. The couple was more saddened by that than any of the girls. They wanted to be together.

When they made their way back to the farm, the marshal escorted them. As soon as they arrived the girls fell to clean up the mess Wharton had made without being asked. Carl looked at Amanda and they smiled at one another. This one simple act proved to Amanda that the girls would be very easy to take care of. Charlie checked the animals and gave them all a good feed which they had missed for a few days. One of the last things the marshal had done before they left town was to pass the word to the ranches in the surrounding area and ask for donations of hay for the orphanage. The day after they got back, the first of the deliveries of hay was made and those continued for the next three days until the loft was full. Each wagonload carried two or three curious men who wanted to see the blood-stained mattress and the tally marks on the post as well as the two portions of hanging rope. One of the first projects Charlie performed was to take the ropes down and burn them along with the straw stuffed mattress. He left the tallies as a kind of memorial.

Harrington was satisfied that everything was going to work out just fine with this arrangement. While he was there, he helped Charlie and Roland build a bed for the boy in Charlie's new room. As the only males in the house, it was only fitting they should be together.

"Well, Ms. Whitaker, I'm going to go back to town and leave you all to it. I've been here going on three days. Hays may be goin' to pot without me being there." The girls giggled at that, and Charlie just shook his head. "Girls, I expect you all to behave yourselves and I know it's a tall order, but I need you to keep Charlie and Roland in line. Boys, you need to act like gentlemen, or you'll answer to me." He mounted his horse and tipped his hat to Amanda. "Ma'am, if you need my help, just send Charlie or Angela to town. They both know the way. Your mother-in-law is closer, and it sounds like she's puttin' together a good work crew at the ranch. Maybe Roland could ride there easier if you needed help."

"No one wanted to work at the ranch for my father-in-law or any of the Whitaker sons," Amanda stated. "Things are different now. Men are showing up from all over the territory to seek employment. Thank you, Marshal. You have been most kind and helpful."

The first night without the marshal was a little scary for

everyone. Charlie talked to Mrs. Whitaker, and they decided he should place some of his weapons around the house in case they needed them. The only ones who knew their location were Charlie, Amanda and Mary. He placed them out of reach of the smaller children and hid them strategically. He made it a point that when he was outside the house, he would wear his belly gun. It made him feel more secure and he took his job as caretaker very seriously. He was the man of the house.

He knew about gardening and wanted to supply the house with lots of vegetables, so he doubled the size of the garden plot behind the house. The smaller girls enjoyed playing in the dirt, so they were helpful at least some of the time. Fruit trees. He had always wanted to try his hand at growing fruit trees. He would talk with Mrs. Whitaker about that when he got the opportunity.

On the third day after the marshal had gone back to Hays, Charlie worked outside until it was too dark to see the garden any longer. He remembered a couple of chores he had put off in the barn, so he grabbed a lantern from the back porch and lit it to see where he was going as he walked the bare path. He was exhausted from his labor and had failed to eat any supper so he could get as much done as possible. Amanda didn't scold him. She was proud of how hard he was willing to work but reminded him not to make himself sick. There were only a couple of things he needed to do, and he completed them quickly and started for the house.

He was halfway to the back porch when he heard voices raised and he could swear he heard a man's voice along with Mrs. Whitaker. Charlie's holster was hanging from a hook on the back porch. He pulled the pistol and walked quietly through the back door. Something was terribly wrong. Some of the little girls were whimpering and he could make out what was being said by Mrs. Whitaker and a man.

"Don't do this!" Amanda cried. "Let her go!"

"All of you need to shut up!" the man screamed. "Where's Charlie? I've been watching the house all day and I know he's around here somewhere." The man was Wharton, and he had his left arm around the torso of Angela who tried to squirm away. Wharton's pistol was pointed at Amanda. His back was to Charlie. "Stop tryin' to get away or I'll raise a knot on your pretty little head!" Charlie placed his index finger over his lips and shook his head at anyone who could see him. He didn't want Wharton to know he was creeping up behind him.

"What do you want from us?" Amanda pleaded. "We keep very little money here at the house. Take it and leave us alone! Give Angela back to me! Give her back right this instant!"

"I talked to some men in Hays that went to the trial of Elmer Bigby. They told me about what went on in the hayloft out yonder. They told me about the six tally marks on a post somewhere up there. Some of the best fun I ever had with a gal was with a young one like this little filly here. I was thinkin' on taking her up to the hayloft and adding a seventh tally mark. If you try to stop me, I'll just shoot her and pick another girl."

Charlie continued to creep up on Wharton. He was afraid if he simply shot him, Wharton's gun might go off and kill someone. Neither Amanda nor Mary was close to any of the hidden weapons in the house. Charlie was walking now between the cook stove and the long table where their meals were served. On the top of the stove was a large, heavy cast iron skillet with hot grease from the evening meal. He touched the handle of the skillet, and it was hot, but he could lift it without burning his hand. The grease, a grayish white, was starting to turn into a solid, but it still swirled inside the pan. Charlie tucked his pistol into his trousers behind him and he took the skillet off the top of the stove. It was difficult for him because of all the work he had done outside all day. His hands were weak from all his labor. He continued approaching Wharton from behind, but he still had the same dilemma as before. What could he do to stop the man but also prevent him from pulling the trigger, even by accident.

"I want you to holler for him, ma'am," Wharton said to Amanda. "Holler for him to come in by the front door. Do it now!" he commanded.

Amanda was shaking so badly she could barely make a sound at first. "Charlie!"

"Louder! He may be down at the barn. Let him hear you!"

"Charlie!" she managed. "Charlie, come to the front door! Please Charlie!"

Charlie switched the skillet to his left hand and was now almost upon Wharton. The situation had escalated to the point where he had to do something to save Angela and stop this perverted man. It became the most important thing in the world for him to prevent the seventh tally.

"Again!" Wharton yelled. "You'd better get that boy in here right now! I ain't warnin' you one more time!"

"Charlie!" Amanda shrieked and at that moment Charlie used his right hand to push Wharton's gun away from Angela's head. The pistol went off just as he had feared but the bullet sailed up harmlessly into the ceiling. Immediately after disrupting Wharton's shooting hand, Charlie threw what grease he could onto Wharton's face. The man screamed and threw both his hands up to his eyes. Angela pulled away and ran into Amanda's arms and Charlie took the skillet in both hands, leapt up into the air and brought it down onto the crown of Wharton's head with deadly force. Charlie heard the familiar cracking of the skull, just like he remembered it when he struck his own father. Wharton dropped to his knees while still clutching his face and then he fell forward. All the little girls including Angela ran to Amanda like baby chicks running to their mother hen and the woman gathered them in to comfort them.

Charlie dropped the skillet and got down on one knee beside the prone figure of Wharton. He checked for a pulse in his neck, and he couldn't find one. Mary walked quietly over to Charlie and embraced him without saying a word. Dixie did the same thing as her sister and Roland came up to the boy with them.

"That fella knew who you were, Charlie," Roland stated. "He called you by name! Where did you know him from?"

Charlie stared at Wharton's body on the floor. "It's

complicated. All you need to know right now is that he was a bad man, but we don't have to worry about him ever again. I'll tell you more about him some other time." Charlie looked at the skillet on the floor next to Wharton and remembered how he had used one to defend himself against his father. The sound it had made on Wharton's skull was the same he recalled from the previous occurrence. "He probably wouldn't have come back here if it wasn't for me. He was after some revenge against me for catching him stealing one time."

"Do you think he was alone?" Amanda asked.

"A man like him doesn't have many friends," Charlie replied.

"Can we at least move his body out of the house?" Mary wondered. "Maybe we could wrap him up in a blanket and move him to the porch."

"That's a good idea, Mary," Amanda said. "I need you to take him to the marshal tomorrow, Charlie."

There was silence as everyone just gazed at the scene. Finally, the quiet was broken from an unexpected source.

"There won't ever be trouble like this ever again in this house." Everyone turned to look at the girl named Dora. She hadn't uttered a word for over a year. "He will be the last one." Amanda strode over to her and embraced her.

"How do you know that dear?" she asked. Dora simply shrugged.

"I just know," she said. Amanda felt she had a premonition, but she didn't think it was wise to press the girl for more of an explanation. She was still fragile after her experience with the Whitaker men. What she said eased everyone's mind. They used the oldest blanket available, wrapped the body in it and moved it to the porch for the night. Roland assisted Charlie in the morning as they struggled to get the large man over his horse. It took them a while and Charlie finally got underway about an hour after the sun came up.

The marshal was surprised to see his young friend again so soon. He was more shocked to see a body lying across a horse led by the boy. He didn't say a word as he approached the dead man. He simply grasped the head of the corpse and lifted it abruptly to see the face.

"Wharton!" he said with surprise in his voice. "Is everybody at the farm alright?"

"He showed up after dark when I was in the barn finishing some chores. I think he wanted to kill me and molest Angela. Somebody must have told him about what the Whitakers had done to the other girls. He even said something about making the seventh tally in the barn loft."

Harrington took control of the horse and started across the street to the undertaker's office. "I'll sell his horse, saddle, guns and tack and use that to pay for his funeral. If anything's left over, I'll deposit it in the bank for the orphanage. It looks like you stove in his head. What did you use?"

Charlie looked a little embarrassed to Carl. "Would you believe I used a frying pan?" That made the marshal stop and look at him.

"You're kiddin' me ain't you?" he asked. Charlie grinned and looked down at the ground.

"He had Angela around the neck with his arm and a pistol pointed right at Ms. Whitaker. I was afraid if I shot him in the back, his gun might go off. I pushed his hand out of the way from behind him and clobbered him over the head as hard as I could. He hit the floor dead."

Harrington smiled at Charlie. "Lord, but you are a caution. Let me take care of this fella and I'll buy you something to eat."

"At the Mexican restaurant?" Charlie inquired.

"Well, I haven't seen my little senorita for two days so I'm past due."

The conversation was one-sided as they ate their meal. The marshal was too distracted by the pretty Mexican girl with her beautiful brown eyes. When at last they finished eating he patted the girl on the rear when he thought no one was looking and left a generous tip for her.

"Do you remember Dora from the orphanage?" Charlie asked.

"Dora? I probably do but go ahead and remind me."

"She's the one who hasn't said a word since last year when… you know," Charlie's voice trailed off.

"Oh, sure. What about her?"

"After I caved in Wharton's skull, I could tell Ms. Whitaker, Roland and the girls were all kind of worried that the bad things that had happened at the farm were always going to keep happening. All of a sudden Dora spoke up and said that was the last bad thing that would ever happen there. It didn't dawn on me for a minute that it was her that said it. I still don't know what to make of it, but it seemed like an odd thing that the first thing out of her mouth for a year was to say that. I think she really believes it."

The marshal shook his head as they walked toward Charlie's horse. He held up his hand. "I vow to never complain about bein' bored ever again," he said, and Charlie laughed at him. "You sure have made life interesting, young man. Do you think I need to come out with you and reassure everybody?"

Charlie considered the offer. "No. I don't think so. They didn't seem too worried about me leaving them alone. Maybe when you do get bored you can ride on out and visit."

Carl shook hands with Charlie. "I'll check the wanted posters and if there's any reward for Wharton I'll keep it for you. Tell everybody back there I said 'Howdy'."

Chapter 28

Six months passed and everyone fell into a fine routine. Charlie had begun the rigorous task of chopping wood for the coming winter. There were plenty of dead trees to choose from and Roland would come along to put the wood into the wagon. The weather was already beginning to cool, and Charlie felt a sense of urgency to get as much wood on the porch as possible before the cold started in earnest. They drove back to the orphanage with a full wagon one day, determined to unload it before a storm swept in. Amanda met them at the back door.

"Charlie, you have some visitors," she announced. "Come on in and I'll send a couple of the older girls to help Roland stack the wood. My! You two have certainly been busy today!"

Charlie's first thought was that perhaps the marshal and Ariana had taken a buggy ride to the farm. He couldn't imagine who else it could be since he didn't know anyone else in town that well. He heard the girls talking excitedly before Amanda shushed them and followed them upstairs. Charlie walked into the drawing room and couldn't believe his eyes. His sister Jane was seated on the couch in front of the fireplace with his niece Rebekah on her lap and his nephew Joshua was at her side, so close he was practically on her lap as well. Jane got up quickly with her daughter to embrace him and Charlie was filled with joy. He thought he would never see them again. He held them both at arm's length to look at them with disbelief and Joshua rushed to cling to his mother's side.

"Oh, my Lord!" he exclaimed. "I'm so happy to see you but how is it you come to find me?"

Tears of joy ran down his sister's cheeks and she smiled a radiant smile. "I sent a letter to our brother, and he sent one back to me telling me where you were. I decided we'd come and see you." She looked around the great room. "You sure landed in a happy place." Charlie knelt to be on Joshua's level.

"Hey, partner. I'm mighty glad to see you. Hey Roland!" Charlie yelled toward the back of the house. Roland walked in to see what he needed. "This is my nephew, Joshua. I'll just bet he'd like to come outside with you and help you stack that wood." Roland held out his hand and smiled at the boy.

"We could sure use your help, Joshua," Roland said. "Those girls out there think they know how to work but we'll show 'em, won't we?" Joshua smiled at him, and the two boys made their way to the back door.

Charlie waited for them to get out of earshot. "What about your husband? I can't believe you got away from him."

The mention of the man brought a tear to Jane's eyes. "I thought about what you said, Charlie. Do you remember? You said if I wouldn't leave Jared for my sake, I should do it for Joshua's sake and Rebekah's sake, too. I couldn't watch him beat my son one more time. My husband couldn't get a job as a preacher, so he took a job in the town saloon as a bouncer. He took up with one of the working girls in the saloon and I took advantage of that and left him on one of the nights he didn't come home. Some very kind people gave me enough money to get to Hays, and the marshal told me how to find you. He offered to be our guide but then something happened in town that he had to take care of, so we came on our own. Are you truly happy to see us, Charlie?"

"Happy? Why, it's like a dream come true!"

"I don't think he'll come here and cause trouble. Do you think he will?" Jane wondered.

Charlie shook his head. "One of the girls who lives here has the second sense," he explained. "She claims there won't be no more trouble at this place and let me tell you, they've had their share of trouble. If he comes here, I'll give him fair warning to leave. When he won't do it, I'll kill him as dead as a doornail." Charlie had a wonderful thought. "You and Joshua and Rebekah should live here with us! I'll talk to Ms. Whitaker. I bet we can work something out. You'll like it here. There's plenty to do and it's a good life."

Dora's prediction of peace and tranquility for the farm proved true over the next three years. Not only was Charlie a good caretaker, but he also became an excellent gardener and hunter. The orphanage added four more little girls to reach the capacity of sixteen. They all thrived under Amanda's tutelage and Mary and Dixie could have struck out on their own, but Mary enjoyed the tender moments she shared with Charlie, and he finally mustered the courage to ask if she would ever think about marrying him. She surprised him by saying yes and on a warm, spring morning they were wed in the church in Hays by Parson Lawrence. They both wanted to stay at the farm, and they were surprised by Corrine Whitaker who gave them the materials and laborers to build a small home for them next to the orphanage. Her ranch was thriving.

Charlie worked for the marshal occasionally if there was trouble anywhere east of town and he saved his money because he didn't need to spend much, and he was able to buy forty adjoining acres for them to start their own little homestead.

Charlie and Mary enjoyed taking walks on their property. Charlie decided a good way to start his farming career was to cut the native grass they walked through for hay and sell it to the orphanage.

On a beautiful spring day Mary announced she was with child, and the news made Charlie happier than he had ever been. However, Mary could tell something was troubling her husband and she reminded him they had decided never to keep anything from each other.

"Something's bothering you, Charlie. What is it?" Mary knew all about how his father abused him when he was younger.

"You know how sometimes I have nightmares?" he asked her. Mary nodded. "They used to be about the beatings my Pa would give me but now they've changed. Now my nightmares are about me becoming like him." Charlie had been looking down at the grass as the wind stirred it around but now he looked straight into the light blue eyes of his pretty wife. "I need to make you a promise and I need you to hold me to it. Here's my vow. I vow never to raise my hand in anger against any of our children. They may misbehave and have to be corrected but there's a big difference in correctin' them and beatin' them out of pure meanness. I promise to never do that. The only thing I learned from my Pa about being a parent is what not to do. I'll be a good listener and a good teacher. I'll love on 'em every chance I get. The chain of abuse has to stop somewhere, and it stops right here with me."

Mary was so proud of her husband. She knew by the way he said it that he meant it with all his heart and soul. He would make a wonderful father.

Marshal Carl Harrington started quite a stir in Hays when he married Ariana, the pretty Mexican girl and he also built a small house for them on the outskirts of town.

Roland and Angela looked forward to their sixteenth birthday so they could also get married and move back to Corrine's ranch and he could work for his grandmother.

From the time Amanda took over the orphanage until she retired many years later, whenever one of her girls reached the age of eighteen and desired to strike out on her own, Amanda would arrange to have a big graduation party, and she would write letters of recommendation for each young lady to carry with them to show possible employers. A handwritten letter from the Hopewell School for Young Girls almost certainly ensured gainful employment.

At Hopewell, joy at last overcame abuse and chaos and everyone lived in harmony. Everyone except Jared Gunderson. He did follow his wife and children to Hays but on the first night he was there he got drunk and became belligerent and threatening and Marshal Carl Harrington had no choice but to shoot him to death. He was buried in a pauper's grave, and no one even knew who he was.

About the Author

A native of Miller, Missouri, Dan Moots inherited his love of writing from his mother, Norma, who enjoyed writing poetry. She was the only person to ever read his first novel which never made it to be printed but she told him she loved it and encouraged him to continue to pursue creating stories for people to enjoy. The next book didn't appear until over thirty years later but now in retirement he has the time to develop more ideas and get those ideas into book form. Creativity runs in the family.

Dan stays very busy as the Director of Missions for his church after serving as a deacon for many years. He also teaches on occasion. Three sons, a daughter-in-law, and two granddaughters occupy some time as do the many golf courses he likes to frequent in the area.